A Liar's Death

(A Detective Jackson Mystery)
L.J. Sellers

A LIAR'S DEATH

Cover art by David MacFarlane
Ebook formatting by Barb Elliott

ISBN: 978-0-9987930-7-8
Published in the USA by Spellbinder Press

A Liar's Death

Detective Jackson Mysteries

The Sex Club
Secrets to Die For
Thrilled to Death
Passions of the Dead
Dying for Justice
Liars, Cheaters & Thieves
Rules of Crime
Crimes of Memory
Deadly Bonds
Wrongful Death
Death Deserved
A Bitter Dying
A Liar's Death

Agent Dallas Thrillers

The Trigger
The Target
The Trap

The Extractor Series

Guilt Game
Broken Boys
The Other

Standalone Thrillers

Guilt Game
The Gender Experiment
Point of Control
The Baby Thief
The Gauntlet Assassin
The Lethal Effect

Cast of Characters:

Wade Jackson: detective/Violent Crimes Unit

Katie Jackson: Jackson's daughter

Kera Kollmorgan: Jackson's girlfriend/nurse

Lara Evans: detective/task force member

Rob Schakowski (Schak): detective/task force member

Michael Quince: detective/task force member

Denise Lammers: Jackson's supervisor/sergeant

Sophie Speranza: newspaper reporter

Jasmine Parker: evidence technician

Joe Berloni: evidence technician

Rich Gunderson: medical examiner/attends crime scenes

Rudolph Konrad: pathologist/performs autopsies

Tayla Holden: murder victim

Tony Barulla: neighbor/suspect

Derrick Jackson: Wade Jackson's brother

Nicky Walker: Derrick Jackson's girlfriend

Samir Thibault: missing woman

Chapter 1

Monday, May 7, 8:45 a.m.

Detective Wade Jackson entered the hospital room, and his stomach clenched. His brother Derrick lay in the bed, pale and still. Jackson had never seen him like this. As a kid, Derrick had been a monkey boy, always running, climbing, and making trouble. He'd been a restless adult for most of his life too. Seeing him so lifeless, with IV lines snaking into his arms, was unsettling. His six-foot frame was now gaunt as well. Jackson walked over and whispered his name.

Derrick opened his eyes, and a funny smile played on his face. "Don't worry, I'm not dying."

"Damn. I wanted your comic book collection." Jackson smiled, then shifted on his feet, not sure what to say next. "Have they figured this out yet?" Derrick had been in and out of the emergency room four times in the last six months. He'd had various symptoms, but mostly a lot of vomiting and gastrointestinal pain. The worrisome elements though were the occasional blood-pressure drops and irregular heartbeat. Yet after dozens of tests, the doctors were still mystified.

"Nope. But I'm feeling better and going home tomorrow."

"Good news." Jackson worried that his brother would lose his job. "Do you need a ride?"

"Thanks, but Nicky will pick me up." Derrick raised his bed to a sitting position as he talked. "She's been great through this whole thing."

"I'm glad you have her." Jackson laughed. "Because I'm not good with sick people."

"That's an understatement."

His brother had met Nicky a year earlier, and they'd bonded quickly, unusual for Derrick. She'd moved in a few months after they got together, and Jackson was glad to see his brother finally settle down after having a dozen girlfriends. Nicky wasn't his favorite, but she was fine, and he didn't see her often because he and Derrick rarely socialized. They had a shaky past that included long periods without speaking.

Derrick chuckled. "I know you hate hospitals, so don't feel like you have to stay."

"I brought you something." Jackson, suddenly embarrassed, reached into his satchel anyway. He pulled out a Butterfinger bar and handed it over. "You'd better hide it from the nurses."

Derrick let out a moan of pleasure. "Awesome! I've had nothing but mashed potatoes and Jell-O for days." He tore into the candy, grinning wildly.

Jackson felt a flush of pleasure. He vowed to make more of an effort to hang out with Derrick. His brother had finally matured in the last few years, especially once they'd resolved the issue of their deceased parents' house. Most of Derrick's problems had been rooted in the way their mother had spoiled him. *God rest her soul.* Derrick was a blond-and-blue-eyed version of himself, but better looking—and more charming. That was why he'd gotten away with everything.

"How are the kids?" Derrick asked, his voice still weak.

"Good. Mostly. Katie is about to graduate, and Benjie is in preschool and loving it." His kids were more complicated than that, but he didn't discuss their issues with anyone but his girlfriend.

"And Kera?" Derrick echoed his thoughts, worry in his eyes.

"Still grieving and caregiving." She'd gone to Redding to take care of her sick parents months earlier, and her mother had recently died. Poor Kera was now caring for her father while dealing with her own loss. He was lonely without her, but he'd started to wonder if their relationship was meant to be. Jackson shifted again, wondering how long he had to stay.

"Either sit down and relax or move along," Derrick said, laughing. "You're making me nervous, standing there."

As Jackson tried to make up his mind, Nicky walked in. She gave him a surprised smile. "Hey, Wade. It's about time you stopped by." Tall and pretty, with long dark hair, Nicky looked great, as always. She was ten years younger than Derrick and always wore fancy clothes and a little scarf around her neck. Jackson sensed she was high-maintenance. "Hey, Nicky. I hear Derrick is getting better."

"Yeah, I was just talking to his doctor. He wants us to come back for more tests in a few weeks."

Jackson glanced at Derrick, and his brother nodded. "I'm trying a new medication. So we need to see if it's working."

"That's encouraging. What are they giving you?"

"It's an ulcer treatment," Nicky cut in. "And I doubt if it will help."

Jackson's phone rang, and he felt a flash of relief. He held up his hand to excuse himself and turned away to answer. The name on the screen was his boss. "Sergeant Lammers. It's good to have you back." She'd been suspended for a while over her medical marijuana use, but now that the substance was legal in Oregon, the department had backed off.

"You won't think that in a minute."

"What have we got?"

"A dead woman. We don't know if it's a homicide yet, but the patrol officer who responded is suspicious."

"Give me a second." Jackson turned back to Derrick. "I have a new case and need to go."

Derrick held up a hand. "See ya. Thanks for the candy."

Nicky gave a small wave too. "Bye."

Jackson patted his brother's arm. "Call me when you get home." It seemed like the right thing to say. He hurried out of the room, glad to be on the move. Derrick probably wouldn't contact him, but that was okay. With new assignments, Jackson tended to work around the clock and could barely stay in touch with his kids. Technically, he worked in the Violent Crimes Unit, but as the senior detective, he rarely handled anything but homicides. Assaults were for newbies.

"What else do we know?" He put in his earpiece and power-walked to the elevator.

"A news carrier spotted the body through the window, a house off West 15th." Lammers gave him the address, then added, "She's been down a day or so, and it's not pretty."

Dead bodies never were. "How did she die?" Jackson pushed the elevator button.

"We don't know. There's no apparent wound."

"Call the team, please."

"I'll give you Schak and Evans to process the scene, but we don't know yet if this is a homicide."

If the patrol cop thought so, it probably was. Eugene, Oregon, the mid-sized college town where he'd lived his whole life, was becoming an easy place to get killed.

Chapter 2

The dead woman lived on a panhandle lot in a quiet, low-rent neighborhood not far from downtown. Jackson rolled down the long L-shaped driveway, parked behind two patrol units, and climbed out. Surprised by the landscape, he scanned the huge property. The front half had been turned into a lush garden, with flowers and vegetables growing side-by-side and ringed by fruit trees. Behind the small cottage, he spotted several structures, which he suspected were chicken coops, and a larger metal building that seemed to be a shop.

A uniformed officer came out of the house and walked toward him. Jackson had worked with her years earlier but struggled to remember her name.

"Officer Whitstone," she offered. Forty-something and petite, the heavy gun, flashlight, and radio at her waist made her walk funny.

"Detective Jackson."

"I remember." She gave him a quick smile. "I was the first responder here, and no one's been in the house but me."

Jackson glanced at the second patrol car.

"Officer Yates is around back," Whitstone said. "It's quite an operation the owner had going out there."

Jackson assumed she was referring to the metal building. "A micro-brewery?" he guessed.

"Nope. A sausage factory." Whitstone rolled her eyes. "If you can label anything made with tofu as sausage."

"Huh?" The idea made no sense to him either. "Did you talk to the person who found the body?"

"No. It was a thirteen-year-old boy." Whitstone glanced at her notes. "Conner Sarkin. According to dispatch, the carrier saw that the homeowner hadn't picked up her paper from the day before. The kid thought it was unusual, so he rang her doorbell to see if she was all right. When Holden didn't answer, he looked in the kitchen window and saw her on the floor, then called 911." Whitstone gave him an amused look. "Then he finished his route and went to school."

Jackson liked the boy already. "Did he go into the house?"

"I don't know. You'll have to ask him. But the side door to the kitchen was unlocked."

"I'll talk to the kid later, but I doubt he has much to add." Jackson started toward the house, walking along a flagstone path flanked by ornamental moss that served as a lawn. "Tell me about the body."

"No obvious trauma and starting to smell."

"I meant the ID."

"Oh, right." Whitstone nodded. "Tayla Holden, age thirty-four. She appears to live alone here."

Jackson realized Whitstone was the one who had reported the death as suspicious. "What makes you think she was murdered?"

The officer led him around the side of the house and opened the door. "I'll show you."

Jackson stepped in, bracing himself. The odor of decomposing flesh was matched by a potpourri of herbal smells. Lavender and mint were all he recognized, but there were more, some of which he associated with Italian food. The bizarre combination made him nauseated.

The woman was face down on the floor in a small dining

area. She wore a loose-fitting purple housedress that had bunched up around her rear-end. His heart ached for her. She wouldn't have wanted anyone to see or remember her like this. He turned to Whitstone. "Did you touch her in any way?"

"No, sir. I could tell by her color and smell that she was dead." The officer stood next to him. "I haven't stepped beyond this point."

Jackson dug through his shoulder bag for a pair of paper booties and slipped them on. "It's best you stay outside now. The ME will be here soon, and he'll be upset enough that I'm near the body." Rich Gunderson was the medical examiner and attended every death within the city limits, even if the deceased was a hundred-year-old woman who'd died in her sleep. With homicides, Gunderson didn't want anyone interfering with the crime scene. But Jackson needed to see the victim up close, to visualize the moments right before her heart had stopped beating.

In this case, he saw Holden sitting at the small round table near the kitchen window, eating dinner from the plate that was still there. *Had someone been with her?* A deep-blue ceramic dish and an empty wine glass sat on the beige placemat. What had she eaten? Where was the fork or spoon? Had someone joined her but not had any food?

Whitstone cleared her throat behind him, so Jackson turned back.

"Look at the floor near her left hand."

A fork lay partially under her fingers. Next to it, the pale-wood floor looked scratched. Jackson took three steps forward and squatted down, the familiar pain in his gut giving him a squeeze. He was due for another MRI, but hadn't made an appointment yet. A closer look at the scratches revealed a crude letter K. What did that mean?

11

"I think it might be a message," Whitstone called out. "Maybe the first letter in the word *kill*."

Or the first letter in the name of the person who murdered her. He glanced back. "I thought you said you hadn't been this far into the room."

"I wasn't. I can see the letter from here."

Damn. Either she had freakishly good eyesight or he needed to start wearing glasses. Jackson pulled a penlight from his satchel and shone it on the letter. The scratch was fresh with no dirt in the grooves.

The rumble of an engine outside made them both turn toward the sound.

"Go see who that is," Jackson commanded. "Nobody but the technicians are allowed in here."

"Yes, sir." Whitstone hurried out.

Jackson stared at the dead woman, whose arms and legs were bare. No bruises or abrasions. The half of her face he could see looked pink, but he suspected it was simply a sunburn. The last few days had been unseasonably warm for early May, and the people of Eugene had gone outside in droves to enjoy it. He'd mowed his lawn over the weekend and could feel the burn on the back of his neck.

Even dead, it was obvious the woman had been pretty in a Morticia sort of way. Jet-black silky hair, a narrow face, and naturally red lips. Another stab of pain in his gut. He could never look at a dead woman without imagining how he would feel if it were Kera. Or Evans. Jackson shook it off, pulled out his camera, and started taking photos. The crime-scene techs would document everything for the official files, but he liked to have his own set. He picked up Holden's hand to see if there were more markings, surprised by how stiff she was. That meant she'd died at least twenty-four hours ago, maybe even Saturday night.

Behind him, a deep voice barked, "Step away from the body."

Chapter 3

Gunderson, wearing his usual black-on-black clothing, entered the kitchen from the same side door.

Jackson stood and tried not to smile. "You cut off your ponytail."

"The wife threatened to leave me."

Jackson stepped aside. "This may not be a homicide."

"Humph." The medical examiner grunted, moved toward the body, and squatted. "She looks too healthy for a heart attack."

"Maybe she choked on dinner." Jackson had visualized that scenario too.

"The odds are against it," Gunderson mumbled. "Very few people actually expire that way, especially women."

"Can you tell when she died?' Jackson knew it was an irritating question.

"Not without a core temperature." Gunderson glared and pulled a probe from his bag of tools. "Go do something else while I cover the basics here."

Jackson moved into the living room, hoping to learn something about the victim. She liked plants, that was obvious. Ceramic pots bursting with foliage were everywhere, with five large ones along the front window. Inspirational sayings in needlepoint adorned the walls, along with herbal monographs. And color everywhere. A bright lime-green blanket lay over the couch, a fuschia seat cushion sat on a rocking chair, and a tangerine-and-sky-blue rug covered the dull wood floor.

"It's quite an eyeful, isn't it?"

Jackson turned to the familiar voice, a mix of emotions surging in his heart. Detective Lara Evans stood with her hands on her hips, a grin on her heart-shaped face. She seemed prettier than usual. More makeup? Or was she growing her hair out? *Not at work,* he chided himself. "Hey, Evans."

"Is this a homicide or not? Lammers wasn't sure." Evans moved toward him, her petite muscular body attractive under her pale-blue blazer.

"We don't know yet. She's on the floor near the kitchen with no apparent wounds, but she scratched a letter K in the wood with her fork."

"That's a new one. Who is she?"

"Tayla Holden, a tofu-sausage maker."

Evans made a face. "Also weird."

"But not for Eugene." Their town was home to a mix of college students, intellectuals, outdoor enthusiasts, cyclists, hippies, and woo-woo types of all kinds, including vegetarians and vegans. Holden had probably bought her bulk tofu right here in town from Surata.

"Is that what's happening in the big metal shop?" Evans asked. "Sausage?"

A patrol officer hustled in from the kitchen. "Yes, and it smells pretty bad. But I didn't see anything suspicious related to her death." The officer towered over him and was forty pounds heavier.

Markham, that was his name. "Have you questioned any neighbors?" Jackson asked.

"Not yet. You got here quickly." The patrol officer

gestured toward the body behind him. "It wasn't clear how she died, so the sergeant only asked for two units to respond. We both felt like we should stay here."

"You handled it fine." Jackson moved to the front door, which looked locked. He turned back to Markham. "Has anyone come in or out this way?"

"No, sir. The side door to the kitchen was open, and we've been using that."

Jackson slipped on latex gloves and checked the knob. It was locked with a dead bolt from the inside. If there had been an intruder, he or she hadn't come in this way. He opened the door, gestured for Markham to follow, and stepped outside. "Do a quick canvass of the neighborhood and see if anybody witnessed anything over the weekend. When I have a time of death, we'll follow up to narrow it down."

"Got it." Markham hustled toward the long driveway, moving quickly for a big guy.

Jackson glanced around the perimeter. The teardrop-shaped property was lined with a greying picket fence hidden mostly by tall evergreen shrubs. He could see the roofs of three neighboring homes, all at different angles. When they'd developed this suburb, this lot had probably been left over after all the cul-de-sacs were developed. So they'd put in a panhandle driveway to access the land. It was rather perfect, a private rural feeling in the middle of the city. But the neighborhood could wait. He needed to know about the victim.

Back inside the house, Evans had donned gloves and was searching the piles of papers covering a large rectangular table. She looked up. "This served as her work desk, and she seems to have had a lot going on." Evans picked up a folder. "These are invoices for her sausage business, which is called

Guilt-Free Goodness. And these"—she shook the manila envelope in her other hand—"are for consultations. I think she's a nutrition counselor."

Jackson walked over. "An evangelical for her vegetarian cause?" Lifestyle advocates, whether it was for exercise or veganism or yoga, could be overzealous in enlightening others.

"Considering what she charged people for her advice, I'd call her a scammer." Evans' eyes sparked with anger. "Two thousand dollars for five one-hour phone conversations!"

Ten times what he made per hour. At least once a week, Jackson vowed to find an easier way to make a living, but being a detective defined him. When he wasn't investigating, he started to feel lost. "Maybe she pissed off a client and they came for revenge. How many people paid her that kind of money?"

"Just two in this batch. But she also has a bunch of smaller receipts for one-time consultations for two hundred a piece."

"We'll question both of her big-money clients to start with." He scanned the table and the area around it. "No computer?"

"Not yet. Check the bedroom." Evans grinned, obviously amused that she'd just given her superior an order.

Jackson smiled back, his heart happy to be working with her again, and started toward the hall. The police department had sent Evans to Costa Rica for three months as part of a Eugene assistance mission to help the country after it was devastated by a hurricane. Doctors, electricians, and construction workers had volunteered too. Jackson was proud of the work she'd done, but having her gone had been emotionally difficult. Her absence had also postponed the decision he faced.

Right before she'd left, they had kissed one evening after closing out a challenging case. He'd wanted to pursue the relationship further—but he also still loved Kera and didn't want to hurt her. Especially when she was dealing with ongoing family heartbreak. Kera's son had died in Iraq a few years ago, and the loss had ruined her marriage. Now her mother had just passed away and her father was fading. Breaking up with Kera seemed cruel, but he didn't know if he was actually *in love* anymore. Whatever that meant. His feelings for Evans were even more complicated, and trying to sort through all of it overwhelmed him. So he'd let things ride, as is, while both women were out of town.

The bedroom door to the left was open, and he stepped through it. Lying on the multi-colored bedspread was a laptop, near a collection of pillows piled against one side of the headboard. Holden had probably been working in bed before having her last meal. A nearly empty bottle of red wine on the nightstand indicated she'd been drinking even before the meal in the kitchen. Jackson picked up the laptop, which was still plugged in and turned on. The screen showed a blog called Guilt-Free Goodness. The photo in the right corner matched the dead woman in the kitchen. Mostly. The publicity image on the blog looked like it had been taken at least ten years earlier.

He scanned the text of her current posting—a discussion about detoxing children in a healthy way. This kind of bullshit infuriated him. Kids didn't need purification. It was bad enough that adults thought they needed to purge themselves, but he hadn't known until this moment that people were forcing it on their kids too. Holden had even referenced the benefits of diarrhea, calling it a "cleansing process." Jackson took a deep breath and let go of his anger. If Holden had been murdered, it was his job to bring her justice and remove the perp from society.

He reminded himself that the victim probably had family members who needed to be notified. The best place to find next of kin was in a cell phone. Where the heck was it? He'd been keeping an eye out for the device since he arrived. A search of the bedroom didn't produce the phone or anything else of interest. He checked the master bathroom. Another potpourri of herbal scents greeted him there too, but no cell phone. The small space overflowed with tiny jars, all seemingly filled with lotions and potions. Jackson suspected she made them herself.

Taking the laptop with him, he headed back to the kitchen. Gunderson was measuring the length of the woman's body. During the autopsy, the pathologist would weigh every organ as well. "Any update?" Jackson asked.

The ME didn't look up. "She's at sixty-five, about room temperature, so she's been dead at least thirty-six hours. I'd put her death between nine and midnight, Saturday evening, give or take a few."

It seemed a little late to eat dinner. Yet the plate was on the table and the fork was in her hand. Or it had been. Gunderson had already bagged and tagged the utensil for examination back in the *dead room* at the hospital. His counterpart, the pathologist, would examine the contents of Holden's stomach and tell his team exactly what she'd eaten. Had the victim accidentally killed herself with a toxic mix of wild herbs? Contrary to popular local beliefs, not everything that grew from the ground was good for you.

Gunderson grunted, staring at the woman's face. Jackson moved closer. "What do you see?"

"Bruising, I think. Around her lips. We'll have to examine it more closely when she's on the table." With gloved hands, he rolled the dead woman on her side, then pried open her mouth. It stayed open, indicating rigor mortis had set in. The purplish color in the part of her face that had been against the floor meant livor mortis—pooling of the blood to the lowest areas—was in effect too.

"And see these faint red marks on her neck?" Gunderson pointed with a gloved finger. "They were probably made by someone pulling on her necklace."

Jackson hadn't noticed the thin chain before, but it had a small silver bird on the end.

The ME pulled out a flashlight, aimed it into the woman's throat, and got in close for a look. "Yep, her windpipe is blocked. She asphyxiated after something lodged there."

"She choked on her meal?" Evans asked, stepping into the room.

Gunderson looked over his shoulder to respond. "I think she had help. That's what the bruising indicates."

"The perp shoved something down her throat?" Jackson and Evans asked at the same time.

"That's my best guess for now. But Konrad will make the final determination."

In other words, they had to wait for the autopsy. But Jackson now assumed Tayla Holden's death had been a homicide. With any luck, the murderer's name started with a K, narrowing down their suspects.

"What are you doing to that poor gal?" They all turned to the gruff voice in the doorway. Rob Schakowski, barrel-shaped and buzz-headed, was the third partner in their core investigative team. The unit had fourteen detectives altogether, but they tended to work in preferred groups.

Gunderson rolled his eyes and went back to work. He was using a pair of tongs to probe the dead woman's throat. Jackson turned to Schak. "Nice of you to show up."

"I was tracking down a witness who's been avoiding me for weeks, but I finally found her at the Pourhouse Tavern in Springfield." He squinted. "What have we got here?"

"We think the perp shoved something into the vic's throat."

"That's nasty."

"Got it!" Gunderson announced.

As he pulled the tongs out of her mouth, the three detectives stepped toward him for a closer look.

The item that had been in her throat was three inches long, cylindrical, and grayish.

"What the hell?" Schak asked.

Jackson and Evans spoke at the same time again. "It's a sausage."

Chapter 4

Evans repressed a laugh. Crime scenes were serious business, and this woman's death was tragic—even if she had been a bit weird and scammy. But the irony of a sausage maker choking on her own product was too rich, and the media would have a field day with it when the news got out. She could imagine the puns.

A ringing snapped her attention back to the floor. The sound was coming from the victim's body. "The phone must be under her," Evans suggested. She squatted down as Gunderson rolled the body on its side. Evans reached into a small pocket in the dress and grabbed the phone before the ME could complain.

Popping up, she glanced at the screen. The blurry image indicated a fingerprint was needed to use the cell. *Damn!* She glanced down at the dead woman. Her fingers were right there. But which one? Either a thumb or index, and probably her right hand.

"No," Gunderson cautioned, but without conviction.

Evans squatted again, grabbed the victim's right index finger, and pressed it into the activation button. The ME groaned.

The blur on the screen sharpened into a caller ID: *Ginger Holden*. Maybe the victim's mother. A sister might have a married name, and they'd seen no evidence that the victim had kids. Evans started to hand the phone to Jackson—she hated notifying the family—but the pained look on his face made her change her mind. She pressed the green icon and said, "May I ask who's calling?"

"Who are you? Why do you have my daughter's phone?" The woman was clearly distressed.

Department policy was to notify the family in person whenever possible, but stalling wouldn't work. "Detective Evans with the Eugene Police."

The mother gasped. "What's going on? What's wrong with Tayla?"

"I'm sorry but I have some bad news."

Another gasp, followed by a small animal-like noise. "Is she dead?" She tried to sound calm now.

The men in the room were all watching Evans, most likely out of respect for the process, but it made her uncomfortable and she turned away. "I'm sorry, but yes, Tayla died late Saturday night. A paperboy noticed her body on the floor this morning."

"But why? She's so healthy." Mrs. Holden burst into tears.

Evans gave her a minute to process the news. While she waited, she walked into the living space and sat in the office chair. She hoped to get past this part quickly. She had questions to ask. When the mother was calmer, Evans gave her the specifics. "She choked on a sausage."

"No! Is this some kind of sick joke? Are you that internet troll who's been harassing her?"

A suspect already? "No, ma'am. This is not a joke. I'm here in your daughter's house with a medical examiner and several detectives. We don't know yet how or why she choked, but we will find out." Evans pulled her tablet computer from her bag and opened a note file. "Tell me about the troll who was bothering your daughter."

Jackson hurried over and signaled for her to put the phone on speaker. Evans complied, setting the purple-cased device on the table.

The mother's voice grew harsh. "He posted horrible comments on her blog until she blocked him, then he started on her Facebook page. She keeps blocking him and he keeps popping up on new sites."

"What's his name?"

"His online ID is FreedomGladiator, all one word." She snorted in disgust. "He's a right-wing asshole who hates all liberals, but especially vegans and gays." The mother started to cry again.

Evans keyed notes into her file as she waited for her to calm down. Jackson did the same, only he still used a small paper tablet. Evans tried to catch his eye. When he looked up, she mouthed, *Do you want to ask the questions?*

He shook his head and gestured for her to continue. A small vote of confidence, but it still made her happy. She'd loved this man since she'd first started training with him years earlier. He'd been patient with her and passionate about his work, a charming combination that had won her over. His dark eyes, strong jaw, and perfect lips had played a small part too. She even loved the little scar over his left eye where a dog had bitten him.

Evans lost patience with the crying woman and cut in, "We'd like to talk to you at length about your daughter. Can you come in to the police department?"

"I live in Portland so I can't do that right now. But soon." She blew her nose. "I can't believe she's dead. Yesterday was her thirty-fourth birthday. That's why I was calling. I tried all day, but she never answered." She let out another quiet sob. "What more do you want to know?"

"Did Tayla have a boyfriend?"

"No. She used to date, but I think she's given up."

"What about close friends?"

"She has a friend from yoga class. Her name's Caitlyn."

Evans made a note. "What about a job?" She decided not to mention what they already knew about the victim's self-employment. The mother might speak more freely if she wasn't prompted.

"Tayla had several of her own businesses. She made tofu products, like sausage, but just for local stores and restaurants. She also did nutrition counseling work, mostly over the phone. She helped people change bad eating habits."

Evans wasn't sure sausage was considered a healthy choice, even with tofu as a base. She ate cheeseburgers sometimes, so she wasn't judging, just being realistic.

"I know the sausage business infuriates a lot of vegan fanatics," the mother said apologetically. "But Tayla's philosophy is to eat what we crave, but to make it as healthy as possible."

Evans couldn't argue. "She craved sausage, huh?"

Behind her, Schak snickered. Evans ignored him and took notes while the mother talked.

"Tayla grew up on a farm where we raised pigs and made our own breakfast meats. As a kid, she hated the slaughter part, and I think that's why she became a vegetarian. But she still loves the taste." A door slammed in the background, and Mrs. Holden announced that she had to hang up. Evans tried to set up a time to talk further, but the woman had already broken the connection.

She turned to Jackson. "I'll try to track down the online troll, but he could be anywhere in the world."

"He only works as a suspect if he's local."

"Or traveled here." Evans wanted to be upbeat.

"If he did, we'll find him."

"Unless he's left town already."

Schak joined the conversation. "I'll check out her clients and customers and see if anyone feels cheated."

"I'll spend more time on her computer," Jackson added. "Plus track down her financial information."

The medical examiner stuck his head out of the kitchen doorway. "Will someone help me load the body? My techs aren't here yet because no one was sure about the nature of this death." He nodded, a confident smirk on his face. "Until moments ago, that is. I called in a team, but we might as well get her corpse out of the way. Whatever trace evidence is on her can be collected before I wash her down."

Evans hoped Schak would volunteer, but he'd already turned his attention to the paperwork on the desk. She stepped toward the ME, but Jackson sighed and said, "I'll do it."

"I'll help." Evans followed Jackson into the kitchen—a large space with slate-blue vinyl on the floor, sapphire-blue and bright yellow tile on the countertops, and pale yellow walls. She found it oddly pleasing and gaudy at the same time. Gunderson had already rolled Tayla Holden into a gray body bag and was zipping her up. "I'll get the gurney," Evans offered.

She hustled out to the white van and opened the back. The rolling transport sat in the middle, surrounded by tools and tripod work lights. At least this death had been in a house and not outside in the dark and cold. As the newest person in the unit, she'd worked her share of scenes like that. In fact, she'd handled two in February, both homeless men. But the perp, a third transient, had been easy to find and confessed to the crimes. Sometimes when people had been on the streets their whole lives, they grew weary of the struggle and deliberately committed crimes that would land them in prison—where they would be warm and fed and taken care of. For the three months she'd been in Costa Rica, she'd seen a lot of people displaced by the hurricane, but at least the temperature there never dropped below seventy, so nobody froze to death or went to jail just to get warm.

She went back into the house, entering through the side door again, and rolled the gurney next to the body. She stood near Jackson, who'd taken the heavier top half, and they squatted down together, brushing elbows. His touch always electrified her.

Gunderson bent down too, groaning as he did. "Ready, set, lift."

They heaved the corpse onto the gurney, surprised by the weight. As the ME pushed her out the kitchen door, the patrol officer came in the front. His eyes were bright with something to share.

"What have you got?" Jackson asked, before she could.

"A creepy neighbor," Markham reported. "Based on a few things he said, I think he's been spying on our victim."

Chapter 5

Evans wanted to be the one to question him. "Where is he located?"

"The brown house on the other side of the west fence." Markham pointed toward the side of the house. "Their bedrooms are only about twenty feet apart, and there's a gap in the hedge where he can see through."

"I'm on it," Evans said, looking at Jackson for approval.

"I'll come with you. I need to see this guy."

They followed the officer outside, and he pointed down the driveway. "Go out to the street and turn left, then left at the corner, then left at the first side street. The house is at the back of a cul-de-sac. You see this metal roof sticking up behind it."

"What's the neighbor's name?" Evans asked.

"Tony Barulla." Markham gave a shrug. "Or at least that's what he told me."

As she and Jackson started to leave, another white van pulled in and parked behind the first. Two crime-scene technicians climbed out. A tall, thin woman named Jasmine Parker and a short balding man named Joe Berloni. They were both excellent at processing trace evidence, and Evans was glad to see them.

She exchanged a quick update with the pair, then kept moving. Halfway up the driveway, Evans had a thought and stopped short. "Let's go look over the fence at his house from this side first."

"Good idea."

She backtracked until she found a path through the garden, then stepped carefully until she reached the hedge. The glaring break in the line of arborvitaes was too well aligned between the houses to be coincidental. The five now-brown shrubs had been cut back to knee-height, and three had been dug out. It looked like Holden had been preparing to replace them.

"What if the neighbor killed the trees to get a better view?" she mused.

"It sure looks that way." Jackson stepped up to the gray picket fence behind the dead shrubs. On his tiptoes, he was just tall enough to see over it. Evans felt a familiar pang of jealousy. She hated being five-five, but she made up for it by staying in excellent physical shape. She lifted weights daily and practiced martial arts. As an expert fighter, she'd taken down perps twice her size, and she was the only woman to have passed the grueling physical test to become a member of the SWAT unit. "What do you see?"

"A second-floor window with a telescope aimed at the vic's house."

A ball of rage burst in her torso. "Fucking pervert." Predatory men were everywhere. She'd always known that—having been sexually coerced into giving an asshole cop a blowjob when she was a teenager—but now that women everywhere were coming forward with their stories, the depth of the problem was painfully obvious. "Anything else?"

"A ladder against the fence too. On its side at the moment, but positioned right below the gap in the hedge." Jackson turned back. "Let's go put the squeeze on him. I'll push to take him downtown in handcuffs, while you do your thing."

"This could be fun." Evans made her way back through the foliage, with Jackson following.

At the sidewalk, they went left, then turned again on the first cul-de-sac. They cut across the middle, heading straight for the two-story brown house. Evans hung back as Jackson knocked and called out, "Eugene Police! Open up!" He was running the case.

From the house next door, they heard someone call out, "He's in there." A middle-aged woman headed toward them across the grass. "I just saw Tony talking to another officer and he hasn't left. I watched. He drives an old black pimp-style car and I didn't see it leave." She stopped at the edge of her own property.

A neighborhood full of spies. That would work in their favor. "Thanks," Evans called back. She moved toward the witness. "What's your name?"

Now the woman hesitated. "Dana Arness. Can I ask what you want with Tony?"

"Just to talk. Why were you watching him?"

The neighbor, wearing sweatpants and no makeup, shrugged. "I saw the first cop and wondered what was going on. Besides, I don't trust Tony. He's really weird."

Behind her, Jackson shouted again. She glanced over to see the door open. Evans spun back to the neighbor. "I have to go, but we'll talk more later. Will you be home?"

"Until three. I work nights."

Evans handed her a business card and hustled toward Creepy Tony's house.

Jackson hadn't gained entry yet, so she joined him on the wide cement step. The man peering through the screen door was short, with a bulging belly and curly hair. His T-shirt was torn in places and stained around the neck. "I don't have to talk to you! Get off my property!" He had a shrill voice and a nervous tongue-flicking habit. Evans would have felt sorry for the guy if he hadn't been spying on his neighbor.

"We're not leaving!" Jackson yelled back. "Either you answer questions or we cuff you and take you into the department."

His volume surprised Evans. Jackson usually tried to reason with people. But that was her job this time.

The guy just stood there, flicking and biting his tongue.

"We know you spied on your neighbor, among other things," Jackson ad-libbed. "You're only digging yourself in deeper."

Barulla started to close the door. Jackson yanked open the screen and shoved a foot inside. "Get out your cuffs," he commanded.

Evans pulled a pair from her inside pocket and stepped forward, peering around Jackson. The suspect's eyes darted around, but he held his ground. Keeping her voice soft, she tried empathy. "Hey, just because we know about the telescope doesn't mean we think you're the bad guy. We're hoping you saw something that can help us."

He leapt on the new subject. "Like what?"

"Like someone coming to visit Tayla this weekend."

His narrow shoulders relaxed a little. "Why? What's going on?" His tone was curious, but Evans thought he might be faking his ignorance. Dark transition glasses hid his eyes.

"Let us come in and we'll tell you about it." She decided to play to his ego. "You'll be the first in the neighborhood to know what's going on."

More tongue action while he considered it, then Barulla let go of the door and stepped back. "I'll give you five minutes."

Jackson surged into the house and Evans followed. The place was a dump. Dirty dishes everywhere, stinky socks on the floor, and enough empty beer cans to fill the back of a truck. The sour smell was overwhelming. She glanced at Jackson, but his face was deadpan and focused on the hallway. He quickly moved his gaze back to the homeowner.

"What do you do for a living, Tony?" Jackson hadn't moved to sit down, because the only available surface was a filthy recliner in front of a massive TV. The appliance looked new and high-end.

"I'm a software engineer with Analytech, but I work at home sometimes." Barulla stood with his legs wide and his arms crossed, as though blocking access to the hall.

Evans gave a quick glance in that direction. A partially open door revealed what appeared to be an empty room. The difference between that space and this shithole living area was stark. They had to get a look inside the spare bedroom.

"So what happened with Tayla? You said you would tell me." The homeowner was tense again.

"She's dead," Jackson responded. "But I think you knew that."

"What are you talking about?" His high-pitched voice was hard to read, because it sounded fake no matter what he said.

"Where were you late Saturday night?" Jackson asked.

"Uh, I was here, probably sleeping." He shifted and rubbed his head. "No, I take that back. I went to a movie."

"What movie?" As Jackson asked questions, Evans eased toward the hall. From her new position, she could see into the kitchen, which was even more disgusting than the living room. But it was the empty room with the bare floor that intrigued her. Whatever was in there had to be important if this otherwise pigpen guy kept it clean.

"Uh, the new Marvel. I got home around midnight."

"Can anyone vouch for that?" Jackson kept up the pressure.

Barulla spread his arms in mock display. "As you can see, I live alone. My choice. I don't have the patience for other people's stupidity."

Arrogance—a red flag for criminal behavior. Evans took another step toward the hall. Barulla shifted to block her path. "You're not searching my house without a warrant. And you have nothing to base one on."

Jackson scoffed loudly. "You have a telescope aimed at Tayla Holden's home, where she was recently murdered. You also have no alibi. I could call a judge right now and get a subpoena delivered here in twenty minutes." Jackson called out to her. "Evans, let's cuff him while we wait for the paperwork."

Rapid blinking as Barulla's gaze shot back and forth between her and Jackson, not knowing who was going to move on him.

She knew Jackson was bluffing about the subpoena, so Evans improvised. "I think I see meth-making equipment. For the safety of the public, I have to check it out." As a detective, she wasn't required to wear a body camera, but she tried to keep her actions reasonable, if not totally by the book.

"Such bullshit!" The homeowner was in full panic.

"Be quiet and step toward me!" Jackson commanded.

"No cuffs, please. Let's just sit down and let me explain."

Evans heard a confession coming. It would start out as a contrived mix of truth and lies, but Barulla would eventually tell them everything. He was hiding something in that room that meant trouble for him.

"Fine. Have a seat on the floor," Jackson ordered.

The man hesitated.

"Now!" Jackson yelled.

Barulla let out a small cry of defeat and clumsily lowered himself.

As soon as he was down, Evans strode for the empty-looking room. She pushed open the door and stopped, her mouth agape. A formica table stood in the center of the room, and a shelf lined the wall behind it. Both were covered with packets of powder, timers, and fuses—bomb-making material.

Chapter 6

Monday, May 7, 1:22 p.m.
On his way back to the department, Jackson bought a chocolate muffin (lunch!) and three cups of coffee at Full City Roasters. He missed working downtown and being able to scoot across the fountain plaza to grab java from his favorite shop anytime. But they'd moved into a bigger, nicer space on Country Club Road. Now that he was used to the new building, he couldn't imagine going back to their cramped quarters in the old City Hall.

Before getting back on the road, he called his daughter and left a message: "I have a new homicide, so I need you to pick up Benjie from daycare. I think I can be home for dinner though. Let me know that you got this message." He hoped Katie would check her messages after school and get back to him. At seventeen, she was driving and helping him raise the boy. He felt guilty sometimes about giving her too much responsibility, but Katie loved Benjie and caring for him kept her out of trouble. They'd had enough of that.

After pulling into the parking lot, he drove around to the back. The Violent Crimes Unit occupied this side of the second floor, and they had their own entrance. He climbed the steps, careful not to spill his tray of coffee, swiped his ID through the security system, and entered the building. Without stopping at his desk, he headed straight for the conference room. He usually took a moment to type up case notes before a task force meeting, but they didn't have much information yet. The bomb squad was processing the materials they'd found at the neighbor's home, but so far, no one had any theories about how it related to Tayla Holden's choking death.

Officer Whitstone had transported Tony Barulla to the department earlier, and he was sitting in one of the interrogation rooms downstairs. Jackson would question him after the meeting. The suspect had demanded to call a lawyer as Jackson put him into the back of the patrol unit, but Barulla hadn't been arrested or charged yet, so his phone call could wait.

Jackson sat at the end of the long table with his back to the whiteboard. If the case became complicated—and it looked like it would—they might have seven or eight people at the next task force meeting, including the new district attorney. But at this point, he was only expecting his core group.

Moments later, Evans walked in and grinned when she saw the coffee. "No doughnuts?"

They both laughed. He sometimes bought meals for the team on the department's card, but junk food was off limits. They were all watching their weight. Schak especially. He'd had a heart attack a few years earlier, and Jackson didn't want to contribute to his already unhealthy diet.

Evans picked up a paper cup and took a seat. "I ran background on Barulla. One arrest for vandalism five years ago, and that's it."

"What did he do?"

"Spray-painted the word *whore* on a woman's front window." Evans shook her head. "I didn't read all the details because I didn't have time, but she was an ex-coworker."

Jackson glanced at his notes. "Barulla currently works at Analytech. Was he at the same company then?"

"No, he worked at SocioSystems then and was fired after the incident."

"What incident?" Schak hustled in and sat across from Evans.

She repeated the vandalism details, then added, "I'll bet he's never had a real girlfriend."

"Ya think?" Schak snorted. "That place was disgusting even by my standards."

"His retaliation against a woman who scorned him makes him a prime suspect in our homicide," Evans said.

Jackson tended to agree, but it was his job to keep the investigation objective. "We don't have a death ruling yet for Holden, and we don't know that the co-worker Barulla harassed had rejected him." Jackson met Evans' eyes. "Unless that's in the report you read."

"I'll find out now." She tapped the keyboard of her tablet computer. "Gunderson thinks she was murdered, so that's good enough for me."

Jackson didn't argue, but he would attend the autopsy conducted by the county's official pathologist and get a full accounting. He turned to Schak. "Will you take the board?"

"Seriously?" His partner looked stunned.

Evans burst out laughing, then went back to reading the file.

"Just kidding." Jackson grinned. Schak's penmanship was worse than a second-grader's on meth.

Evans slapped the table. "I was right. The woman Barulla targeted with vandalism claimed he asked her out several times and she told him no." She jumped up, grabbed a marker, and moved toward the whiteboard. At the top, she wrote

Tayla Holden (choking victim), then drew a line down the right side. In that space, she listed their main suspect, *Tony Barulla*, then wrote *disgruntled clients* halfway down, as possible secondary suspects. She went back to the first listing and underneath jotted *vandalism, bomb material, revenge.*

"You think Barulla killed Holden to retaliate for rejecting him?" Jackson asked, for clarity.

"Possibly. Or maybe for something related to their properties. Neighbors really get into disputes sometimes." She chuckled. "A U.S. senator was assaulted over a shrubbery argument, so if Barulla is mentally ill—as the bombs indicate—then he might seek revenge for any kind of offense."

Detective Michael Quince, another member of their investigative team, was working with the bomb squad to investigate the suspect and would report to them soon. Jackson had wanted to search Barulla's home himself, but the sergeant who supervised the SWAT unit and bomb squad outranked him and had taken over the scene on arrival. Bruckner considered Barulla to be a terrorist and was running a separate investigation that would probably involve the FBI as well.

Schak shook his head. "The wacko neighbor may not be our murder perp. The MOs don't mesh at all."

"I don't buy that," Evans argued. "Writing *whore* on a coworker's window and shoving a sausage down someone's throat are very personal attacks. Especially since they're both women."

Schak crossed his arms. "It's the bombs that don't fit."

The door opened and Detective Quince—who looked like a model for men's suits—walked in.

"Good timing," Jackson said. "We're talking motive and method."

"I heard." Quince took a seat near the board. "Our preliminary investigation indicates that Barulla is a complex deviant." He looked around the table. "No coffee for me?"

"Sorry," Jackson said. "I didn't know when you would show up."

"I'm kidding." Quince reached out and touched Evans' hand. "Good to see you. How was Costa Rica?"

A pang of jealousy surprised Jackson. Quince was happily married and just being friendly.

"Beautiful and ghetto at the same time," Evans said. "It's lush with trees and palms and bright flowers, but the stores and houses—or what's left of them—are funky and rundown." She snorted. "And many don't have a fourth wall. They're big on open-air living."

"Aren't there a lot of bugs?" Schak scowled. "I mean, considering the lack of walls."

"Oh yeah. Mosquitoes sampled me for breakfast, lunch, and dinner when I was outside, and I saw cockroaches the size of mice. But the house I stayed in had a solid screen so it wasn't bad. No air conditioning though, which is why they leave out the fourth wall, to catch a breeze."

"Not for me," Schak said. "I live for winter, when I finally stop sweating."

Jackson cleared his throat. "Let's get back on track." He focused on Quince. "What do you mean by complex deviant?"

"At Analytech, where Barulla works, they've had a series of weird attacks on employees—all in their homes." Quince opened his briefcase and pulled out his case file. "The company's PR person suspected Barulla, because of a previous conviction, but the patrol officers investigating have never been able to prove anything."

"What kind of attacks?" Jackson was thinking about the

poor woman with the sausage in her throat . . . and the bombs next door.

"One guy found shit in a pair of shoes he'd left on the porch." Quince paused to make a face. "A female supervisor had her car keyed in her driveway, and the CEO had a pipe bomb go off near his front door." Evans turned from the board, her mouth open. "Did they analyze the shit? Was it human?"

"No, canine."

Jackson shook his head. This was a first for their team. "When did all this happen?"

"Over the last eighteen months," Quince said. "The first victim, with the shoes, didn't talk about the incident at work, so seven months later, when the supervisor had her car damaged, it seemed like an isolated incident. The CEO's incident wasn't until five months after that. He thought a neighbor had done it, so the company didn't realize they had an internal problem." Quince shrugged. "The patrol team didn't figure out the crimes were related until they had a third vandalism victim who worked for Analytech."

Evans had been scribbling notes on the board, but she spun around. "What about the bombs? Was Barulla planning more property crimes? Or was he going to hurt someone?"

Quince raised his brows. "We don't know. But he kept a digital journal that the technicians are trying to access. We're hoping it will tell us everything."

"You got a subpoena for his files already?" Now Schak was open-mouthed. The suspect's computer had been locked and inaccessible.

Quince grinned. "Bomb-making material gets a judge on board quickly."

Jackson itched to get downstairs and question the perp.

Barulla's criminal escalation could have easily progressed to murdering a neighbor. He glanced around the room. "What else do we know about either Holden or Barulla? Any property disputes? Did they ever date?" While he'd coordinated with the bomb squad, Schak had talked to neighbors, and Evans had gone back to continue searching the victim's house.

"I didn't find any contact from Barulla on Holden's computer or social network sites," Evans said. "But she could have deleted it, so we'll have the tech guys do their magic."

Schak jumped in. "I've got a little oddity too. One of Holden's neighbors claims she was burying raw chicken parts in the corner of her property. The neighbor says she knows because her cat digs them up sometimes."

"That's weird and disgusting." Evans made a face, then wrote the detail on the board. "I thought Holden was a vegan."

Jackson found it odd as well. "She must have been trying to hide the chicken because she's supposed to be a vegan role model and nutrition consultant." He glanced at Schak. "Did the neighbor seem upset about it?"

"Sort of. But I don't see chicken parts as a motive for murder."

Jackson wasn't so sure. "Unless she was putting poultry in her sausage, which was labeled vegan." *Could someone be angry enough to kill over that?* They had to start digging. "Schak, get Holden's financial records and start looking at her business dealings." He turned to Evans. "Talk to her friends and see if we can find a love interest. Male or female."

"I'll keep working with the bomb squad on Barulla," Quince offered.

As they started to get up, the district attorney walked in. Jim Trang was forty, but with his flawless Asian skin looked twenty-five. He'd been an assistant DA for about ten years, then their DA had gone off the rails and killed someone. For once, the city manager had done the right thing and promoted from within.

"Am I too late?" Trang asked. "Sorry."

Jackson gave him a brief rundown. "I'm getting ready to interrogate Tony Barulla now."

"I'll watch from the monitor," Trang said, still standing. "Bruckner is headed down there now to get started."

Jackson bolted to his feet, annoyed that the sergeant was charging forward without him. "Schak, I want you on the monitor too." When experienced detectives observed an interrogation, they sometimes picked up facial or physical reactions that the questioner might miss—because they were looking at notes or focusing on what to ask next. Those little tics could lead to a confession.

Pounding down the stairs, Jackson cringed at the pain. His retroperitoneal fibrosis was a chronic condition that he managed with intermittent steroid use—after an initial surgery when he was first diagnosed. He was supposed to have another operation to remove more of the growth, but he kept putting it off. Without Kera to nag him about his health, he'd fallen into some bad habits. Maybe after he wrapped up this case, he would call his doctor.

Chapter 7

The foyer at the bottom of the stairs contained two solid doors, each with a small monitor mounted on the wall next to it. The cameras in the interrogation rooms also fed into the conference space above. Jackson glanced at the view of the first room and saw the suspect seated on the far side of a metal table. When he entered the small space, Sergeant Bruckner stood up from the chair near the door. He looked like a weightlifter stuffed into a business suit.

Bruckner nodded at him, then turned back to Barulla. "This is Detective Jackson. We're going to record this conversation."

"That's not legal!" Barulla tried to stand, but he was shackled at his ankles and wrists.

Bruckner ignored him and sat down. So did Jackson. At some point, they would take the cuffs off the suspect so he would be free to make gestures and telegraph when he was lying. But they would wait and give him the freedom as a reward for cooperating.

Jackson took the lead before Bruckner could start asking about the explosives. The murdered woman was their priority. "How well did you know Tayla Holden?"

"I didn't know her. I didn't kill her. Can I get a Coke?" His tone was deadpan and his cadence unusual.

"In a while. We need some answers first." Jackson gave him a hard stare. "This will go better for all of us if you provide as much detail as you can."

"Why should I? My lawyer wants me to keep my mouth shut."

Jackson didn't believe Barulla had one. He might have worked with a public defender years ago when he was charged with vandalism, but that didn't mean anything now. "What's your attorney's name?"

No response.

"That's what I thought." Jackson leaned forward. "You're in a lot of trouble. The DA plans to charge you with plotting terrorism, and I'm trying to pin a murder on you, so if you have an explanation for all the bullshit we found in your house, now would be a good time to tell us."

Barulla blinked rapidly. "I'm not a terrorist. I just like explosives. So what? Lots of guys do."

Bruckner jumped in. "But most men don't harass their coworkers. Considering your pattern of vandalizing people at Analytech, we have to assume that you planned to hurt people with your bombs."

"No." Barulla shook his head. "You can't prove any of that."

"You've been convicted of harassing a coworker in the past," Bruckner reminded him. "Now that we have access to your home, I'm sure we'll find evidence that links you to the three new incidents. So just tell us who you planned to target with the bombs."

"Nobody!" Barulla shouted. "I'll sue you for illegal search and seizure."

"We have a subpoena, and the technicians will find traces of whatever you used to kill your neighbor's hedge." Bruckner's tone held an edge now.

Jackson didn't care about the vandalism. He wanted to get to the murder—and make Barulla uncomfortable. He cut in. "We know you were spying on Tayla Holden. Did you watch her get undressed?"

No response.

"That means you did. She caught you, didn't she? And confronted you?"

"I never had a conversation with the woman." His voice was still deadpan and his body perfectly still. He was trying hard to seem believable.

Jackson wasn't buying it. He decided to use a false statement, hoping to trigger a revealing response. "What made you use a phone cord to strangle her? Convenience?" Jackson watched the suspect's eyes, hoping he would signal surprise.

Barulla was quiet for a moment, then said, "I don't know what you're talking about."

Damn. He needed more leverage. "You squeezed Tayla hard enough to leave bruises on her lips and chin. Our tech people can pull fingerprints from skin, you know." It was rare, but he and his team had earned a conviction once with that type of evidence.

"I never touched her." A flicker of anger. "She was a bitch."

Now they were getting somewhere. "What makes her a bitch?" Holden had probably rejected him, but Jackson didn't expect Barulla to admit it.

"I said hello to her a few times and she ignored me."

"Tell us more about that." Jackson stood and uncuffed the suspect's wrists. Behind his back, he signaled the monitoring team to bring in the Coke Barulla had requested. Now that the suspect was talking, he wanted him to be relaxed and comfortable. Bruckner didn't interfere.

"What's to tell?" Barulla rubbed his wrists. "Tayla thinks she's special. She was like that with everyone."

Everyone? They were neighbors, not coworkers. How much spying had he done? "Who is everyone?"

"The UPS guy. The landscaper. She flirted with all of them."

"But not you?"

Silence.

Time to push his buttons. "What made you think you even had a chance with her?"

Barulla bristled. "Why not? I'm smart, I make a good living, and I'm decent looking."

"So you *did* ask her on a date. Was she out in the yard? Or did you see her on the sidewalk?"

"I didn't ask her out. She wouldn't even say hello when we met at the mailbox."

"I can tell that made you angry. When did you start plotting to kill her?"

The suspect shifted in his chair and his eyes narrowed. "You can't trap me with that bullshit."

Next to him, Bruckner's phone beeped. The sergeant read a lengthy text, then asked, "Did you leave a pipe bomb in Ron Durkin's driveway on the night of May first?"

Barulla blinked. "Of course not. He's my boss, but I don't know where he lives."

A lie. Jackson could tell. The subject was clearly making the suspect uncomfortable.

Bruckner let out a grunt. "Durkin's neighbor just identified you as the person he saw in the vicinity the night the explosive went off. At this point, you need to cooperate, because you *are* going to prison. It's just a matter of how long." The sergeant's voice grew cold. "Or maybe you'll get the death penalty for murdering that poor woman."

The perp was silent for a long moment.

They waited him out.

Finally, Barulla leaned forward and the words came out in a rush. "I may have messed with a few of my arrogant coworkers, but I never hurt anyone. I didn't kill Tayla, and I can prove it."

Chapter 8

Monday, May 7, 8:02 a.m.
Sophie Speranza trudged across the newspaper parking lot, dreading the meeting that awaited her. Whenever the publisher called the whole staff together, it was always bad news. Usually another round of layoffs. The 400-employee paper was down to 157, and that included press operators and route supervisors.

She stopped by her desk to turn on her computer and drop off the oversized bag that weighed nearly as much as she did. She'd had to retire the red leather one that matched her hair, but the new one was a lovely deep maroon. She'd briefly considered dying her hair the same color, but her girlfriend had objected. Jasmine was the only reason she stayed in the area, working for a dying print newspaper. That and the crime beat she covered. For a mid-sized college town, Eugene had more than its share of bizarre violent crimes.

She made mint tea in what served as a break area, then carried her mug into the open space where employees had gathered. The room buzzed with nervous people gossiping about who would get laid off and what they would do if it were them. The publisher walked in at fifteen after the hour—late to his own meeting—and the crowd settled into a quiet murmur.

James Brewer, an attractive man in his mid-fifties, stood on a folding chair he'd brought with him. "Thanks for your time and attention. Today's news has been a long time in coming, and my heart is heavy."

Groans rippled through the room.

"No, we're not closing down. I always said the newspaper wouldn't go under on my watch, and it won't. But it will change ownership. The *Willamette News* has been bought by Skytop Media, and a new publisher will take the helm. This is my last day here. Over the week, the publisher will introduce herself to small groups and make structural changes. Some of you will be let go."

Another round of groans.

"Skytop runs a tight ship, so those that remain will probably face increased workloads."

Fuck! Sophie wanted to run from the building. She was already doing two jobs. In addition to the crime beat, she had to write monthly articles for a supplement that featured advertiser-driven content. This month's assignment was to feature a group of women who'd recently started their own businesses that were doing well. Salespeople would then pressure those startups into running ads in the supplement.

The publisher droned on for another five minutes about keeping their spirits up and maintaining high standards for the newspaper regardless of ownership. She snickered, along with the financial reporter who stood next to her.

"Too bad they won't let me report the details of this bullshit acquisition," Abby whispered. "This is the one story I'd care about high standards for."

"I just hope I don't end up covering Springfield again," Sophie whispered back. The publisher had once re-assigned her to the drudge beat, hoping she would quit—so he could replace her with an entry-level intern who would cost half as much. But Sophie had helped the police catch a sexual predator and had won a prestigious award for a previous story about an eco-terrorist. Readers had pressured the paper's management to let her keep covering crime stories. That was the highest honor writers could attain—loyal readers who wanted more of what they did best. But she didn't think that would save her this time.

People shuffled off, and she realized the meeting was over. Sophie carried the tea she hadn't touched yet back to her desk in cubicle world.

Her neighbor, the financial reporter she'd stood next to, stuck her head over the half-wall. "I think both our jobs are safe, but I'm still going to look for another gig."

"I'll probably be fired before the week is over. Brewer tried to replace me with an intern last year, so clearly my position isn't valued."

"Yeah, but you're writing those pieces for the supplement now." Abby grinned, her wrinkled face clearly amused. "So you're bringing in advertisers and paying your own way."

A repulsive thought. "That means they might lay off someone with seniority instead. Which doesn't really cheer me up."

"It's all bullshit now. Just keep cashing the checks until they walk you out the door with a box of your personal items." Abby disappeared behind the wall.

That could happen at any moment. Sophie had seen dozens of coworkers experience it, and she'd cringed for all of them. Most were stoic, but one older woman who'd worked classified ads for twenty years had cried loudly.

Sophie opened the file she had started on the female entrepreneurs. She'd already interviewed a woman who built high-end custom bicycles for competitive cyclists, and another who was a chocolatier. Today she was scheduled to talk to Tayla Holden, who made vegan sausages that were reportedly so good they'd won over some meat-eaters. Her business was growing so rapidly, Holden was rumored to be looking to upscale and hire employees.

Sophie made a list of questions, then set them aside. Her interview wasn't scheduled until ten. She spent an hour writing the piece on the bike builder and looking over her shoulder, expecting her supervisor to be there with an empty cardboard box. At nine-thirty, still employed, she hurried out to her car. As compensation for the anxiety she was dealing with, she ate a granola bar from her car stash on her way to Tayla Holden's home. The businesswoman lived just west of the downtown area, in a neighborhood where large, pretty oak trees hid a swath of older homes that were showing signs of wear.

Sophie turned onto 15th Avenue and immediately spotted three dark-blue police SUVs. Something big was going on, and her interview with the sausage maker might have to wait. She parked as close as she could to the cop cars, climbed out, and hurried toward the officer standing on the sidewalk. As she approached, she realized the panhandle driveway where the cop stood matched her address for Tayla Holden.

What the hell?

Sophie hurried up to the officer and tried to introduce herself, but he barked at her to leave the area. "This is a crime scene. Do not interfere."

"But I was scheduled to interview Tayla Holden right now. At least tell me if something happened to her."

"She's dead. That's all I know. Now please leave the area and let us do our job."

Dead? Too stunned to move, Sophie tried to process the

news. She hadn't known Tayla personally, but they had exchanged emails and one brief phone call. The woman had seemed vibrant and passionate, and it hurt to know her life force was gone.

Sophie started back toward her Scion, but before she reached it, curiosity overcame her. Tayla was too young and vibrant to have just died unexpectedly. The police presence meant she'd been the victim of a crime. Her story subject had probably been murdered. Sophie stopped in her tracks. She couldn't leave the area without figuring out what she could.

Might as well call Jackson and see if he would share any information. When she'd interviewed him for a feature story years ago—a PR piece his boss had made him do—he'd been openly hostile. Over the years, she'd proved herself to be a resource, and he'd started to return her calls. Not surprisingly, he didn't answer, so she left him a message: "Hey, Jackson. It's Sophie. I'm out here on the sidewalk in front of Tayla Holden's house. I was supposed to interview her today, and now I hear she's been murdered. If I can help your investigation in any way, let me know."

Offering to dig up information for the task force was the best way to ingratiate herself and get pertinent details in return. She'd conducted background research on Holden, but the story was supposed to be a fluff piece that would sell ads, not investigative journalism, so she hadn't gone very deep. But she would now.

Meanwhile, cops and crime-scene techs were probably at Holden's home. What if she could at least get a photo? That would help fill out the otherwise barebones story she would upload this afternoon. Sophie visualized the neighborhood, seeing it in her mind from a bird's eye view. Panhandle homes were typically surrounded by other properties. If she could get into a neighbor's backyard and peek over the fence...

The home she'd stopped in front of looked occupied: a Volkswagen van in the driveway and lights on inside. She backtracked to the corner and headed down a side street, looking for a house with no cars and no lights. The second property had a For Sale sign and appeared vacant with no furniture showing through the open curtains. Sophie marched up to the front door with confidence, just another homebuyer wanting to peek in the window.

She knocked, and when no one responded, she trotted around to the backyard. A lot of grass and not much else. Could she see over the fence? No. It wasn't that tall, but neither was she. She glanced at the slab of concrete that served as a back patio. A realtor had staged it with a beach chair and a funky wood-spool table. The table would be perfect to stand on—if it were only near the fence. She couldn't move it by herself though. Unless...

Sophie used all her strength to tip it onto its curved side, then rolled it slowly toward the back of the yard. When it banged into the fence, she simply released the big spool and let it flop over. Perfect! She hopped up on the table and gazed easily into the next yard. Actually, she could see two properties with a hedge running perpendicular to the fence she was looking over.

To the right, Holden's half-acre took up most of her view. A female officer stood near the side door of the house, and directly in front of Sophie was a metal building with a small window. Inside the structure, a male cop seemed to be searching the premise. At first, what she saw confused her, then Sophie remembered the subject of her story. This was a sausage-making operation.

She pulled her camera out of her bag and shot some quick photos of both officers, using her zoom lens. She had to be her own photographer most of the time now too, especially on these fluff pieces. Noise from a nearby house made her spin in that direction. A police officer moved quickly to search the other home's backyard. What the heck was going on? Especially out front of that brown two-story home. From her vantage, she could barely see along the side of the house, but she spotted part of a large vehicle parked on the street.

Sophie jumped down and ran back to the sidewalk. Heels clicking on the cement, she strode to the next corner and rounded it. The department's bomb squad vehicle sat two houses away. Patrol SUVs blocked both ends of the street from traffic, but no officers were in sight. She kept moving, expecting to be challenged any moment.

Seconds later, she was. From behind her, a booming male voice commanded her to stop. Sophie pulled her camera, the zoom lens still in place, and took three quick images of the blocky rig that the squad used to detonate bombs when they found them. She'd seen the vehicle up close when she took the citizens' police academy.

Footsteps pounded behind her, pinging her nerves. She spun to face the officer. He'd likely been sitting in the unit at the end of the street when she passed it.

"Journalist!" she shouted, tucking her camera back into her bag.

The big guy, in his late forties, grabbed her arm and started dragging her back the way she'd come.

"Let go of me! I can walk on my own." She propelled herself forward to show she wasn't resisting.

The pressure on her arm let up, but the officer didn't

release her.

"Let go! I know Sergeant Lammers and I'm personal friends with Ed Barnes, the police auditor."

The officer released her arm. "Stay out of this area until it's clear. For your own safety."

Sophie walked away, too pleased with her scoop to even ask the man his name. Maybe she could leverage the photos to get more information about the murder. Now she just needed to find a busybody neighbor who wanted to gossip.

Chapter 9

Monday, May 7, 4:05 p.m.

Jackson strode back into the conference room, noticing that the DA and Quince had left. Schak and Evans, still standing near the monitor, turned.

"You and Bruckner tag-teamed him well," Evans said. "But Barulla is definitely a freak, so I'll check out his alibi as soon as I leave here."

Schak made a scoffing sound. "A hooker isn't much of an alibi, even if she does back up his claim."

"He's still our main suspect." Jackson picked up his satchel. "But we need to check into disgruntled clients as well. I'll get started on those." He nodded at Schak. "Check with the lab and see if they can give us a quick rundown on the contents of Holden's sausage. If there's chicken in it, that opens up a gaping hole for hundreds of possible suspects."

"You think being tricked into eating meat could make someone mad enough to commit murder?" Schak didn't sound skeptical; he was just clarifying.

"It's certainly possible."

"After reading some of the comments on the victim's blog, I think so too," Evans added. "Her followers consider animal protein to be a toxin and refer to it as *death*."

"But how would a consumer know?" Schak scowled. "I mean, unless they had the product tested."

"Maybe the neighbor who told you about the chicken

went public. Follow up with her and ask." Jackson made a mental note to search for the neighbor on social media sites when he was looking for the victim's consulting clients. "Let's get to work, then meet back here around seven."

"Are you buying pizza?" Schak raised an eyebrow.

"Sorry, no. I have to have a quick meal at home with the kids. Benjie still gets stressed if he doesn't see me all day." He had found the young boy at a crime scene, next to his dead mother. The toddler had bonded to him on sight, and when Jackson couldn't find any relatives, he'd felt compelled to adopt him.

Schak started for the door. "I think we have our perp in custody, so I'm not working late."

Jackson nodded, not wanting to push Schak too hard. They often worked around the clock during the first few days of a homicide, but they weren't young anymore—except Evans. Still, he was skeptical about Barulla as the killer. Jackson had the same doubt Schak had expressed earlier at the meeting. The murder had been up close and personal, and Barulla's pattern was to strike indirectly and from a distance, a cowardly MO. "See you at seven."

When Schak was gone, Evans touched his shoulder, caressing it seductively. "Let's have a drink after the meeting tonight and catch up."

His heart leapt in his chest. Finally, they would have a private moment. But what would come of it? Would she invite him home? Heart pounding, he smiled, unable to speak at first. *Keep it simple. Honest.* "I'd like that."

Her eyes held his long enough to convey that she'd missed him, that she wanted him. The urge to kiss her overwhelmed him and he turned away. Never at work. The department had cameras and people everywhere. "See you tonight," he called over his shoulder as he walked out.

In the hall, he headed for the area at the front of the building. Normally, the tech people didn't work late, but tonight they would at his request. The first day of a homicide investigation was critical. They had to find evidence before the perp destroyed it, then question him while he might still have remorse about the crime.

Officer Delarosa stood as he entered. She was young, wore her hair buzzed along the sides, and had never worked a patrol shift. When she was first hired, Schak had mocked her behind her back. But her computer forensic skills were so damn good, they'd started to call her the Hack. Jackson nodded. "Thanks for working late."

"No problem. This victim is interesting. I mean, she's kind of a nutcase." Delarosa grabbed a chair from the empty desk and pulled it over near hers.

Jackson sat. "Did you find FreedomGladiator?" When he'd dropped off Holden's phone and laptop earlier, he requested that Delarosa focus on tracking the troll who'd harassed the victim.

"Sort of. His posts originate out of Dallas, Texas, but it's likely a proxy server, and he could be anywhere. I haven't nailed down his profile yet." She glanced at him with sincere eyes. "Don't worry. I will."

Liking her passion, Jackson gave her a small smile. "Show me some of his messages."

"Here, I've got a printout. I bolded the worst of his threats." She handed Jackson a stapled report. "I know you old guys like things on paper."

That stung—but it was true. He needed copies of everything for task force meetings and to present to the district attorney. He started reading the comments.

FreedomGladiator had called Holden *a libtard, idiot vegan, piss-stained snowflake*, and *human cancer.* He'd also ranted about how people like her were *fucking up the American way of life* and *pushing their agenda on everyone.* Jackson scanned down, numb to the vitriol.

At the top of the second page, a post was printed in bold: *Real Americans arnt gonna take it anymore. Were coming 4 U and bringing the guns U hate so much.* Jackson ignored the typos and focused on the threat. Was it just online intimidation or something more serious? He thumbed through the stack of papers. Nine pages of comments, with five more that were bolded. He went back and read just those posts.

"None of the threats seem specific or indicate plans to travel here," Delarosa said, leaning toward him. "These all came from the victim's blog, by the way. She had deleted them, but the digital record was still there."

"Nothing to help ID the guy?" Jackson skimmed through the vague threats, thinking FreedomGladiator probably wasn't their perp.

"No, but I'm still working on a digital trace." She ran a finger along her earlobe. "Should we ask the FBI for help? Can they pressure Twitter to identify him?"

Jackson scoffed. "The bureau can't even locate potential school shooters from their tweets." He stood. "Don't waste too much time on this guy, since he's probably not local."

"I've got more." Her tone held a teaser of enticement.

Jackson sat back down. "Tell me."

"A local man named Aidan Emmerson sent Holden an email accusing her of fraud." Delarosa clicked keys on the victim's laptop as she reported the information. "Strange as this sounds, he claims she puts meat in her vegan sausages."

The technician opened an email and turned the laptop toward him. "He was pretty upset."

"Was?" Jackson made a note of the name.

"Holden responded and denied it, claiming she used paprika and fennel as flavor.

Jackson leaned in to read the message: *Why? Really, I want to know. Why would you put animal meat in a vegan product? Is it greed? Hoping to sell more? Or are you a carnivore who's trying to fuck with healthy people and feed us death? I CAN TASTE IT!*

The message wasn't signed, but the sender's email address was Aidan_Emmerson@hotmail.com.

"How do you know he's local?" Jackson asked.

"I found him on Facebook." Delarosa grinned. "No tech skills required."

"Show me his profile."

Delarosa quickly loaded the page. "He belongs to a community called Fruitopia, and it's located outside of Veneta."

A solid suspect to check out. Sometimes vegetarians and animal advocates valued animals' lives more than humans. Passion for a cause could cloud a person's judgment. "Text me the address or nearest locators."

"His Facebook posts are pretty weird," Delarosa commented. "But he doesn't seem angry or violent in that space."

"What kind of weird?"

"Stuff about how a fruit-only diet can heal any health issue, including cancer. And several discussions about purging toxins and going for weeks with no solid food at all, just smoothies."

"Maybe a lack of nutrients affected his brain," Jackson

mused, somewhat serious.

Delarosa chuckled. "People do get cranky when they're hungry."

"Have you copied all the laptop files? I'd like to take it and read some of the victim's posts. Get to know her a little."

"She's flaky." Delarosa flashed a smile. "But yes, I've copied the files. The phone data too, so you can have both." She handed him the laptop, and Jackson slipped it into his satchel.

He started to get up, then glanced at the technician. "Anything else?"

"Maybe." Her eyes twinkled with amusement.

Oh boy. This wouldn't be good. He eased back onto the chair. "What is it?"

"Photos of naked men on her phone. Maybe previous boyfriends?"

"Are you thinking blackmail?"

Delarosa shrugged. "It's just info. You're the detective."

"Any texts to go with the images? Any idea who the men are?"

"Not really." Her cheeks flushed pink. "But one of them looks like you."

Jackson felt his own face get warm. "You're not suggesting it's me, are you?"

"Oh no." She shook her head. "But seriously, if he wasn't blond, he could be your twin."

Dread filled his stomach. "Can you show me just his face, please?"

Delarosa picked up the purple-cased phone and scrolled through some photos. She covered the bottom half of the screen and held it out to him. "See what I mean?"

Oh crap. It was his brother Derrick.

Chapter 10

Monday, May 7, 6:05 p.m.

Evans stopped for a cheeseburger at the Five Guys deli near the expressway entrance and took the food to her car to eat. She had skipped fries so she could indulge in a little dark chocolate after her shift. She might still go for a late-night run . . . unless the drink with Jackson led to something much better. She wolfed down her meal, trying not to think about what it would be like to finally get naked with the man she'd loved for years. Jackson was unattainable. She'd learned that the hard way. They'd gotten close before, but something always interfered—usually his dedication to his family. The last time, he'd caught her off guard with a passionate post-case kiss, and the very next day, the police chief had asked her to represent the department in a team traveling to Costa Rica for hurricane-relief assistance. She hadn't been able to say no. She wanted the chief's job some day.

Evans wiped her hands, started her city-issued dark-blue sedan, and drove three blocks to the Whitaker neighborhood. The Whit, as the residents called it, was a odd mix now. Twenty years earlier, the area had been nothing but cheap-rent housing on the edge of the tracks, populated by low-wage earners, sex workers, and heroin addicts. Now breweries and restaurants occupied the main thoroughfare and brought in customers from nicer neighborhoods. But the hookers and druggies remained.

Right now, she was looking for a prostitute named Sunni. "With an I," their suspect had said. Fortunately, Evans had an address and a description. Sort of. Barulla the Bomber had described his supposed alibi as "kind of short with blonde hair, but dark on top. And nice breasts." He hadn't known her eye color or had any idea how old she was. But the prostitute lived in an "upstairs apartment in a big house on the corner of Third and Adams."

Evans made a quick right, confident she could find the place. The hooker might be anywhere at the moment, so this could turn out to be just her first effort. Sometimes she had to return multiple times to pin down a witness or suspect. She approached people where they worked whenever she could, but in this case, the alibi conducted her business at home. As Evans approached the next intersection, she groaned. All four corners held older two-story homes. She might have to knock on a few doors.

The curbs at the intersection were painted yellow and had No Parking signs. Evans pulled over anyway. She climbed out and looked around, grateful for the warm air and muted daylight. This assignment would have been more challenging in the winter. The house to her immediate right was the nicest of the four and didn't show any indication of being subdivided. Probably a single-family unit. She walked around the corner to check for exterior stairs, but didn't see any. She also didn't notice lights or hear any sounds. She would save this one for last.

Evans crossed the street, taking in the details of the second house. Faded off-white paint, top and bottom porches with wood railings, and a tall hedge blocking her view of anything but the front. She scooted to the right and searched for a break in the foliage. Not finding one, she backtracked and went around the front end of the hedge to enter the yard. As she made her way down a path of mossy concrete pavers, she smelled dog shit just before the barking started. The sound came from inside the house, so she kept going, her hand on the Sig Sauer under her jacket. She checked her inside pocket to make sure the cuffs were still there.

Rounding the back corner of the house, she spotted stairs leading to a door on the second floor. This could be the apartment. With a quick glance around for the dog—or anyone with an attitude—she bounded up the steps. The door jerked open before she could knock. A woman with harsh blonde hair and dark roots stood there, her mouth open in surprise.

Clearly, she'd been expecting someone else. "Detective Evans, Eugene Police."

The woman clutched the front of her faded-pink sundress, started to speak, then changed her mind. She stepped back and pushed the door.

Evans lurched forward and got her knee in the space before it latched. "Hey, you're not in trouble."

"Good. I'm still not talking to you."

But she didn't resist when Evans pushed the door back open. "What's your name?"

"Sunni. Why?"

"I need to ask you about one of your clients."

"What clients? I work at the Taco Bell down the street."

Evans glanced around at what she could see of the living room. A low-to-the-floor sofa bed, a prehistoric TV, and a kid's toy box. But no John or pimp that she could see. But having a kid didn't stop anyone from turning tricks. "Can I come in? I need to ask you about something really important. I don't care that you're a sex worker. A woman is dead."

Sunni blinked and her lower lip trembled. "Who? Someone I know?"

Evans waited.

The woman finally stepped aside and let her in, closing the door behind her.

"Who's dead? Tell me." Fear in her voice now.

"A vegan blogger. I'll show you her photo." Evans took out her tablet, loaded up Facebook, and opened the page she'd bookmarked earlier. She turned the screen toward Sunni. "Do you know her?"

The woman shook her head, relieved.

Evans logged into the county's jail records and did a quick search for Tony Barulla. He looked as ragged and stone-faced as everyone did in their mugshots. Evans held out the phone again. "Do you know him?"

For a moment, the hooker didn't respond. Then she let out a quick breath and asked, "Is Tony dead?"

Progress, finally. "No." Evans slipped her tablet back into her shoulder bag. "When was the last time you saw him?"

"Saturday night. He's a regular."

Damn. "What time was he here?"

"Around nine, like usual."

"When did he leave?"

"Before ten. I had another appointment."

So Barulla *could* have killed his neighbor. The ME's time-of-death window wasn't absolute. "You're certain about the times?"

"Yeah. I told you, he's a regular."

Even if the Bomber hadn't committed murder, they still needed to nail him for all the vandalism and maybe plotting something bigger. "What do you know about him?"

"Tony's nice to me. He often brings little gifts, like candy

65

or flowers he picked."

Huh? "Does he ever talk about himself or his hobbies?"

"Not really." Sunni plopped down on the couch, her hands clenched. "Is Tony in trouble? I don't believe he killed anyone."

Behind Evans, the door burst open. She spun, reaching for her weapon.

A skinny guy with neck tattoos charged into the room. "What the fuck is going on?" He stared hard at Sunni. "You're supposed to be workin' now."

"Stay back!" Evans yelled. "Eugene Police!" She scanned his body, looking for weapons. His hands were balled into fists, but she didn't see the bulk of a gun anywhere.

"Get the fuck out!" The pimp pointed toward the door. "This is my place and there's nothin' going on here."

"You get out! I'm talking to Sunni and I need five more minutes." Evans stepped toward him. "Now!" She gripped her weapon but didn't want to pull it yet.

The pimp ignored her and moved toward the woman. "Get in the bedroom. You ain't talkin' to no cops."

Sunni stood and scurried toward an open door near the tiny kitchen.

Evans tried to make up her mind about the situation. Technically, she was done questioning Sunni, but she wanted more information about Barulla if she could get it. And she hated pimps as much as she hated sexually abusive men, especially cops. "Get out or I'll arrest you for interfering with a police officer."

He pivoted toward her. "Don't be a bitch."

Wrong thing to say. "On your knees! Now!" Evans moved toward the pimp, ready to take him down and cuff him.

"Daddy?" A child's scared voice made them turn. A little

boy, too young for school, stood near the hall.

The pimp's shoulders slumped and his face softened. "Hey, Bubba. You should go back to bed. There's nothin' goin' on." He stared at Evans. "Five minutes," he said and sauntered out.

Chapter 11

Monday, May 7, 6:23 p.m.

Jackson pulled into the driveway and a wave of nostalgia hit him, followed by a vague sense of despair. He'd lived in this house as a kid, moving out during his marriage to Renee, then ending up back in the home after his parents were murdered. He'd also spent his whole life in the city of Eugene. What did that say about him? He liked to think he was loyal to his hometown, but maybe he was just boring and unambitious.

His son burst out the front door and ran toward him, smiling so big it made Jackson's heart melt. He climbed out and scooped up the boy in a tight hug. "Hey, Benjie. Did you have a good day?"

"I am now." The boy grabbed his face in both hands and kissed Jackson, a gesture he was still getting used to. His own parents hadn't shown him much physical affection, and even though he'd tried to do better with his own daughter, she tended to need a lot of body space. Benjie was the other extreme and had clung to him from the moment Jackson had pulled him out of the crawlspace at the crime scene.

"What did you do in school?" Jackson walked toward the house, carrying the boy and his shoulder bag. His whole body let him know how stupid that was, but he ignored the pain.

"We played with blocks and said letters." Benjie recited the alphabet as they entered the house, getting as far as M.

"Good job." Jackson detached himself, sat the boy at the table, and put his service weapon on top of the refrigerator. A delicious aroma filled his senses and his stomach growled. Something cheesy was in the oven.

Katie slipped into the room behind him. "Hey, Dad. You're kinda late."

He turned and grinned. "Maybe five minutes."

"What are you smiling about?" She pretended to be annoyed but didn't pull it off. With her short dark hair and upturned nose, his daughter looked so much like her mother now it unnerved him. But she was thinner than Renee and more striking. "You're cooking dinner. What is it?"

"Lasagna!" Benjie yelled from the table. "I grated the cheese."

"Thank you." Jackson gave Katie's forehead a quick kiss, then did the same with Benjie. "Sorry, but I have to go back to work later."

"Boo!" His son folded his arms across his tiny chest.

Guilt flooded Jackson. He'd never felt this bad about leaving Katie so he could work, but she'd had a mother. Now Katie was acting as Benjie's part-time mother and it wasn't fair. But it kept his unpredictable daughter out of trouble. He rumpled Benjie's hair. "I'll be here for awhile, so we'll have time together."

Jackson took a diet Dr. Pepper out of the fridge and downed a third of it.

"Right before dinner?" Katie scowled.

He burst out laughing and his daughter did too. Benjie joined in, just for fun.

"I'll save the rest." Jackson winked at Katie. "Should I set the table?"

"Please."

Halfway through the meal, Benjie realized he had to pee and ran to the bathroom. Katie took the opportunity to announce "I'm having a problem at school."

Another one? Jackson tried to keep his face sympathetic. "What's going on?" She'd been bullied for shaving her head in sympathy with a sick friend and had almost dropped out.

"Jason Rothwell is sexually harassing me and lying about it." His daughter's tone was matter-of-fact. When she'd lost her mother, Katie's innocence had died along with Renee, pushing his daughter into an early maturity that bordered on jaded.

"What exactly is he doing?" The term *sexual harassment* was so broad that it caused a lot of social confusion, especially for young men.

"He squeezes my butt and kisses me on the mouth. But he's careful to not ever do it in front of other people."

A flash of anger. "Where are you alone together?"

"Why? That's not the problem." Katie was defensive now. "The problem is that his mother is a teacher at the school so the principal downplayed the whole thing when I reported it."

Jackson tried not to sigh. "We'll go into his office together tomorrow after school." He realized his mistake immediately. "I mean *her* office." He'd met the woman when they discussed the bullying problem. His daughter had grown into a beautiful young woman in the last three years, and it created more problems for her than opportunities. She hadn't figured out yet what she wanted to do with her life, but she had no interest in being a cheerleader or model and he was glad for that.

Katie nodded. "Yeah, I would expect that kind of bullshit from a male principal, but not Mrs. Mayfair."

"Professional coworkers tend to protect each other—

until they're called out."

"You mean like cops do?" Katie gave him a disappointed look.

"Yeah, like that."

Benjie rejoined them at the table. "What's sexual harassment?"

Oh crap. Jackson grinned at the boy. "It's an adult thing. You don't have to worry about it."

"That's bullshit." Katie crossed her arms. "He goes to preschool, and the world is full of predators. We need to teach him about inappropriate touching."

Jackson sighed and patted Benjie's shoulder. "It's pretty simple. If someone touches your private parts and makes you uncomfortable, you need to tell me about it."

"And don't touch anyone else's private parts without permission," Katie added. "He might as well learn that early."

Benjie was quiet for a moment, then blurted out, "What if it's an accident?"

"Then say you're sorry and get back to playing." Jackson gave Katie a hard look. "Let's talk about something else."

After dinner, he put together puzzles with Benjie for a while, then explained that this was the first day of a new assignment and he had to get back to work. Benjie wasn't happy but he didn't complain. They'd met at his mother's homicide scene, so despite his young age, the boy understood what his dad did and why it was important. Jackson made promises to both kids about when he would spend more time with them, re-holstered his weapon, and hurried out.

At the department, he opened his case-note file and keyed in the information about Aidan Emmerson. Then he stared at the monitor for a long time. The other new information was about his brother. He knew in his heart

Derrick had nothing to do with the victim's death. And no one would ever identify his brother from the picture in Holden's phone. *Was he obligated to report the ID to his team?* He'd never left information out of a case file before. Because everything mattered. Sometimes the smallest details led them in a new direction that brought justice to the victim. What if all the men in the photos knew each other? Maybe they all worked out at the same gym. Maybe Derrick knew the killer. Jackson keyed in the Derrick detail, printed the updated file, and headed for the conference room.

As he stepped inside the long, narrow space, Schak lifted his head from the table. "Hey, I was just resting for a minute. I haven't been sleeping well lately."

Was he drinking again? Jackson pushed the thought aside. He'd had many sleepless nights himself, and most days, strong coffee was all that got him through. Besides, Schak was ten years older. "I could use a nap myself. Everything okay with you?"

"I'm good. It's Tracy. She gets up three times a night to pee, then I can't get back to sleep."

"Try the couch." Jackson laughed. "I can't believe she hasn't put you out there yet."

Evans walked in and slapped Schak on the shoulder. "Are you in the doghouse again? What did you do? Pee on the floor?"

"Funny." Schak didn't smile.

Jackson moved to the whiteboard, leaving his case notes on the table. "Let's make this a quick meeting. I want to put in a few more hours on the case tonight." He turned to Evans. "What have you got?"

"A sticky mess. I talked to the sex worker Barulla claims is his alibi. She confirmed that he was at her place Saturday night, but says he left before ten. That late, it's only a seven- or eight-minute drive. So technically, he could have gone straight home, then jumped over the back fence to Holden's place just in time to kill her."

"Unless the pathologist narrows the time-of-death window," Jackson said, trying not to swear. Ambiguity was such a time-suck. He needed Barulla to be either in or out as a suspect.

"Would she let him in?" Schak countered. "Unless they knew each other and were friends? There were no signs of forced entry and no signs of a struggle."

"Gunderson said he saw bruising around her mouth," Jackson reminded him.

Schak scowled. "I meant no jimmy marks on the front door or chairs turned over."

Now Evans jumped in. "She could have known the killer and invited him in. Maybe things went badly after that, and he shoved a sausage down her throat in rage."

A quiet moment while they all considered it.

Evans shook her head. "No, this doesn't seem like a crime of passion. More like a calculated murder, even though using the sausage was likely a spontaneous decision."

"We obviously need to dig deeper into her personal life." His brother's photo flashed in Jackson's mind. Time to tell his team. "Speaking of which, I have an odd detail to report." Jackson pulled in a breath. "There are images of naked men on the victim's phone. One of those men is my brother Derrick."

After a split second of silence, Schak burst out laughing. "I wish I could have seen your face when you caught sight of that."

Evans turned to him, her look and tone more serious.

"We have to put him on the suspect list. As well as identify and question all those guys." She winked. "I'll handle these leads."

"His name is Derrick." Jackson turned and wrote his brother's full name on the whiteboard, unease filling his stomach. "But he's been in the hospital, so he's not much of a suspect."

"What's going on with him?" Evans looked concerned.

"They don't know. He's had all kinds of weird issues in the last six months."

"Was he in the hospital Saturday night?" Schak asked.

"I think he went in early Sunday morning, but he'd been sick for days."

Schak was no longer amused. "Still, he's a viable suspect. What if our victim was blackmailing the men she had naked photos of?"

Evans locked eyes with Jackson. "I'll question Derrick tonight. Is he still in the hospital?"

"I assume so. He was there earlier today when I visited." *Had that really only been this morning?* It seemed like days ago. He stepped over to his shoulder bag and handed the victim's phone to Evans. "Delarosa copied all these files, and she might be able to help you identify the other men."

She grinned. "After dealing with a pimp and a hooker, it'll be nice to have a fun assignment."

Jackson smiled to be polite, but he wanted to stay focused. "You'll see in my notes that we have another suspect. Aidan Emmerson emailed Holden and accused her of putting meat into the vegan sausages she made. He seemed pretty angry, so I plan to question him as soon as I find him."

"We need to send a sample to the lab," Evans said. "They should be able to determine the contents."

"They have the sausage that the ME pulled from her throat," Jackson reminded her. "But they have to process trace evidence first so we won't likely get the food analysis for days." Ready to wrap up, he glanced back and forth at his team. "Anything else?"

"Not yet." Schak closed his notebook and stood. "I'm going home. I'll check back with more of the victim's neighbors in the morning."

Schak needed more than that on his plate. What else still needed to be assigned? "I want you to track down and question the clients that paid Holden thousands for nutrition counseling." Jackson flipped through the stack of papers he'd taken from the victim's house. "Paul Stagado and Flora Ardt." He handed Schak the invoices. "There are no addresses, but I'm guessing they both follow Holden on Facebook. We need to find out where they live and how they feel about the money they spent."

"Will do. Are we meeting tomorrow?"

"Let's gather for lunch here at noon. I have to attend the autopsy in the morning and track down Emmerson."

"See you then." As Schak walked out, Jackson gathered up his notes.

When they were alone, Evans whispered, "Are we still having that drink?"

Chapter 12

Jackson slid into a curved booth at Sixth Street Grill, and Evans eased in on the other side. He wanted her to scoot around beside him, but they were in public, and that would be stupid. The darkness of the bar offered no real privacy because other detectives, including those from the fraud and sex-crimes units, hung out here too. *Damn!* They should have gone somewhere else. Had he picked this place because he didn't trust himself to be alone with Evans? No, it was just habit from when they worked two blocks away.

"It's strange that your brother knows the victim." Evans broke into a grin. "Yet it's not. This is Eugene, where the connection threads pop up everywhere."

A server stopped at their table and asked what they wanted to drink. The skinny young guy was probably the only non-female on staff. Jackson started to order a beer, but Evans talked over him. "We'll have the house-special peach margaritas."

He never drank hard liquor and wasn't likely to finish his, but he didn't want to be a boring date. *This wasn't a date,* he reminded himself. They were colleagues, discussing a case. He gave Evans a small smile. "Are you celebrating something?"

"Being here with you. Especially after three months in rural Costa Rica. I got lonely. And I struggled with the language barrier. And the poverty."

"Do you feel good about what you accomplished though?"

"Yes and no. I spent a lot of time teaching basic safety practices to homeless women, so that was a positive. But there's so much damage and reconstruction that still needs to be done that it felt overwhelming. After a month, I just wanted out."

Jackson reached over and touched her hand. "I'm so glad you're back. I've been lonely too."

A pause. "Kera's still with her parents in California?"

"Yes. She wants me to take a week off to spend with her, but I'm not sure I can."

"You mean you don't want to."

He had mixed feelings, for sure. "I can't leave the kids, and I don't want to take Katie out of school." He laughed. "She wouldn't go with me anyway."

Evans leaned forward and spoke softly. "I'm glad you don't want to go see Kera. That means you're letting go of the relationship."

Jackson struggled for the right thing to say. He still loved Kera, but not in the same way as he had at first. They'd met on a homicide case he'd investigated, and he'd had to rush her to the hospital when she'd been attacked. They had both been newly divorced and vulnerable and needed each other. But so much had changed since then. "I think it's time."

"Before I left, you told me you loved me," Evans whispered.

He did love her, but he didn't know what it meant. He was afraid to get her hopes up . . . because he might get bogged back down in his own family drama. For reasons he didn't understand, letting himself love Evans and be with her felt selfish.

The server stepped up with their drinks, giving him

another moment. Finally, he said, "I do love you. But starting a new relationship feels unfair to Kera and my kids."

"How long are you going to put your life on hold for her?" Evans scooted toward him and placed a hand on his leg. "I'm here . . . in the flesh . . . right now." Emotion crept into her voice. "Our jobs are dangerous. We've both been shot, for Christ's sake. If this was your last day on earth, wouldn't you come home with me?"

Hell yes!

But it wasn't his last day and he had obligations. "You know I would. But I have to break off with Kera first. I owe it to both of you to be straight about this."

"So do it."

"I will." Jackson sipped his drink. "But we have to wait. This is already day two of a homicide, and we owe it to the victim to get back out there while the perp might not have covered his tracks yet."

Evans tipped her margarita back for a long slug, then nodded. "I knew you would stall again."

"Hey, we shouldn't even be sitting here like this in public. Especially with my brother as a possible suspect. I'm already going to be under scrutiny for how I handle this investigation. If anything goes sideways . . . " He trailed off, not sure how to clarify what he was thinking.

"I know. We have to be careful." Evans scooted back to her side of the booth. "So let's work for a few more hours, then meet back up at my place. I'll question Derrick at the hospital, and you can call Kera before you start tracking down Emmerson."

Jackson let out a soft laugh. Evans' tenacity was a big part of what made her a good detective, as well as strong enough to keep her place on the SWAT team. "We shouldn't make a plan. It's just asking for something to come up. A new suspect. An active shooter scenario. Maybe a riot in the university district."

Evans laughed too. "You're right. Let's get beyond the first few days of this investigation." She finished her drink. "Any advice on dealing with Derrick?"

"Flatter him; he's vain."

"If he looks anything like you, complimenting him will be easy." She stared into his eyes. "Any chance he had anything to do with Holden's death?"

"No. Our perp is someone with a fresh passion to hurt her, or at least shut her up."

"Is Derrick involved with anyone now?"

"A woman named Nicky Walker. They've been together about a year, a new record for him."

Evans cocked her head. "Why would a man who's old enough to know better let a woman take a picture of him naked?"

He shuddered a little at the thought. "I don't know why women do it either. They have more to lose."

"What do you mean?"

Jackson realized he'd stepped on thin ice. "I just mean men are more likely to share an image like that with their friends, or online."

"Good save." She smiled and reached for her jacket. "We should go. If I'm not getting laid tonight, I'm not investing any more time in this date."

That made him smile. *Damn,* he loved her honesty and humor. As they stood up together, he whispered back, "If you really care about me, you'll wait until I'm ready."

Evans laughed. "Three years and counting."

In the parking lot, she hugged him around the shoulders.

"Call me if anything comes up on this case."

"You know I will." Once, he'd pulled his team out of bed in the middle of the night to pursue a new lead. That was the nature of their job. He wanted to kiss her again, but resisted the urge. Not in a well-lit downtown public parking area. "See you soon."

"I hope so." Evans sauntered toward her car.

Jackson turned toward his, wondering if he'd made yet another mistake with Evans. As he climbed in his sedan, his phone rang. The name on the screen made his heart miss a beat: *Kera Kollmorgan*.

His hand trembled and he nearly dropped the phone. *Was he ready to tell her that he was moving on?* Maybe she was calling to tell him the same thing. He put in his earpiece, pulled in a deep breath, and pressed the answer button. "Hey, Kera."

"Wade, I have both good and bad news."

She rarely called him by his first name. No one did. But she sounded calm. Maybe too calm. "What's going on?"

"My father died this morning."

"Oh no. I'm so sorry. Are you doing all right?"

"Strangely, yes. It's mostly a relief for both of us at this point."

"Still, I wish I was there for you." He meant it—in theory. Yet he was grateful he wasn't actually dealing with her pain. Then immediately felt guilty for thinking that.

"It's okay. Dad's been slowly dying since I got here." She let out a short, controlled breath. "His memorial service is tomorrow, then I'm coming home."

Taken aback, Jackson floundered for the right response. "That's great news. I've missed you." The thought of holding her in his arms made his heart surge, then ache with more guilt.

"Good, because you know I sold my house, so Micah and I need a place to stay."

Chapter 13

Jackson pulled into his driveway and sat for a few minutes, his thoughts racing. Kera would be here the day after tomorrow. Three months ago, that news would have been joyful, but now it terrified him. Impatient with waiting, he'd decided in his head that she wasn't coming back at all. So he'd shut down part of his love to protect himself. Now Kera was about to sleep in his bed—and he had just told Evans he planned to break things off with his estranged girlfriend. For months, neither woman had been in his life and he'd been painfully lonely. Now they were both present, and it terrified him. If he messed this up, he could hurt both women and end up alone. Maybe that's what he deserved, but they didn't.

Just be honest.

With that decided, he headed inside. He needed to focus on the investigation and not let his personal life distract him. A woman had been murdered, and they'd already passed the forty-eight hour window that was critical for finding the suspect. Now his team was working against the odds to close this case.

The lights were on, but the house was quiet. Jackson put his service weapon into the locked case on the bedroom dresser. It opened with the press of his finger—and only his—so he could access it quickly. He tapped on Katie's door to let her know he was home. Or more honestly, to hear her voice and know that she was all right. She had been doing well—and staying sober—for nearly a year now. Before that, she'd scared the hell out of him by running away from home so she could drink through her grief.

He took off his shoes, then grabbed his phone from his jacket pocket before hanging it up. A quick glance through the calls he'd ignored revealed one from his doctor and one from Sophie Speranza. He would get back to both of them tomorrow.

He pulled the victim's laptop from his shoulder bag and settled into his recliner to work for a few hours. Normally, he would have searched the device already, but finding the explosives at the neighbor's house had focused the whole team on Barulla as a suspect. After leaving Evans earlier, he'd driven out to the Veneta area where the Fruitopia community was located. But in the dark, he hadn't been able to find the turnoff road, so he would try again in the morning.

Holden's Facebook page opened with a colorful banner and *Tayla's Tribe* in a large, script-style font. Combined with her four-thousand friends and followers, the label indicated that Tayla considered herself a guru or spiritual leader of sorts. He scanned through her posts to get a feel for what she offered her tribe and discovered mostly deepisms—meaningless feel-good messages—as well as encouragement to "eat clean." He'd heard the expression but suspected that everyone used it in a different way.

A glance at a few dozen comments revealed that her followers were mostly loyal and supportive but tended to be illiterate. Some seemed to have taken eating clean to an extreme and had posted about eating nothing but apples for three days or *dry fasting* for a week, whatever that meant. A guy named Pom bragged about becoming a *breatharian*. No food or nutrients at all? *Really? Darwinism at work.*

Even after scrolling back a week, the FreedomGladiator troll didn't show up. Holden had probably deleted his comments and blocked him. Jackson logged into her messages, still hoping to find a boyfriend or a female friend who would know who Tayla had been dating. Most of the texts were questions about nutrition or requests for vegan recipes. But he came across one from a woman named Flora who was upset about the nutrition coaching she'd paid for. She claimed that eating vegan had made her lifeless and depressed, and she wanted her $2000 back. Tayla had agreed to refund half, and Flora had eventually settled for it. Jackson wondered if Holden had actually given the money back. He clicked to her Facebook listing and noticed that she was in Germany. Not a likely suspect.

Back on Holden's page, he accessed the link to her blog and skimmed through a few essays. When he landed on the one he'd seen earlier about safe detoxing for children, his disgust reached a peak and he had to close out. Tayla Holden had taken the natural lifestyle to an extreme. Or at least she pretended to online so she could cultivate a following and extract money from gullible people. But he couldn't let his personal feelings interfere with his investigation.

He shut down the browser to search through the personal files on her hard drive. Most were business-related: tax documents, promotional material, and letters to clients. A subfolder revealed a collection of other people's blogs pasted into Word documents. She plagiarized her content? No wonder Holden didn't seem to have any close friends. Unlike her online followers, the people who got to know her in person probably didn't like her.

A file marked *Medical Stuff* caught his eye. He scanned through PDFs of hospital bills, feeling like he was wasting his time. But a Word file triggered his curiosity and he opened it. Holden had written a passionate letter to a doctor, describing her intense chronic pain and pleading with him not to end her Percocet prescription.

Was the victim an opioid addict?

Jackson made a note of the doctor's name, then checked the date the letter file had been opened. Nearly two years earlier, so it wasn't likely relevant anymore. At the scene, he had searched her bedroom and bathroom and hadn't seen any prescription bottles. Had she found another way of treating her pain or had it diminished? If he had time, he would search her house again, keeping in mind that a woman who preached the natural way might feel compelled to hide her pharmaceutical stash.

Chapter 14

Tuesday, May 8, 5:55 a.m.

Evans woke before the alarm and bolted out of bed. As she hurried to the kitchen, she listed her tasks for the day: question Derrick Jackson, talk to the technician about identifying the other images from Tayla's phone, and figure out who the victim had been sleeping with. Intimate partners turned out to be the perpetrators at least seventy percent of the time.

Her new single-cup coffeemaker was ready to roll, so she added hot water, then sat at the table and turned on her tablet to scan the news headlines. She'd made a trip out to the hospital the night before, but Derrick had already checked out. After considering a trip to his house, she'd decided to skip it and go for a run instead. Besides the fact that she didn't really think he was guilty, he would probably be more cooperative this morning.

The national news had another headline about a famous actress coming forward with a me-too account of sexual harassment. A not-so-well-known executive had too. Evans was pleased every time a woman spoke out. For each one who talked about it, there were dozens who suffered in silence. At eighteen, she'd been physically abused and sexually coerced by a police officer who'd threatened to send her to jail if she didn't give him a blowjob. She'd left Alaska shortly after, straightened up her act, and instead of hating all cops, she'd decided to become one. Law enforcement needed more women and people of good character.

Evans poured coffee, then signed into the department's incident log, scanning for anything else of interest. Another robbery in the campus area and a local hospital employee accusing her boss of sexual assault. The movement was still gaining momentum. Evans hoped it would discourage predators. But some men, especially those in power, felt invincible.

She changed into workout clothes, then entered the bedroom she'd turned into a kickboxing area—by padding the floor and walls. Headphones in place, she cranked up her electronic dance music and sparred with an imaginary partner for thirty minutes. The firefighter she'd dated recently had occasionally worked out in here with her, but she hadn't fought any real matches in years.

An hour later, she parked in front of a quaint house in the River Road area. Built in the fifties, the style was boxy with painted shutters and a small covered porch. An older white truck and a red Mazda took up every inch of the driveway. That meant Derrick and his girlfriend were both likely home. She would question them separately. Talking about an ex-girlfriend in front of the current one could be volatile.

A bizarre thought hit her as she hustled up to the front door. Derrick's current girlfriend—Nicky, she remembered—might have killed his ex out of jealousy. Especially if she found out that Holden still had Derrick's naked photo on her phone. *Oh boy.* This would be a fun conversation.

The woman who answered her knock scowled at Evans through the screen door. She had long thick hair, lush pouty lips, and substantial cleavage. Her face wasn't all that pretty, but most men would find her attractive anyway. "Detective

Evans, Eugene Police. I need to speak with Derrick Jackson."

"What about?"

"I'll tell him when I see him. Step aside, please."

The woman hesitated, then pushed open the screen. "Please make it quick. He just got home from the hospital."

Evans moved inside, asking, "What's your name?"

"Nicky Walker. I'm Derrick's girlfriend and roommate."

"Do you know someone named Tayla Holden?"

"No. Should I?"

The girlfriend sounded calm and confident but didn't look Evans in the eyes. Time to push her buttons. "Have you ever heard Derrick talk about Tayla?"

Nicky's eyes narrowed. "No. Who is she?"

"You can ask Derrick after I talk to him." Evans glanced around, not seeing him. The house was cluttered but tidy and smelled like cat. She turned back to Nicky. "Where were you Saturday night?"

"What?"

"Saturday night between nine and midnight. Where were you?"

Her brow crease deepened. "Right here, taking care of Derrick. He finally let me drive him to the hospital around three in the morning."

For the moment, Evans believed her. She wanted to move on, but Nicky was still talking. "The doctors were so glad I did. Derrick's blood pressure was scary low. I may have saved his life."

A drama queen? Evans gave her a supportive look. "Where is Derrick? I need to see him now."

"This way." Nicky gestured for Evans to follow. They walked through the kitchen toward a side door. "We converted the garage into a bedroom to have more space for our king-size bed," she explained. "The rooms in the house are too small for anything but storage." As she opened the door, she called out, "We're coming in."

The man in bed sat up, looking pale but otherwise physically fit. His bare upper body was skinny but he still had a six-pack. Evans caught herself staring. He looked a lot like Jackson, only with dirty-blond hair and hazel eyes. Her attraction to him surprised her.

While he pulled on a T-shirt, Evans introduced herself and glanced around. The room had pale yellow walls and thick chocolate-colored carpet. Kind of nice for a garage.

Evans noticed the girlfriend still hovering. "Will you give us the room, please?"

Again Nicky hesitated before complying. "Don't over-stress him," she pleaded on her way out.

Derrick gave a half-smile "She worries too much about me." His eyes were dull, like someone who'd had the flu.

"Since you're not well, I'll get right to the point. Where were you Saturday night between nine and midnight?"

"Uh, home. Puking and shaking."

The couple was consistent in their response, but they could have rehearsed it. "What's wrong with you?"

"They can't seem to figure it out." A edge of worry. "Why are you asking about Saturday night?"

"I'll get there. When was the last time you saw Tayla Holden?" Evans shifted, feeling uneasy. She'd never questioned someone in their bed before.

"More than a year ago. What is this about?"

"Your naked photo is in her phone."

"Oh shit. She took that without my permission."

Nicky burst into the room. "Another woman has a picture of your junk? Why didn't you tell me?"

Evans stepped over, blocking Nicky from approaching the bed. "Just get out. You can talk to him about this later." The new girlfriend started to seem viable as a suspect, except for her alibi with Derrick. Evans softened her tone. "You and I can talk about Tayla in a moment too."

Nicky's eyes flashed with conflicted emotions. "Okay. I'm sorry. I'm just tired. I haven't slept much since Derrick got sick." She backed out the door.

Evans closed it and refocused on Derrick. "Did you fight with Tayla about the photo?"

Confusion twisted his pretty face. "Well, yeah. At the time. We broke up soon after."

"Did she ever blackmail you with it?"

"What? Of course not." He made a scoffing sound. "Even if she did threaten to post the picture, I wouldn't care enough to pay her off. Tayla is weird, but she's not a blackmailer."

"Weird how?" Evans noticed a small trunk, pulled it over, and sat down. She didn't mind being on her feet, but she liked to make eye contact with people she questioned.

"She's a vegan, but she makes exceptions. She's emphatic about not putting any chemicals on her skin, but she smokes pot." Derrick rolled his eyes. "And she purges all the time. I couldn't take it."

Evans guessed at what that meant, and it wasn't a pretty image. Derrick seemed sincere, but she didn't trust her judgment about him. "Do you know anyone who might want her dead?"

"What? Tayla's dead?" His eyes registered surprise.

Oops. She hadn't handled that well. "Yes, I'm sorry to have to tell you that she was likely murdered."

Derrick's face went blank and he was silent for a long moment. Finally, he shook himself as if to snap out of it. "We only dated for a few months, and I haven't seen her in over a year. So sorry, but I can't help you."

Evans stood. "If you think of anything important, let me know." She pulled a business card from her bag and handed it to him. As he reached for it, color drained from his face, and he started to shake. The card dropped to the bed. Alarmed, Evans asked, "Do you need medication? An ambulance?"

Derrick's body convulsed and he abruptly vomited—right on the bedspread.

Startled, Evans jumped up. Nicky rushed into the room, yelling, "This is your fault! I told you not to stress him."

Jackson's brother vomited again, then blacked out, and fell over.

Evans grabbed her phone and called 911.

Chapter 15

Tuesday, May 8, 7:55 a.m.

Jackson took the elevator down to the basement of the old hospital. The cool, stagnant air made him miss the spring sunshine he'd just left outside. As he walked the short hallway, he braced himself, then pushed open the door at the end. The room's white paint, bright lights, and gleaming stainless steel made him blink. The smell of decaying flesh and powerful disinfectant burned his nostrils.

Called "Surgery 10" for unknown reasons, the morgue was one of his least favorite places. But attending autopsies didn't feel optional. Especially when the *manner* of death was uncertain. Tayla Holden's *cause* of death was obvious: asphyxiation, or lack of oxygen to the body. But whether the sausage in her throat was accidental or homicidal would be determined by the pathologist. If he couldn't find enough physical evidence either way, he might even label it "undetermined."

"Good morning, Jackson. Thanks for being on time." Rudolph Konrad's deep voice contrasted with his fleshy baby face, but his demeanor was consistently deadpan and precise.

"Hello, Konrad." Jackson grabbed a paper gown from the shelf and pulled it on. He donned booties, gloves, and a mask too. The barriers protected him from anything the corpse might give off and kept the trace evidence on the body from being contaminated.

Konrad handed him a small bottle of mint oil. Jackson removed the stopper, put a few drops inside his nose, and handed it back. The intensely pleasant smell didn't cover the rot, but it helped. "Where's Gunderson?" The medical examiner usually attended the autopsies as well.

"He's out on another call. Death never rests." The pathologist gestured to a bank of large metal drawers against the end of the narrow room. "Shall we?"

Damn. Gunderson usually helped prep and move the bodies. Jackson nodded and grabbed one side of the wheeled table. They rolled it to the wall, and Konrad opened the top drawer on the left. Together, they slid the corpse out of its cold storage and onto the autopsy gurney. After they moved Holden under the bright exam lights, Jackson stood near the end of the table, distancing himself from her face. Dead bodies were evidence, facts to process. Dead faces were people whose lives were gone, individuals who would never laugh or smile again. He'd seen enough.

The pathologist reached for his tool tray and rolled it Jackson's way. Konrad was about to began the inch-by-inch search of the victim's skin, starting with the feet, as usual.

"Can we start with her head? I need to know if this was just a choking accident. I can't let my team waste time tracking down leads for a crime that didn't happen."

Konrad gave him a frustrated look. "All right." He rolled the tray back into place at the other end and searched the victim's long hair and scalp. "She has minor swelling in her squamous bone at the hairline." He pressed his gloved hands against the dead woman's nose. "Some swelling in her bridge too. Both probably caused by falling face first to the floor." He looked over at Jackson. "Based on what I saw in Gunderson's death-scene photos."

Jackson forced himself to nod and be patient.

The pathologist examined Holden's eyes, noting, "Subconjunctival hemorrhage," the technical term for broken blood vessels, which were always evident in asphyxiation. Konrad reached for a large magnifying glass to examine the area around the woman's lips, then stretched her lips to look inside her mouth. After a moment, Konrad took a thin pair of tongs and retrieved a small piece of trace evidence from her throat. He carefully placed it into a small glass container and screwed on a lid. "There's bruising around her mouth, caused by pressure and a tear on the inside of her cheek, mostly likely caused by her own capped tooth."

"Are you saying someone held her mouth open and shoved a sausage into her throat?"

"That's what the evidence points to." Konrad squirmed, something Jackson had never seen him do.

"But?"

"It's not an easy thing." Konrad put down his tools and acted out a demonstration on the deceased. "You only have one hand to control the person because you have to hold the choking item in the other. And the victim will fight you." The pathologist stepped back, thinking it over.

Jackson tried to visualize himself pulling that off with an average-sized adult woman. *Maybe.* "The perp would have to be really strong, or she would have to be sedated. Or both." He remembered the half-empty wine bottle in Holden's bedroom. Was that enough alcohol to make the victim compliant? Or had it been combined with another sedative?

"It could have been initiated as sexual foreplay," the pathologist said, still deadpan.

"What?"

"Some people feed each other as sexual stimulation."

Konrad gave a small shrug. "Knowing these things is part of my job."

Jackson visualized the scene again. "You think the victim might have allowed the perpetrator to put the sausage into her mouth, thinking he meant it as seduction? Then he forced it into her throat and held her mouth closed?"

"Or it became lodged in her trachea by accident."

"What about the bruising? And the inner cheek bite?" Jackson imagined the man in a panic when his lover started turning blue. If it had been an accident, he would have given Holden the Heimlich maneuver.

Konrad nodded. "The evidence points to homicide as a manner of death, but I want to see her blood toxicology before I make a final determination."

Jackson was convinced. Someone had murdered Tayla Holden. The K scratched in the floor made more sense than ever. Suddenly impatient, he wanted to bolt from the room and get back to the investigation. But he owed it to the victim to see what else her body might reveal. "What about time of death? Can you narrow the window Gunderson gave us?"

"Not until I see her organs."

Jackson didn't want to stay for that.

Konrad moved on, gently probing her neck. "No bruising or abrasions on her carotid and no other signs of struggle." He kept going, making verbal notes into a mounted recorder as he went along. While he waited to hear something significant, Jackson kept his brain busy thinking about the investigation, making lists and observations in his head. He was still waiting for the tech specialist to get back with information about the online troll who'd harassed Holden. Law enforcement across the country was finally waking up to the realization that online threats could quickly turn into real-life crime.

"There is lividity in her breasts, confirming that she fell and lay face down while dying."

Jackson glanced at the pale body, noting the purplish discoloration in her belly and thighs, where blood had pooled after her heart stopped beating. But feeling voyeuristic, he quickly looked away.

After a few more minutes, Konrad announced, "She has surgery scars on the inside of her left knee and calf area. They are consistent with the bone scan I did this morning, showing a titanium plate on her tibia. She broke her leg a few years back and also had an arthroscopic knee surgery. Both could have resulted from a skiing accident."

The letter she'd written came to mind. No wonder she'd been in chronic pain and had pleaded with a doctor for pain meds. Yet none of that information was helpful. Jackson started to tune back out, but Konrad wasn't done. "She also has a C-section scar that looks about twenty years old."

That was news. Despite having no photos or references to a child in her personal things, Tayla Holden had given birth. Unless the child had died, he or she was still out there somewhere. The long-ago birth wasn't likely relevant, but it could be. Many children given up for adoption sought out their biological parents as adults. And often, those parents didn't want to be found.

Chapter 16

Tuesday, May 8, 8:05 a.m.

Sophie checked her email and ignored all of it. Nearly every message was from a public relations person. The few from newspaper readers could be dealt with later. Eager to find the occupant of the house where she'd seen the bomb squad vehicle, she opened Google Earth and searched for the property. She had wanted to get it done yesterday, but after writing a short piece on Tayla Holden's death, she'd had to attend a department meeting, then, as directed, find a new female entrepreneur to feature.

On screen, she counted three houses from the corner she had approached from, then zoomed in on the address. This was the easy part. Getting the county to give her the owner's information over the phone would be more challenging. She called the property-tax assessor's office and let it ring eight times before hanging up.

A trip down to the courthouse seemed necessary, but she'd only been at work a few minutes, so she felt a little weird about leaving just yet. She opened a file and started to write a follow-up piece about Holden's murder but realized she didn't have any new information. She called Jackson again, left another message, then tried Detective Evans, who was sometimes more cooperative. Evans didn't answer either.

Feeling shut out, Sophie contacted her girlfriend in the crime lab. Jasmine had worked late the night before—as she always did when they had a new homicide—so Sophie hadn't seen her or talked to her yet.

Jasmine picked up, sounding rushed. "Sophie, you know I'm swamped, so I'll see you later this week."

"Dinner Thursday?"

"Probably."

"Can you please give me something on Tayla Holden's death? I can't get the detectives to return my calls."

"They're very busy." Jaz lowered her voice to a whisper. "She asphyxiated on a sausage."

Seriously? "You mean her own product?"

"Probably."

A salacious detail for her write-up. But the cop stationed in front of Tayla's house had said *crime scene*. "Did she choke on it by accident? I thought this was a homicide."

"It is. We'll talk more later." Jasmine hung up.

Sophie fleshed out her story with the new information, grabbed her bag, and headed downstairs.

The property-tax office took up a large space in the lower level of the county courthouse and usually had a long line. Not this morning. All three counter windows were occupied, but only one person stood waiting. Sophie went past the counter to the archive area, logged on to the county database, and plugged the Grant Street address into the search field. A file loaded seconds later, another surprise. The homeowner, Anthony Barulla, had purchased the house five years earlier. Sophie jotted down the sale price and tax lot information, knowing none of it would matter.

On her way back to the newspaper office, she cruised by the house and it looked quiet. Crime-scene tape crossed the door, but no police cars or activity were evident. Now that the law enforcement people were gone, she could try interviewing neighbors. Sophie parked in Barulla's driveway and walked next door. No one was home, so she tried the house on the other side.

The older woman who answered claimed, "Tony was a quiet guy who kept to himself," then closed the door in Sophie's face. She had no luck across the street either, so she got back into her car and drove around the block. The police vehicles were gone from this area as well. Out of curiosity, Sophie pulled down Tayla Holden's driveway, wanting to see the house and the business operation she had intended to write about. An orange portable police barrier had been moved off the concrete and sat next to the fence on one side. She rounded the bend and saw a small white car parked in front of the house. A woman with long silver hair leaned against the hood, staring at the home. She parked and walked over. "I'm Sophie Speranza, a reporter with the *Willamette News.*"

"Ginger Holden. This is my daughter's house." Late fifties and pretty, the woman's eyes were full of pain.

Finally! Someone who might answer questions. "I'm so sorry for your loss. Tayla's death is such a tragedy."

"It's heartbreaking. But Tayla attracted such vitriol for her beliefs that I've been worried about this for a while." The mother's lips trembled as she fought to control her emotions.

"Vitriol from who?" Clearly, she hadn't done enough research into her subject's personal life.

"You know, the ugly trolls who hate anyone unconventional. A guy named FreedomGladiator, in particular."

Sophie wondered if she could subtly pull a notepad from her purse. Or maybe just get out her recorder. "You think he killed her?" At least she had a new detail for her article.

"I don't know." Tears filled Mrs. Holden's eyes. "Tayla was such a vital woman. At least until her motorcycle accident."

"When was that?"

"About five years ago. It almost killed her, then left her in chronic pain." A small smile. "I'm so amazed that she managed to start a business."

Damn. Maybe she would write a posthumous profile. "I'd love to know more about your daughter. I was scheduled to interview her for a feature about local women entrepreneurs."

"I'm not sure I'm ready to talk yet. My grief is still raw. I just came down from Portland to be near her." She wiped away her tears. "I had hoped to stay in Tayla's house and start sorting through her things while I planned her memorial service."

Sophie glanced at the cottage. "It's locked?"

"Yes."

"Call Detective Evans and see if she'll let you in. The team seems to be done here."

"Evans. Got it. Maybe later." The mother sighed. "Poor Tayla. She tried so hard, but men could never be serious about her, so she gave up. The pain changed her personality. Then she went through so many doctors after the accident, trying to deal with the aftermath." She tugged her sweater closed, in spite of the warm sun. "But because of the addiction epidemic and the damn DEA, doctors are all paranoid now about prescribing opioid medication. It's so unfair to people who live in daily agony."

Sophie sensed there was more to the story. "Did Tayla finally get help? I mean for her pain?" She didn't want the grieving mother to think she had called her daughter an addict.

"She went to a pain clinic and things got better for her. That's when she started the vegan-sausage business." The mother choked out a half-laugh, half-cry noise. "My girl was full of surprises."

Sophie's phone rang in her purse and she considered ignoring it. But what if Jackson or Evans were finally returning her calls? Sophie excused herself and slipped the cell out. Jasmine. She turned to Mrs. Holden. "I have to take this."

"That's fine. I'm leaving anyway."

"Nice talking to you." Sophie answered her phone as she walked to her car. "Hey, Jaz. What's up?"

"A little detail I picked up this morning from the autopsy report." Her girlfriend was whispering again. "Tayla Holden had a C-section scar, so she has a child that nobody seems to know anything about."

A secret child? Plus an online harasser, a possible drug addiction, and death by murder. A surge of excitement pulsed in Sophie's veins. This was starting to shape up as an intriguing profile piece.

Chapter 17

Tuesday, May 8, 9:35 a.m.

In the bright, blue-sky morning, the drive out to Veneta was more pleasant than it had been the night before. The blink-and-you'll-miss-it town was ten miles from Eugene on the way to the coast, and the commune he was looking for was a few miles south. Now that he was out of town, Jackson put in his earpiece and called Southside Medical again. A Google search that morning had connected the doctor on Holden's letter to this practice. His earlier effort had gotten a recorded message.

This time a receptionist answered and put him on hold. He glanced over at the reservoir he was passing and noticed that someone was out sailing. When the woman came back, Jackson cut in. "I'm a detective with the Eugene Police and I need to speak with Dr. Obbert."

"I'm sorry, but she retired a year ago."

"What happened to her patients? Did they transfer to another doctor?"

"Yes, but they all went to different family practitioners. Why do you ask?"

"I'm trying to find Tayla Holden's doctor. Is she still a patient there?"

"I can't release that information."

"The woman was murdered and I'm trying to find out why. Just tell me if she was a patient."

"Spell her name, and I'll check with my supervisor." She sounded as cranky as he had.

While he waited, he sped past two slow-moving cars and thought about what he would ask the new suspect. The receptionist was suddenly back in his ear. "Tayla Holden hasn't been a patient here in the last two years, so we have no medical records for her."

A dead end. "Thanks."

Jackson slowed, turned on Crow Road, and tapped his phone. The GPS directional voice told him to make a right in "two.point.five" miles. He'd keyed in the address before leaving his house. A few minutes later, the voice gave him a "five hundred feet" message so he slowed down. The access was barely visible as a break in a large patch of blackberry shrubs. No wonder he'd missed it the night before.

After he bounced through a series of deep ruts, the dirt road smoothed out. He passed an apple orchard and a large pond with a handful of ducks. Up ahead, the lane ended with a cluster of buildings. As he drew closer, he realized it was a patchwork of houses, all different sizes and styles, with a large flat-roof structure in the center. He had checked out their website, and they claimed to be a "supportive community dedicated to living a natural lifestyle." Some of the occupants were renters, but most had bought land ownership during the founding phase. He parked in front of the first home, a faded two-story farmhouse that was likely the original building. As Jackson climbed from his vehicle, a man stepped out the front door.

"This is private property. How can I help you?" Tall and balding, he sported a long beard and cut-off jeans.

"Detective Jackson, Eugene Police. I'm looking for Aidan Emmerson."

The man stared, silent, for a long moment. "Aidan's a good man and you can find him in that blue house." He pointed down the dirt road to a structure three-hundred feet away. The home was dome-shaped and constructed of triangle-shaped components.

Jackson decided to leave his car where it was parked and walk over. It might be his only opportunity to stretch his legs today. His intestinal pain flared up halfway there, and he started to wonder about his ability to function as an effective police officer. Investigative work usually didn't require much physical exertion, but occasionally he had to chase someone down. And if the city experienced an emergency—such as an active shooter or unruly protest—then every officer was called out. Was he still fit to serve?

Ignoring the pain, he pounded on the suspect's door. "Eugene Police! Open up!"

A moment later, it flew open. The man's fearful expression gave Jackson pause. He introduced himself in a calmer tone, then said, "Tell me your name."

"Aidan Emmerson." Wearing only baggy shorts, his ribs stuck out of his tanned bare chest and he looked about thirty. But it was hard to tell under the three-day stubble.

"I have some questions for you." The stink of clove incense wafting from the house made Jackson glance at the porch chairs. "Let's sit out here."

Emmerson perched on the edge of a wicker chair, his thin face still worried. His curly shoulder-length hair made him look harmless.

Jackson didn't let that disarm him. "When was the last time you saw Tayla Holden?"

"From Tayla's Tribe?"

"Yes."

"I don't know her. We're just online acquaintances." He scratched his beard and looked away.

Jackson didn't believe him but decided to circle back to it later.

"What's this about?" Emmerson tried to sound calm, but he was clearly nervous.

"Your angry message to her."

His body tensed. "Tayla is a fraud and her product is poison. Someone needed to call her out."

"You mean her vegan sausages?"

"They have meat in them!" he shouted. "I can't prove it but I can taste it."

"This is very upsetting to you."

"Of course it is. Food politics are my life."

Would he have admitted that if he were guilty? "Where were you Saturday night between nine and midnight?"

"For most of the evening, I was at a friend's house, celebrating his birthday. I got home around eleven."

"Give me his name and address." Jackson pulled out his notepad.

"I only know him as Tree."

Oh boy. "Where does he live?"

"Somewhere in Noti. I rode out there and back with another friend and wasn't paying attention to street names."

"What were you high on?"

A flash of panic in his eyes. "Nothing. Please tell me what this is about."

"Are you sure you've never met Tayla? She seems to think you did."

His shoulders slumped. "Okay, I did. But it was a brief introduction at an herbal conference. I don't know her personally."

"Why lie?"

"I didn't lie. I said I didn't know her, and that's true."

"But you hate her." It wasn't a question.

"She disgusts me. And she made me hate myself for eating an animal's dead flesh."

"Have you fantasized about killing her? Maybe feeding her some of her own sausage as you strangle her?"

His eyes popped open wide. "What are you talking about? Did something happen to Tayla?"

"Someone killed her with her own product, and you are a likely suspect."

"No. Just no." He stood, his hands flailing.

Jackson stood too. "This conversation isn't over."

"I've never hurt anyone. I don't even kill flies. I just shoo them outside." Tears rolled down his face. "You have to believe me."

The theatrics seemed overplayed. He would have to check out Emmerson's alibi and question others in the community to see if the man had ever talked about hurting Holden. Jackson's phone beeped, and he pulled it from his pocket. A text from Evans. "Excuse me." He stepped off the porch and read the message: *Derrick is back in the hospital and not doing well.*

Damn! Jackson turned to the suspect and handed him a business card. "Find the address of the party you were supposedly at and text it to me. Along with the names of three people who were there and their phone numbers. I want it all before the day is over or I'm coming back to arrest you."

Emmerson blinked rapidly but didn't respond.

Jackson hurried to his car, his pain escalating. He vowed to get his prescription for prednisone refilled before he ended up in the ER too.

When Jackson walked into Derrick's hospital room, his brother was sitting up and flirting with a pretty nurse in blue scrubs. Or trying to. His voice was weak and the skin on his face slack. Nicky stood nearby talking intently with a guy who looked too young to be a doctor.

"I see you're feeling better," Jackson joked.

"Sort of." Derrick smiled, but his eyes were pinched.

The nurse turned to Jackson. "We gave him Zofran to stop the vomiting, and his blood pressure is back to normal too."

"All good news. But still, why does this keep happening?" Jackson stepped toward the doctor, wanting his attention.

"We still don't know," Nicky said, getting in between them. She introduced him to Dr. Tedesco, then kept talking. "A woman detective came to the house this morning and upset Derrick. I think that's what triggered this episode."

Dr. Tedesco gently disagreed. "No, the vomiting and diarrhea are not psychological. But he may have cyclic vomiting syndrome, even though it's almost always diagnosed in teenagers. Another possibility is that he's severely allergic to something in his environment."

"But you already checked him for allergies," Nicky said.

"Those skin-patch tests are limited to a short list of common allergens," the doctor said, rushing the words. "I've also consulted with an immunologist, and he'll stop by any moment."

"You think he has an autoimmune disease?" The thought surprised Jackson.

"Like what?" Nicky asked. "I've never heard of vomiting associated with immune issues."

Another physician stepped in, and Jackson was relieved

to see that he was older, despite his dyed hair. The new doctor, a big man, glanced around the room, looking displeased, possibly by the number of visitors. Nicky didn't look happy to see him either. "I'll put in a request for a home-toxin analysis," he announced. Then he mumbled something to the young doctor and left the room.

Tedesco patted Nicky's arm. "We'll get this figured out. Kettering is the best in the state. Or we can send Derrick to OHSU in Portland if we have to. They have an outstanding diagnostics team."

Nicky seemed distracted for a moment, her mouth tight. Then she crossed her arms. "That sounds inconvenient."

"The intermittent nature of his symptoms makes this challenging." Tedesco nodded at Jackson. "But since he's feeling better, your brother can go home." The doctor abruptly left. Jackson suspected he was tired of dealing with Nicky.

She looked at him with an open mouth. "Neither of his doctors seem invested in Derrick's case. Maybe we should take him to the big hospital in Portland. I'm sure they have more people on staff."

"Let's wait and see," Derrick said. "I can't afford to make trips to Portland or spend weeks in the hospital up there while they figure this out."

"But maybe you should," Nicky said, abruptly changing her mind. "You need the additional attention." She squeezed Derrick's hand. "I can't believe they want to send you home already."

"That surprises me too," Jackson commented.

Nicky grabbed her purse from the chair. "I'm going to talk to someone in the administration office about this." She flounced out.

Jackson was relieved to be alone with his brother. He pulled up a chair. "I'm worried about you."

"You and me both. I've lost twenty pounds in the last six months, and I'm about to lose my job too."

Derrick worked nights as a machinist in a small shop. "Did your boss explicitly say that? I don't think they can fire you for being sick."

"Yes, they can. And I don't have a union."

"Well, hell. Do you have money saved? Is Nicky working?"

"Nicky gets a small inheritance thing every month, but she also launched a GoFundMe campaign." Derrick looked sheepish. "It's bringing in money."

White-collar charity. Those efforts often annoyed him, but Jackson was glad his brother wouldn't end up homeless. "You must be racking up some outrageous medical bills."

"Oh yeah. But it will be much worse if I lose my job and health insurance."

Jackson wanted to tell Derrick that he could stay with him if things got rough, but he wasn't prepared to take in Nicky too. He also had no idea how long Kera and Micah would be in the house. "The home-toxin analysis sounds promising."

Derrick shrugged and reached for his water. "I'm skeptical. But I feel like I'm bouncing back quickly this time, so maybe the thing will just go away as mysteriously as it started."

"I hope so." Jackson wasn't optimistic. By Derrick's expression, he wasn't either. "Can I get you anything?"

"No. Just talk to me about something non-medical." His brother closed his eyes for a second, sounding weary. "I'm so sick of discussing this illness, whatever it is."

"The Cubs are looking good this year." Jackson had heard

another detective say it recently.

Derrick laughed weakly. "You really should watch baseball every once in a while."

"I know. I work too much." Jackson didn't know what else to talk to him about, except the case. "I attended Tayla Holden's autopsy this morning."

The smile disappeared from his brother's face. "Jesus. That's dark."

"I know, but I want to find her killer. She has a C-section scar. Do you know anything about her child?"

Derrick sighed. "Just that she had her very young, fifteen I think, and gave her up for adoption."

"A daughter?"

"She named her Grace, but her adoptive parents may have changed it." Derrick squirmed. "This isn't what I had in mind for light conversation."

Feeling guilty, Jackson decided to share his personal situation. *Why not?* Derrick had plenty of experience with women. "Kera's coming home in a few days."

"About time." Derrick held up his hand.

Jackson high-fived him.

"It's rough going that long without sex," Derrick added. "I don't know how you do it."

"Work hard and don't think about it."

His brother shook his head. "You're too damn serious."

"I think I have a problem though."

"What? My perfect brother? Tell me. I could use the distraction."

Jackson wasn't sure how much he should say. "I don't think I'm in love with Kera. I love her, but it doesn't feel the same."

"Hmm. Do you still want to fuck her?"

He'd known Derrick would be blunt, so he let it go. "She's gorgeous. And if she crawls naked into my bed, what else am I going to do?"

"So what's the problem?"

"I'm not sure I want to live with her. Or be a father to her grandson."

"I can't blame you for that." Derrick reached over and squeezed his shoulder with a weak grip. "Just get laid a few times before you tell her."

Jackson laughed, hoping it was meant as a joke. But he regretted sharing and decided not to mention his attraction to Evans. "I'm not sure that's fair. But if she insists . . ."

Derrick let out a full-bellied laugh, then coughed like a tuberculosis patient. Jackson pressed the call button, afraid of what might happen next.

Chapter 18

Evans got in her car, eager to leave the hospital. Derrick's illness was disturbing, but not her problem. She had to focus on the case, especially if Jackson was distracted by family stuff. For now, she would cross Derrick off her list of suspects, despite how Schak felt, but she was still betting on a past or current lover as the perp. The act of shoving the sausage into the victim's throat seemed personal.

As she started the engine, her phone rang, and she checked the ID: *Captain Stricklyn.* A wave of emotions rolled through her. They'd dated for six months, but neither had wanted to commit to a serious relationship. Then Ben had been promoted from Internal Affairs to management, and his new authority had changed him. They'd ended their relationship on mostly good terms, but she'd heard rumors that he was drinking heavily and had become hard to get along with.

On the fifth ring, she finally picked up. "Hello, Ben."

"It's Captain Stricklyn, and I need you in my office ASAP."

Asshole. This wouldn't be good. "Yes, sir. I'm in the field, but I'll be there as soon as I can." She hung up before he could respond. What the hell could this be about? Her trip to Costa Rica? Evans buckled up and headed out. She had done the department, and the city of Eugene, a favor by going to the disaster zone and charitably representing both. Chief Owens had asked her because she was single and childless. She always worked holidays for that reason too, giving officers with families the day off instead. So she should have points on her side. Ben wasn't even her direct boss. So if there was a problem with how she did her job, Sergeant Lammers should be the one to tell her.

Once Evans was on the expressway, she tried to stop thinking about it. She would know soon enough. But that proved impossible, and by the time she reached the department, her nerves were pinging. She pounded up the stairs and trudged down *management hall*, the corridor lined with captains' offices. Chief Owens occupied the corner office at the end, and she almost wished she'd been summoned there instead.

Stopping at the second door, Evans knocked boldly, trying not to feel intimidated. The door, which wasn't fully latched, pushed open. Ben Stricklyn looked up and barked, "Come in and close it."

His looks seemed different, but she couldn't tell why. His shaved head was still sexy, his chiseled face still attractive, and his body as buff. Did his suit look loose? Maybe it was his eyes. They looked stressed.

Evans stepped inside but didn't sit. She stood with her feet apart and shoulders back, ready for anything. Or so she thought. Her ex-lover jumped to his feet, came around the desk, and pulled her into him. With both hands on the sides of her head, he pressed his mouth into hers. Too stunned to react, Evans processed a barrage of thoughts and emotions. *What was he doing?* His lips and tongue were so familiar, her body responded the way it had when they were intimate. But this was too weird. And wrong. Jackson was finally coming around, and she didn't want to blow it with him. Plus Ben's breath smelled like alcohol.

She tried to pull back, but he had a grip on her head. *What now?* He was her boss and an old friend. Kneeing him in the balls didn't seem like an option. Finally, he ended the kiss but didn't let go. "I've missed you so much."

"I see that." She pretended to chuckle, trying to keep it light. Ben wasn't thinking straight and she had to humor him. Evans pulled free of his grip. "This isn't the time or place. Why did you want to see me?"

"For that kiss. To convince you to start dating me again."

Not a chance. She scrambled for a way to be diplomatic. This man could derail her career in a heartbeat. "I'm flattered by your interest, but I'm not really available."

For a long moment, he stared, his dark eyes boring into her. "I saw you with Jackson last night at the Grill. I know you started sleeping with him. That's why I had to act now."

"Ben, our relationship didn't work. You were committed to your son, and I was still—" She paused, not wanting to admit she loved Jackson. "Still thinking about someone else. So just let it go."

"I can't." He grabbed her again, forcing another kiss.

Anger flared and Evans jerked free. "Stop! I'm not interested."

"I don't believe you." His mouth twisted into a strange smile. "I know how sexual you are. I know you find me attractive. I felt it when I first kissed you."

Evans stepped back. Everything he'd said was true, but none of it mattered. She'd been attracted to a lot of men she would never sleep with. Her body and brain functioned separately sometimes. "I'm leaving now." She pivoted toward the door.

Stricklyn grabbed her shoulder and spun her back. "I'm your boss. You don't leave until I dismiss you."

He had crossed too many lines! "Your behavior is inappropriate. Don't force me to report you."

His eyes flashed and his voice dropped into a menacing tone. "Don't even think about telling anyone. If you do, I'll report Jackson for fraternizing with a subordinate and he'll be fired."

She started to swear but caught herself. Instead, she took a big step toward the exit. As she grabbed the doorknob, Stricklyn called out, "I may report him anyway, unless—" He left the rest unsaid.

Evans spun back, her mind reeling. "Unless what? I sleep with you? That's sexual coercion."

Stricklyn's lips pulled back in a sick smile. "You've willingly sucked my cock. No one will ever believe you."

Evans snapped her mouth shut and bolted from his office.

Chapter 19

Tuesday, May 8, 2:35 p.m.

Jackson walked through the parking garage, trying to look normal despite the pain. He felt selfish about leaving Derrick, but even worse about being distracted from the investigation for hours. They were already three days out from the time of death. They had suspects, but nothing solid on any of them, and he worried they might not close this case. He reached his car, still thinking about the victim. Because she was attractive, Holden had drawn the interest of a creepy, potentially violent neighbor. But the woman had also generated conflict with various people who might have been angry enough to kill her. She also seemed to lack real-life friends. Still, Holden hadn't deserved to die, and every victim needed justice. Just as important, if her killer was walking around free in Jackson's jurisdiction, he posed a threat to others. His team had to dig in and get what they needed to nail the guy. Or woman, he reminded himself.

Halfway to the department, he remembered his promise to Katie and made an abrupt left turn. *Damn.* More time away from the investigation. He checked his phone and decided he had time to stop for a chicken sandwich and quell the riot in his stomach. He downed the late lunch in the school parking lot with a cup of coffee, then took another Aleve and texted his daughter. He waited five minutes but she didn't respond.

Maybe she was sitting in the administration office

waiting for him. Jackson got out and headed toward the building. He heard teenage laughter and a wave of nostalgia hit him. He'd gone to high school right here, nearly thirty years ago. Not much had changed except the color of the paint and the style of the cars in the parking lot. He missed driving the gorgeous midnight-blue GTO that he'd restored. Benjie's adoption lawyer had been expensive, and he'd had no choice but to sell the one valuable thing he owned. But he and Benjie would rebuild another vehicle when the boy was older.

Inside the main doors, he veered toward the office, not seeing Katie in the throng of kids hustling to get outside after a long day of classes. An older woman and two high school students were behind the counter, and three young people sat in the chairs. Katie wasn't one of them. Jackson texted her again, then leaned against a wall to wait.

The older receptionist caught his eye and called out, "Can I help you?"

"I'm not sure. I'm meeting my daughter and we planned to speak with Mrs. Mayfair." He walked toward the desk as he spoke.

"What's your daughter's name?"

"Katie Jackson."

The receptionist's brow puckered. "She was sent home earlier. The system should have emailed you about it."

He hadn't checked his personal messages all day. "Why was she sent home?"

"She had an altercation with another student."

Oh crap. "A boy?" Jackson couldn't remember the name of the guy Katie had said was harassing her.

"Yes, but I'm not at liberty to discuss any of this." The receptionist pursed her lips. "You should talk to Katie."

"I want to see Mrs. Mayfair."

"She's not here, but I can make an appointment for you."

He didn't have the patience to go through the process and didn't know his own availability without calling up the calendar on his phone. He also suspected Katie may have decided to short-circuit the proper channels and simply deck the guy. She'd done it before. "You said *sent home*, but not expelled?"

"Yes, as far as I know."

"Okay. I'll get back to you about the appointment." Jackson left the office.

In his car, he called Katie and left a message: "Please contact me and let me know you're okay." He wasn't terribly worried. She'd been doing volunteer work with a women's advocacy group after school and sometimes turned off her phone. She'd also become interested in photography and often tuned out when she was shooting or modifying images. For the most part, he was delighted that she willingly exited the digital world on occasion.

But not right now. His immediate concern was Benjie and whether Katie would pick him up from preschool. If she didn't, he would have to drive to the center, then take the boy to his ex-wife's sister who sometimes babysat for him, the way she had when Katie was young. The big-picture worry though was whether Katie would finish high school. She only had a few weeks left. *Please let her make it through.*

Jackson decided to get back to work. Benjie still had another hour at school, so Jackson didn't have to stress about him just yet. He had time to search Holden's home again before their task force meeting.

Ten minutes later, he pulled into the panhandle driveway, noticing the barrier they'd left to keep neighbors away had been moved. At the side door, he lifted a ceramic flowerpot and retrieved a key. He'd found it on a hook in the house the first day he'd been here and had placed it where the forensic techs could use it if they needed to return. No one was here now, but the crime-scene tape across the door hung loose on one side. Maybe Schak had stopped by when he questioned the neighbors.

Someone had left the kitchen window open to air the place out, and Jackson breathed a sigh of relief. He headed straight to the bedroom he'd checked the day before—in his quick effort to find electronic devices—and began a more thorough search. Where would she keep prescription medications or illegal drugs? If Holden lived alone, why would she even hide them? Maybe this was a waste of time. The letter he'd read mentioning the Percocet had been written years ago. But he kept looking. If Holden hadn't been able to get a doctor to refill her prescription, she might have bought pain meds on the street. Getting involved with a drug dealer could turn out to be deadly. Food choking didn't fit a dealer's typical MO, but in the crime world, anything was possible.

He searched every drawer, including the tiny slots in her jewelry box. He checked for false bottoms and hidden side pockets and looked behind a painting for a safe. He started to move toward the bathroom, then turned back and lifted the top mattress.

A small black handgun lay near the top right side. Jackson lowered the mattress, pulled on latex gloves, and retrieved the weapon. He didn't recognize the model, but she most likely kept it for protection. Still, he had to turn it into the crime lab and ask them to run the serial number for criminal activity. Or whether it had been reported stolen. He made sure the chamber was empty, then placed it into an evidence bag and labeled it.

Jackson checked his phone to see how much time he had. It was nearly four, but Katie had texted to say she would pick up Benjie as planned. He sent her a quick *Thanks*. They needed to discuss today's incident, but it could wait. If she'd punched a guy for grabbing her ass? *Oh well.* At least she wasn't letting herself be victimized. She had gone to the principal first. Jackson couldn't wait for her to be out of the high school environment.

The bathroom search went more quickly but didn't produce anything useful. He went back to the living room and started pulling out couch cushions and looking under lamps. Nothing. The kitchen cupboards were more interesting and introduced him to a variety of foods and substances he'd never heard of—powdered monk fruit, raw cacao, and spirulina, for example. Except for a bottle of aspirin, he didn't find any medications. Discouraged, Jackson stared out the open kitchen window and wondered where else a person might keep medications.

The victim's car, a mint-green Subaru wagon, sat under the carport. Had anyone searched it yet? Evans' discovery of the crazy-neighbor suspect had interrupted their normal thorough search of the victim's home and belongings. He stepped outside, hoping the vehicle was unlocked. He had no idea where the victim's keys were. Maybe in a purse or travel pack of some kind. Neither of which he'd seen yesterday or today.

The passenger door opened and Jackson searched the glove box. Nothing but warranty papers and a packet with insurance and registration. The console was crammed with a typical collection of car junk: flashlight, sunglasses, bandaids, chapstick, and napkins. But no medication.

Backing out, he spotted a pink sweater on the rear floor. He reached for it, thinking it might have pockets. Underneath was a small handbag. Jackson pulled the bag into his lap and dumped the contents. A small plastic bottle lay between her car keys and a wallet. Through the clear amber, he saw round white pills. Based on what he'd learned, he figured they were some kind of pain medication. But the container had no label, so the drugs hadn't been purchased in a pharmacy. Or the pills had been transferred to another container for unknown reasons. He would have to drop them off at the lab for analysis, even though they probably weren't important.

He put everything back into the purse and shoved the bag into his own large satchel. Jackson dug out his phone and called the state lab to request an expedited toxicology report on Holden. He wanted to know what else Holden might have had in her system before he let go of this line of inquiry.

Chapter 20

Jackson drove to the evidence lab on Garfield and pulled up to the security post. The gray-brick building, with its lack of windows and signs, wasn't intended for public drop-ins. He waved his barcode ID in front of the camera and waited for the metal gate to open. When it did, he drove around to the back and parked in front of the big bays.

With the intention of making this a quick stop, he tried to hurry into the building, but the searing pain slowed him down. He took deep breaths and powered through. Inside, the steps to the second floor were even harder. Sweat broke out on his forehead as he reached the landing. *Crap!* He understood how Holden must have felt and why she had ended up with illegal pain meds.

Jackson stopped, thinking about how sweet relief would feel. Those pills were right there in his shoulder bag. He could take one right now and no one would ever know. He could even pocket some to help him get through the next few days of the investigation. Then, after they had a suspect nailed down, he would get another CT scheduled. If the fibrosis was growing again—and he knew it was—he would consent to a second surgery. He'd rather take a few weeks off to recover than have to give up his career. Right now, he needed to be functional.

He looked around, but the halls were as quiet as always. He unzipped his satchel, then opened the small handbag inside. For a long moment, he stared at the pill bottle while the throbbing subsided. *No.* He couldn't. Not without knowing for sure what they were. It was stupid to even be in this mode. His doctor would write him a script for Vicodin or Oxy; all he had to do was ask. Why was it so damn hard to admit to anyone, especially another man, that he was in pain?

Trying not to shuffle, he headed to Joe Berloni's door and knocked. After a moment, Jasmine Parker stepped out of the next office. "Hey, Jackson. Joe's in the lab. What have you got?"

"Some medication I need tested." He pulled out the pills and stepped toward her. "They were in the victim's purse, which I just found in her car."

"I thought your team had searched it yesterday, or I would have. Sorry." She reached for the bottle. "No label? Interesting."

"Can you get these tested soon?"

"I'll do what I can."

"Thanks." He moved past her, heading back the way he'd come.

Downstairs, he entered the evidence-processing room. Joe stood next to the downdraft table, dusting a detached steering wheel for fingerprints. The short man with a boxer's body called over his shoulder, "Hey, Jackson. I'll be with you in a moment."

Jackson waited, his anxiety growing.

Several minutes later, the technician set the wheel aside. "These prints are from the carjacking near campus." Joe grinned. "But I just pulled Holden's necklace out of the superglue box, and we've got a partial print to work with. I'll run it through the database as soon as I can."

Maybe their first break in the case. Fingerprints could make a conviction—but you had to find the right person first.

"You're sure the print doesn't belong to the vic?"

"Positive." Joe wiped his hands on the rubber apron he wore. "I also tested the sausage link for animal protein, and it's definitely got chicken in it."

"So our victim is guilty of fraud." *Crap.* He already disliked the woman for taking his brother's nude photo without permission, but now that this accusation was confirmed, the list of suspects could grow. Did he have an obligation to notify the public about this finding?

"Anything else I can help you with?" Joe asked.

"I have a handgun that needs processing." Jackson pulled the heavy plastic bag from his overstuffed satchel. "Where do you want it?"

"Can you run it upstairs to my desk?"

No, that would be excruciating.

The thought must have registered on his face, because Joe changed his mind. "Uh, just leave it on that table by the door."

"Thanks. I have a task force meeting to get to."

At his desk, Jackson keyed the new information into his case document. It boiled down to Aidan Emmerson as a viable suspect and some negative information about the victim. She took illegal meds for her pain, she fed animal meat to unsuspecting vegans, and she kept a handgun under her mattress—but maybe none of it mattered. Holden had probably been killed by Barulla, the Peeping Tom neighbor who harassed coworkers and made small bombs for fun. *Damn!* People seemed more fucked-up than ever. Was it bad parenting? Too much crap on the internet? Or chemicals in the water?

Jackson laughed as he got up to collect the printouts. He

sounded like a grumpy old man. When he crossed the open space to the printer, he had to fight the urge to double over in pain. Good thing he kept Aleve in his desk drawer. He downed two, then moved slowly across to the conference room, hoping to get there before anyone could watch him walk in.

Evans was already at the table. "Hey, Jackson." She stared as he moved past her to the chair at the end. "What's wrong? Is your disease acting up again?"

"A bit." He sat down. "Will you take the board?"

"Of course. Who else are we expecting?"

"Schak, Lammers, maybe Quince."

"Let's order pizza. I've had a stressful day." Anxiety in her voice.

Jackson searched her eyes. *A little anger too?* "Everything okay with you?"

"I'm not sure. But let's get this done." She pulled out her phone and pressed a contact in her file. "Hand me your expense card."

Jackson dug for his wallet and the card he used occasionally when his team worked overtime and needed some compensation. Evans ordered two large pizzas, one with pepperoni only for Lammers, and a meat-lover's with the works for everyone else. When they finished off the good one, they would dig into what was left of the pepperoni.

As Evans ended her call, Schak came into the room. "Yes!" He made a forearm-to-knee victory gesture, then grinned sheepishly. "I haven't had pizza in months." He patted his belly. "Tracy's not happy with the weight I've gained back."

Evans didn't take the opportunity to zing him, which made Jackson even more worried about her. But now wasn't the time to ask. "Let's get started." Evans moved to the whiteboard as Jackson summed up what he'd learned. He paused to let her catch up, then continued. "The new suspect is our biggest concern. He belongs to a commune, so he doesn't strike me as a runner. I'll see if I can get him to come in and give us a fingerprint."

Schak laughed. "An anti-establishment type? You might be able to trick him into it, but he'll never volunteer."

Evans cut in. "The fact that Holden was producing a fraudulent product might actually be a bigger factor. How many other customers did she piss off?"

"They would have to know that it was falsely labeled," Jackson argued—even though he'd had the same thought earlier. "No one else has contacted Holden about it. I've searched her recent emails, and Delarosa has skimmed through the last three months. There's plenty of conflict about food choices and what she charges, but no one else mentioned meat in her sausages."

"Good." Evans' tone was abrupt. "We have two viable suspects and a fingerprint. Maybe we'll wrap this up soon."

Jackson turned to Schak. "Did you get Holden's financial records?"

"The bank faxed them early this afternoon, and I spent the last two hours staring at numbers." He pulled a stack of papers from his briefcase and removed the one on top. "Three transactions stand out. Two deposits that match the dates and amounts on the receipts we found. Two thousand each, one by PayPal and the other a cashier's check."

They already had those client names on the board. The bank statement just confirmed that Holden had indeed been paid an outrageous amount of money for weird food advice. "And the third?" Jackson asked.

"And a thousand-dollar transfer through PayPal to a

weird Hotmail address." Schak sounded tired. "I haven't been able to figure out who it is yet."

"It's a good chunk of money, so stay on it."

Sergeant Lammers, who was Jackson's size, walked into the room with a scrawny pizza guy behind her. "Look who I found wandering the halls."

The skinny young man put the boxes on the table.

"Your tip is on the card," Evans said.

He thanked her and left. Lammers took a seat across from Schak and reached for a slice of pepperoni. "What did I miss?"

"Everything." Evans gave a curt smile.

"I'll get you caught up," Jackson offered. While the others chowed down on dinner, he summarized their findings. "We have two suspects. One is a Peeping Tom neighbor who spied on the victim and also harassed his coworkers with vandalism. The other is a customer who's pissed off that Holden put chicken in a product she sold as vegan."

"Holden died with a sausage in her throat, correct?" the sergeant asked.

"Yes, and the pathologist confirmed that it was forced."

"Focus on the angry customer," Lammers directed. "The poetic justice is too perfect."

Jackson concurred. "The neighbor is in jail for bomb-making, so we have him on hold anyway." He reached for a slice of the loaded pizza. He had to get something into his stomach to settle down the anti-inflammatories. That reminded him of the pills he'd found in Holden's purse.

"Another thing. I found an unlabeled bottle of pills in Holden's purse. I think they're opioids, because I also discovered a letter she'd written to a doctor about chronic pain. But that was two years ago and the doc has since retired, so I hit a dead end there."

"But the lack of a label could mean street meds," Evans said. "If she's involved with a dealer, that opens up a whole new avenue of investigation."

"I know. But dealers don't usually kill their clients," Jackson countered. "Especially someone like Holden, a thirty-something, middle-class woman who's a reliable source of income."

"Good point."

"I found a handgun under her mattress too, but she's a woman living alone, so it's not unusual."

"A woman with a lot of conflict in her life," Evans commented as she stood to update the board.

The room was quiet while they ate for a moment. Jackson read over his notes for details he might have forgotten to mention. *Oh yeah, the autopsy.* "Hey, this may not be important, but Holden has a C-section scar, so she had a baby at one point. It's a little weird only because we didn't see any evidence of a child in her life."

Evans put down her pizza. "I just remembered that Derrick told me Holden gave up a baby girl for adoption at fifteen."

"How old would she be now?" Lammers asked.

"Nineteen or twenty." Jackson tried to visualize a young Tayla Holden. Would she have her mother's dark hair and pale skin?

"I'll call Holden's mother and ask her about the child," Evans offered. "I can also talk to Emmerson's friends and check his online postings. He might have bragged about going after Holden."

"Great." Jackson wished he had done that already. But he'd spent time with Derrick in the hospital and had wasted an hour driving to Katie's school. He started to take another bite and his phone rang. He checked the ID: *Delarosa*. He took the call, put the phone on the table, and said loudly, "It's our tech specialist, and I've got her on speaker."

"Hey, Jackson. I found FreedomGladiator, the troll who stalked and threatened Holden online."

"Where is he?"

"Cheshire."

Damn. A rural town about twenty minutes away. "It looks like we have another suspect."

Chapter 21

After the meeting, Evans drove west on the old highway, battling the glare of the setting sun. The tiny town of Cheshire was apparently home to FreedomGladiator, AKA Larry Alder. She'd volunteered to check him out, thinking he might be more open to a woman than to Schak, an older male cop with an attitude. Jackson hadn't wanted her to go alone and had given her a printout of the troll's comments—to give her background on who she would be questioning. Gladiator had called Holden *a libtard, idiot vegan, piss-stained snowflake*, and *human cancer.* He'd also posted: *Were coming 4 U and bringing the guns U hate so much.* Jackson had planned to go with her, but his daughter had called as they walked out of the conference room, so Evans had waved at him and jogged out to her car. She'd noticed that he was in pain and wanted him to go home and rest.

But she wasn't ready to call it a night. Rage at Stricklyn still burned in her belly and she was spoiling for a fight. Trolling people online with hate messages wasn't illegal, but it was just as bad as sexual harassment. She wanted all those men to experience consequences for their behavior. She couldn't confront her boss, but if Larry Alder threatened her in even the smallest way, she would hit him with a Taser, cuff him, and take his sorry ass to jail.

Unless he lived with a house full of gun-owning men. In which case, she would walk away and call for backup.

The address Delarosa had provided turned out to be a mobile home park just off the main road. Evans slowed for the speed bump in the entrance, relieved that the suspect had close neighbors. If anything went down, she didn't want to end up locked in a pig farmer's shed in a remote location. She checked her Sig Sauer, then pulled the Taser from under the seat before stepping out of the car. Dread filled her belly. A few months earlier, when she'd tried to rescue a trapped child, she'd been taken hostage by a bitter old white guy. Angry people had become unhinged and unpredictable, making law enforcement more dangerous than ever. She blamed it on the political culture.

Alder's trailer was near the front. Although it was at least forty years old and coming apart at the seams, potted plants with beautiful blooms surrounded the home. That surprised her. Evans knocked on the thin metal door, and a woman answered. Gray-haired and soft everywhere, she peered over her glasses. "Are you a cop?"

"Detective Evans, Eugene Police. Do you know Larry Alder?"

"He's my son."

Of course the troll lived with his mother. "I need to speak with him."

"About what?"

"Homicide. You don't want to be charged as an accomplice, so don't cover for him." Evans pointed at the faded-black Dakota truck in the driveway. "That's his vehicle, so I know he's here. I need to ask a few questions, so let's get this over with."

The woman glared and stepped aside. "My Larry didn't kill anyone, so you're wasting your time." She shouted down the hall. "Larry! Get out here!"

Evans took two steps into the house, widened her stance, and waited. The room appeared clean but reeked of cats and garlic. Had she ever walked into a house that didn't smell like anything? Not on the job. She'd once attended an open house for a million-dollar property that was on the market, just to take a peek inside, and it had been odor-free. Could rich people afford better ventilation?

The man who skulked into the room was her same height and only twenty pounds heavier. All of that weight was in his stomach, leaving him with pencil-thin arms and legs. His thin face looked about thirty, but his hairline had disappeared. Evans looked him over. His elastic-waist pants and snug yellow T-shirt didn't seem to conceal a weapon. "Do you own any guns, Mr. Alder?"

"No, why?"

She handed him the printout of his online comments to the victim. "You threatened to come for Tayla Holden and bring your guns." She'd done a quick search of the database before leaving and hadn't found Larry Alder in the system anywhere. Not as a perp or accomplice or witness. He looked like he hadn't left the house since high school. "I'd like to see those weapons you mentioned."

"I don't allow guns in this house." His mother's arms were crossed, her T-shirt straining against a big belly too.

"Will you please go outside for a minute so I can talk to Larry alone?"

"This is my house and I'm not leaving."

Evans grabbed the suspect's arm. "Come outside with me."

He didn't resist. "Hey, look. I know I gave that lady a hard time online, but she's crazy," Alder whined as they stepped onto the closet-sized front porch. "She pushes people to eat only fruit, which is just stupid, then she makes tofu sausages.

That is messed up."

Interesting that he focused on the sausage. "Why do you care?"

"I just hate bullshit. Especially all that feel-good nonsense that says if we just love each other and eat only plants everything will be fine. Humans are hunters and have been for millions of years, and love doesn't pay the bills. People have to work. Other people get sick and die for no reason." A tiny catch in his voice.

He might have a reason for his bitterness, but she couldn't let herself feel anything for him. "Do you hunt?"

"Not since my dad died." He shivered in the cool evening air.

"Where do you work?"

"Bartell's meat-packing plant."

That might explain his touchiness about vegans. "Where were you Saturday night between nine and midnight?"

"Right here."

"Can anybody vouch for that?"

"My mother. She got home from bingo around nine-thirty."

Of course she did. Evans held back a sigh. To break his alibi, she would have to question his neighbors and see if anyone saw him leave. She wanted to glance at the time on her phone but resisted. Larry Alder was less viable as a suspect than Holden's bomb-crazy neighbor or the vegan hippie who discovered chicken in the sausage he'd eaten. But she would talk to a few people while she was out here.

A few more questions first. "Did you ever meet Tayla Holden in person?"

"No." He belched as the word came out.

A waft of sour beer hit her face and Evans stepped back. "How did you connect with Holden online?"

133

"I don't know. I think I saw some stupid thing she posted on Twitter."

And that was all it took. "Then what?"

"I commented back."

She waited him out.

"Then I got curious and checked out her blog and Facebook page."

"You stalked her."

He scowled but let it go.

"How deeply did you investigate Holden? Do you know where she lives?"

"No! She's a freak. I don't want to know her."

Did he protest too much? "But you find her sexually attractive?"

"Not really. I prefer blondes."

Evans would have bet he was a virgin. "Don't leave town, because I'll be back with more questions."

Keeping an eye on him, she stepped off the porch and strode to her car. She climbed in and waited for Alder to go back inside, then pulled forward to the next mobile home. She knocked on three doors and only found one person home. An older man who didn't know Larry Alder and hadn't been home Saturday night to watch comings and goings.

On the drive home, Evans' phone beeped. She looked at the ID and answered her headset. "Mrs. Holden. How are you?" She'd been intending to call the mother.

"Stressed out. I drove down from Portland to be near my daughter. But when I tried to get into Tayla's house, it was locked and someone had moved the key. Where is it?"

Too soon. "The house is still a crime scene, so you'll have to wait a few days to start sorting through her things."

"Can I just sleep there and save money on a hotel? I won't

touch anything but the coffeemaker."

"Uh, I'll ask my boss." The sun had set and the drive back was dark. It bothered her to be on the phone so she looked for a place to pull off.

"I went to the morgue to see my daughter's body too. I can't believe they already did the autopsy."

"I'm sorry, but it's part of the investigative process. It's how we determine manner of death."

"Was she murdered, for sure?"

"Yes." Evans spotted an abandoned grange and slowed.

"By whom?" The mother was fighting back hysteria.

"We don't know yet, but we have several suspects." She pulled over and put the car into park but left it running.

"Did you find the horrible man who harassed Tayla online?"

"Yes, he's been questioned, but he has an alibi." Technically, she still had to get Mrs. Alder on record, but she wanted to wait and catch her off guard. At the moment, she needed information from the victim's mother. "Do you know anything about the child your daughter gave birth to?"

A long silence. "She gave her up for adoption. Tayla was only fifteen. I wanted her to have an abortion, but she wouldn't do it."

"Has the daughter ever tried to make contact with her mother?"

"I don't think so." Her voice dropped. "What does this have to do with Tayla's murder?"

"Probably nothing. But we try to explore all possible motives." That reminded Evans to get to the important question. "We need to talk to Tayla's friends. Or better yet, her lover. Do you know who she was close to?"

"Tayla didn't have women friends. She tried, but they

always got jealous and petty with her."

Yeah, right. "Who was she dating?"

"She'd pretty much given up on men, but the last I heard about was named Derrick."

Oh hell.

Chapter 22

Wednesday, May 9, 5:17 a.m.

Jackson woke to the sound of his phone—the ringtone he'd set for family members. He looked at the clock and his heart skipped a beat. Where the hell was Katie if she was calling at five in the morning? He snatched his cell off the nightstand and saw the contact was his brother. This could be almost as bad. "What's going on?"

"She's dead." Derrick could hardly talk through his own loud sobs.

Jackson didn't know what scared him the most, the words or hearing his brother cry. "Who's dead? What are you saying?"

"Nicky."

"How? Where are you?" His brother had been in the hospital yesterday afternoon.

"I'm home. They released me last night."

Oh yeah. Jackson put on pants and shoes while he waited for Derrick to get control. "What happened?"

"I don't know. When we got home, I was tired and went to bed. When I got up this morning to pee—" He broke off again, but only to take a long breath. "I found Nicky on the kitchen floor."

"You're sure she's dead? Maybe she's just passed out."

"I think she was strangled." Derrick cried softly this time. "I was right here the whole time. Sleeping!" Guilt and distress in his voice now. "But our bedroom is in the garage and I was medicated, so I didn't hear anything. Can you come over, please?"

Jackson was already strapping on his weapon. "I'll be there in ten minutes. Stay away from her body."

He yanked on his work jacket, put in his earpiece, and strode out into the hall. Katie stood by her door, looking worried. "What's wrong with Derrick?"

"His girlfriend is dead." Jackson kissed his daughter's forehead, wishing he hadn't been so blunt. But Katie didn't know Nicky. "Go back to bed. Your uncle will be all right."

As Jackson ran out of the house, a terrifying thought hit him. Two women were dead now, and Derrick was the only connection between them. Had his brother lost his mind and done these things? "No!" He said it out loud, the only sound in the quiet neighborhood. He didn't believe Derrick was capable. But one of his colleagues might.

He raced toward his brother's home, running red lights at dark, empty intersections and playing out scenarios in his head. As he turned on River Road, he realized he needed to call Lammers and report the incident. She would then assign someone else to lead the investigation. If the two deaths seemed linked—and they did on the surface—the cases would merge into one, and he would lose his leadership, maybe even be kicked off the team. He'd never had a case taken away before, and he would fight to stay on this one as a supporting investigator.

As he turned on Derrick's street, he pressed the voice-help button on his phone, which he'd just learned to use. "Call Lammers."

After five rings, she groused, "What the hell, Jackson?"

His boss was used to middle-of-the-night calls, so she was

just giving him a hard time. "We have another death. My brother's girlfriend. I'm on my way there now."

"Oh, for fuck's sake. Please tell me it was an accident."

"I haven't seen the body." He didn't want to tell her Derrick had mentioned strangulation.

"I'll call Gunderson. We're keeping him busy this week."

Jackson pulled up in front of Derrick's house. "I'm at the scene now. I'll text you in a moment if it looks like we need a team."

"Be smart, Jackson. Everything by the book. Don't let your relationship to the witness derail you. And if this woman was murdered, your brother is the prime suspect, so I'll have to let someone else take the lead."

"Understood. I'll be in touch." He hung up and called 911, just in case Derrick hadn't. He gave a brief rundown, then hurried toward the small house.

As he reached for the doorknob, he abruptly stopped and sucked in a long breath to slow himself. This was a crime scene. In his satchel, he found his last pair of gloves and pulled them on. He also retrieved his penlight and examined the doorknob plate. No sign of forced entry. He glanced at the driveway. Two vehicles in place. He hurried over and felt both hoods. Cool to the touch. No one had driven them recently.

The front door opened and Derrick stepped out. "Wade? What are you doing?"

Jackson strode over. "My job. Which protects you as well as me."

"The other detectives will blame me, won't they?" Wearing only pajama bottoms, Derrick shivered.

"Let's go inside," Jackson said, grabbing his arm. "We don't have much time to talk before the first responders get here."

The tidy cottage smelled like cinnamon—and human excrement. *Oh no.* Sometimes bodies released the contents of bowels and bladders when muscles loosened after death. The last one he'd seen like that had been a naked old man who'd been stabbed by his fifty-year-old son as he got out of bed. Blood, piss, and crap everywhere!

Jackson saw Nicky on the floor in the truncated space between the kitchen and small dining area. A nearly identical placement to Tayla Holden. He turned to Derrick. "Did you touch her?"

"No. I knew she was dead. Look at her face. And the smell." His brother had control now, thank goodness, but his shirtlessness kept reminding Jackson of the photo he'd seen on Holden's phone. "Go get dressed while I look at her body."

Derrick glanced down as though he didn't realize what he was wearing and gave a small shrug. He shuffled past his girlfriend's body, then moved slowly through the kitchen and through a back door. *Was he medicated?* Jackson wondered. Or just weak from his illness? And where the hell was he going? Jackson remembered that Derrick had mentioned their bedroom being in the garage. He and Nicky must have remodeled. He'd only been to this house once for Derrick's birthday barbecue.

Focus! Pivoting back to the body, Jackson recited a mental list of procedures. He couldn't get anything wrong here. But the supplies in his satchel were low, and he couldn't find any paper booties. But it didn't matter. First responders almost never put them on before entering a crime scene either. He pulled out his camera and shot several images of the corpse in relation to the rest of the house, then moved in and took a dozen close-ups. Derrick was right about the manner of death. Nicky had been strangled with her own scarf. He touched her arm. Even through the gloves, the coolness was obvious. Bodies dropped three degrees every two hours, so she had most likely been dead since midnight.

Derrick came back into the kitchen dressed in jeans and a T-shirt, but he was still shivering. Jackson called out, "If you're sick, go get into bed." It would look better for his brother too. "I'll come talk to you in a moment." He heard a vehicle stop in front of the house. Probably a patrol officer. Jackson hurried after his brother. The converted garage was cooler than the rest of the house, but the carpet was thick under his feet.

Derrick sat on the edge of the bed with his head in his hands. "What is happening to me? I have this fucked-up disease no one can figure out and now my girlfriend has been killed right here in my house." He looked up at Jackson and pleaded, "Don't let them put me in jail. If I start puking or my blood pressure drops, I'll die in there before a doctor responds."

Jackson put a hand on his shoulder. "I'll do everything I can to help you. But you have to be honest with me."

"I have been!"

"What time did you get home last night?"

"Around nine. We left the hospital at eight or so, but we stopped at a pharmacy for anti-nausea medicine, then hit KFC to get Nicky some dinner."

"What did you do when you got home?"

"I took one of the pills and went straight to bed. I watched TV for a few minutes, then nodded off."

"What about this morning?"

"Like I said, I got up to pee and had to go into the house. There she was . . . on the floor." Tears rolled down Derrick's face.

Jackson had seen his brother cry more in the last half-hour than the rest of his life combined. Derrick's grief was real. But he knew from experience that it didn't necessarily mean he was innocent. Perps often felt grief and guilt too. Still, he believed Derrick. Something else was going on here.

A patrol officer burst into the room. Jackson stood and reached out his hand. "Detective Jackson, Eugene Police." He didn't want to get shot by an officer who didn't know him.

"Carlos Marina." Young and stocky, his grip was almost painful.

Jackson gestured toward the bed. "This is my brother, Derrick Jackson. He woke up and found his girlfriend dead, then called me."

The expression on the officer's face sent a wave of fear through Jackson's gut. Marina thought the story sounded like horseshit. In his shoes, Jackson would have been skeptical too. "I called Sergeant Lammers on the way and notified the dispatch center too. Other detectives should be here soon."

"Sir, I know you outrank me, but I think you should leave the scene."

Had he messed up by coming inside? He'd been so worried about Derrick, maybe he wasn't thinking clearly. "Now that you're here, I will." Jackson squeezed his brother's shoulder again. "It's going to be okay."

Jackson stepped toward Officer Marina. "Derrick has been very sick. He was in the hospital over the weekend and again yesterday. If his blood pressure drops or if he starts vomiting, you have to call for an ambulance immediately."

Confusion in the young officer's eyes. "Yes, sir."

Not wanting to pass by Nicky's body and disrupt the crime scene further, Jackson looked around for a door leading outside. But a tall wardrobe dresser stood in front of it. He nodded at Marina and walked through the open door to the kitchen.

Another patrol officer stood near the corpse, snapping photos. They'd been on the SWAT unit together years ago. "Hey, Jackson. This your case?"

"Sort of. It's my brother's home and girlfriend, and he contacted me. I'm going out to wait for my team."

"Good call."

Outside, Jackson pulled in long breaths of cold morning air. The sun peeked over the hills, spreading a faint glow across the valley. The light gave him an inexplicable hope that everything might turn out all right for Derrick.

But not for Nicky. Jackson finally felt a sense of loss. Another young life snuffed out. And for what? Because she knew Derrick? Was someone killing these women to frame his brother? If so, they picked a really bad time, considering Derrick's illness. Jackson vowed to find the killer—even if Lammers took him off the case. He could still do legwork. If Evans or Schak took the lead, they would keep him informed.

Schak drove up a moment later and parked across the street. He walked over carrying a travel mug, and Jackson could smell the coffee. *Damn.* He could use a cup himself. "Hey, Schak. I know it doesn't seem possible, but this case just got weirder."

His partner stared for a long, silent minute. "I have to take Derrick in for questioning."

Dread filled his belly. "He's too sick. He's been in the hospital three of the last four days."

Another long silence. "Then we'll do a recorded interview here, with a paramedic on standby. Derrick wasn't in the hospital when both of the victims were killed."

"Did Lammers put you in charge?"

"Yes. Because I'm already familiar with the first case."

"Please promise me you'll investigate other leads and other connections between the women."

"You know I will." Schak nodded to give his word. "Now tell me you were smart and didn't go into the house."

More unease. "I'm sorry. I was responding to a family member in distress. But I was only in there for a moment."

Schak shook his head, obviously upset. "If I do find another perp, you just gave his defense lawyer a solid argument." He lowered his voice to a mock judicial tone. "Your Honor, we contend that the real killer's brother, a police officer, tampered with the crime scene to frame my client."

A cloud rolled across the sun, darkening the sky again. Jackson wondered if he would lose his job.

Chapter 23

Schak stared at Jackson and tried to put himself in his friend's shoes. Would he have done the same thing if it was his family? He'd been through something sort of similar with his cousin, and no, he hadn't been protective.

"I can talk to neighbors and see if anybody witnessed a visitor coming to the house last night," Jackson offered.

"No, you can't. You have to leave the scene and let us handle this." Schak sounded gruffer than he meant to, but he had a nasty headache. And Jackson needed to understand how serious this was. Police officers were under more scrutiny than ever, and his partner may have already poisoned the well on this one. Schak was inclined to think Derrick had committed both murders—for reasons that weren't obvious yet. But Jackson would never see the crimes clearly. "Just go, please. You can work on the Holden case for now."

Schak rushed into the house before Jackson could argue. It would be strange to work a major case without him, but Schak knew he could handle the investigation. It was the stress that had him worried. Lately he hadn't been dealing with it well. He stopped inside the door to pull on gloves and booties. A patrol officer stood about six feet from the body, which lay near the kitchen floor.

"I'll take it from here," Schak said. "I need you to canvass the neighbors. Ask if they saw any cars or visitors last night.

Or heard anything suspicious from this house anytime in the last twelve hours." Schak handed him a business card. "If they're not home, check back at the end of your shift and report to my number directly."

"Yes, sir." The officer started toward the door. "Do we know the victim's name?"

"Nicky Walker." Schak wasn't sure about her age, but it didn't matter at the moment. He knelt next to her body and took photos, trying not to think about the person she used to be. The perp, probably her boyfriend, had used a scarf to strangle her. The weather seemed too warm for her to have been wearing the garment at the time, but it was possible. Some women wore scarves year-round for fashion. The detail mattered. If she hadn't been wearing it, then the scarf might belong to the killer. On the off chance that an intruder had done this, he or she might have brought the scarf with them. Or been wearing it themselves. The garment needed to be bagged and sent to the state lab for DNA testing, but he would let the medical examiner handle it.

Schak touched the victim's hand. Cool and stiff. She'd been dead for at least eight hours.

He stood up and looked around the kitchen and small dining area. Nothing out of place or broken. If Derrick and Nicky had had a fight, they'd kept it verbal. Why the kitchen though? Domestic murders almost always happened in the bedroom or living room—because couples fought over sex or money, and occasionally the remote control. He needed to let the ME and the techs handle the evidence while he questioned Derrick. When the obvious suspect was still at the scene, that was the best time to get a confession. But where was he? Schak glanced in the two bedrooms. The larger one held a desk and shelves, and the smaller space had been crammed with storage items such as camping gear and sports equipment.

When he entered the kitchen again, Evans stood near the body. "What the hell?" She looked at him with worry.

"Nicky Walker, Derrick's girlfriend." Voices on the other side of the wall surprised them both. "He must be in the garage. I'm going out to question him. Look for the victim's purse, phone, and computer." Schak hustled toward the exterior door, wishing like hell someone would bring him more damn coffee. Starting his day at six a.m. with only one cup was almost torture. How the hell was he supposed to kill his hangover?

The converted garage held a chill from the concrete, but Schak didn't mind. The damn suit jacket he wore on the job was too hot most of the time, and before the day was over, he would be sweating. A young Hispanic officer stood near the door, keeping his eyes on the man in bed. Derrick sat with his back against pillows and his eyes closed.

The officer nodded. "Carlos Marina."

"Detective Schakowski." He gestured toward the suspect. "Is he okay? Anything I should know?"

"He's Jackson's brother and he's been sick. But he says they don't know what's wrong with him." Marina sounded deadpan, but his expression suggested skepticism.

"Do you have a phone with a camera?"

"Of course."

"Get ready to record this interview." Schak grabbed the only seat in the room, a vinyl-padded trunk and dragged it next to Derrick. For a moment, he just stared. This guy looked so much like Jackson, only blonder and thinner.

The suspect opened his eyes and seemed startled to see Schak's face so close. Derrick blinked a few times. "Sorry, I nodded off for a moment. Who are you?"

"Detective Schakowski. At the moment, I'm your best friend. If you tell me the truth, I can help you."

"Where's Wade?"

For a moment, Schak didn't know who he was talking about. Then he remembered it was Jackson's first name. "Your brother isn't working this case and he can't help you. But if you tell me everything that happened, I'll get you the best deal I can." Plea agreements weren't under his control, but most suspects didn't know that. "Tell me your name."

"Derrick Jackson. And I don't need a deal, because I didn't do anything wrong."

"Your girlfriend, who lives with you, is dead on your kitchen floor, and you're the only one here. But I'm sure you didn't intend to kill her. It was probably an accident." Schak just needed him to admit that they'd fought. Once he had a crack, he could worm through. "Was she giving you a hard time?"

"No! Nicky takes care of me. When I got home from the hospital, I went straight to bed. She brought me my medicine and a glass of water because that's how she is." Tears welled in his eyes. "She's been amazing through this whole ordeal, and I would never hurt her."

Shit. This wasn't going well. "What ordeal?"

"This illness that started last November. The symptoms come and go, but they're bad. I've been hospitalized four times, and they still don't know what it is."

The suspect was trying to generate sympathy, but Schak wasn't buying it. "What time did you get home?"

"Around nine."

"Your girlfriend died shortly after that. No jury will believe you slept while someone else killed her."

Derrick burst into tears.

Schak waited for him to get calm, but Derrick started choking instead. Another sympathy ruse? The man was too comfortable in his own bed. Time to make him sweat. "Get up. We're going into the department so you can make a formal statement." He signaled to Marina to stop recording.

"This isn't a good idea," Derrick whined. "My blood pressure sometimes drops without warning."

"I could book you into the jail instead. They have a staff doctor."

Derrick silently swung his feet to the floor. "Can I take my medicine?"

"Show me what you need and I'll bring it." He wasn't about to let the suspect trigger a medical event as a distraction, or worse yet, get himself sent to the hospital.

"That one is the anti-nausea." Derrick pointed to a plastic bottle on the nightstand. "My blood-pressure pills and the new autoimmune medication are in the kitchen." He stood slowly and trembled like an old man.

A flash of doubt gave Schak pause. Over six feet and muscular, Derrick looked like a powerful man. But if he was really that sick, did he have the strength to strangle his girlfriend? Maybe if she had made him mad enough to get adrenaline flowing. At the moment, he looked feeble.

"I need my jacket too," Derrick said, shivering.

Schak considered cuffing him, then changed his mind. He wanted to let Derrick keep what little dignity he still had on the off chance that he would get careless and say something incriminating.

When Schak escorted him through the house, Gunderson had arrived, and Jasmine Parker, a tech, was collecting trace evidence from the body. He nodded at both but didn't stop to chat. All the responders needed the house clear so they could do their jobs. He hated leaving the scene, but Evans was on site and he trusted her to track down the important stuff. With this case, there didn't seem to be much to solve. They just needed to prove that no one else had been in the house, so by default, Derrick was guilty.

Schak felt bad for Jackson. Having a killer in the family was especially hard on cops. Only a year ago, he'd been through something similar and had wanted to quit the department. That's when the heavy drinking had started. He'd managed to quit for six months, but doing this job without a shot of bourbon to look forward to at the end of the day was asking too much.

They crossed the street, and Derrick climbed into the back of Schak's sedan without protest. As Schak scooted around to the driver's door, he spotted the patrol officer he'd sent out to canvass the neighbors. The man jogged toward him at a good clip and raised a hand. Schak stopped and waited for him to approach.

"We have a witness who saw the couple come home last night just before nine," the officer reported. "The neighbor, Patty Sedarish, was just getting home too."

"Did she see or hear anything after that?"

"No, but her son stopped by around ten, so he might have. She gave me his contact information, and I called, but he didn't answer."

"Stay on it. Thanks." Schak climbed in and glanced back at Derrick. He'd stopped shaking but still looked out of it. "Are you all right?"

"I need to eat. Can we stop for doughnuts?"

What did he think this was? An upscale Uber ride? But Schak was secretly pleased. He could go for a cinnamon roll and a tall cup of coffee. Just thinking about it made his head feel better.

Chapter 24

At the department, Schak took Derrick to one of the holding cells on the main floor instead of an interrogation room. The claustrophobic spaces downstairs were more intimidating, but they were also more isolated. He wanted Derrick to be able to call for help and be heard. He couldn't allow Jackson's brother to die in his custody. Still, he wanted Derrick to get a taste of being locked up. After a few hours of incarceration, he might decide to cooperate. Maybe plead guilty but claim he was out of his mind from the medication he'd taken. That's what a smart lawyer would advise him to do. But Derrick hadn't asked for one, and Schak hadn't read him his rights because he hadn't officially arrested or detained him. The suspect had come with him voluntarily.

He led Derrick into the larger of the two cells and told him to stretch out on the bench if he needed to. While his suspect stewed, he planned to return to the scene and coordinate the investigation. "I'll be back to talk to you in an hour or so," he said, gesturing at Derrick to sit. "If you need anything or feel sick, just call out to Officer Casey. She's in the front office and will hear you." Schak hurried out, not wanting to answer any questions. Officer Casey had worked as a paramedic before joining the department, so she had basic medical skills too. Schak stopped to chat with her before heading out to his car.

He checked the time on his phone. Not even nine o'clock

yet. Way too early to take a nip from the flask under his seat. The device rang in his hand, startling him. *Jackson.*

"Hey, Wade," he said, trying to keep things light. "What have you got?"

"Just checking on Derrick."

"He's in our big holding cell and Casey is watching him."

"The one who used to be a nurse?"

"Paramedic. And I've got an officer talking to Derrick's neighbors about last night's activity. If a witness can put someone else at the scene, it will take some heat off Derrick." He was doubtful but wanted to ease Jackson's mind.

"What about Nicky's phone? Did she get any late calls?"

"Evans is on that, and I'm headed back out to the scene now. I transported Derrick personally just to make sure he got here safely. Later." Schak hung up. Some officers were rough on known criminals and suspects, and he hadn't wanted to take a chance. He had mixed feelings about the rough treatment. Most officers had earned the right to be jaded and bitter. But the code required respect for everybody, and Schak did his best to comply. As he backed out, he laughed at some of the exceptions he'd made. All verbal though. He'd never hit anyone in custody. Not even as a young hothead patrol officer.

As Schak neared the crime scene, he saw more patrol units crowded into the short street and two officers canvassing the neighbors. He parked behind the medical examiner's white van and climbed out. Gunderson and his two lead technicians stood around a gurney near the back doors. The body, zipped into a white body bag, lay on top. As Schak walked over, Gunderson called, "Can you give us a hand?"

He obliged and helped lift the gurney and corpse into the

van, grunting at the surprising weight of it. As the ME closed the back door, Schak asked, "What's the TOD window?"

"Nine-thirty and eleven."

Like Holden's, only narrower, because the death had been reported sooner. "Anything else you can tell me?"

"We know the perp is taller than the victim because of the upward pressure on the scarf he strangled her with. And he's a powerful man. She had no defense wounds, but I took scrapings from under the vic's nails just in case she got her hands on the killer. See you at the autopsy." Gunderson climbed into the van.

He didn't want to attend the damn postmortem, especially since the perp was sitting in a holding cell, but he probably would anyway. *Shit!* He needed to get Derrick's DNA. If the trace evidence on the first victim matched his profile, the case was all but over.

Standing on the sidewalk, sweating in the late-morning sun, Schak called the department's front office and got Officer Casey on the line. "It's Schakowski again. We need DNA from the suspect I asked you to watch. Any chance you can talk him into a swab?"

"I don't have to. He vomited right after you left, and I had to clean it up. I'll pull the paper towels out of the trash and slide them into an evidence bag."

"Thank you. By the way, how is he now?"

"I checked on him a minute ago, and he seems better. He asked for water and I gave him some."

"Bag his drinking cup too."

"You got it."

Schak scooted into the house. Evans stood in the living room, supervising a search. She directed a female officer to check every drawer and shelf in the office, then sent Marina to open every box and bag in the bedroom used as storage. As they walked away, she grinned at Schak. "I've already searched the bathroom and kitchen, and now I'll start on the bedroom."

"You have her electronics?"

"Just a phone and a small tablet." She pulled a plastic evidence bag from her satchel. "The cell was on the kitchen counter, and the mini iPad was in the bathroom. Both are password-protected."

Shit. A tech guy would be able to get into both, but that meant a delay. "Will you drop them off with our tech unit?"

"I'm on it." Evans stepped toward him. "Have you talked to Jackson?"

"Briefly." He understood her concern and half-suspected she was in love with the guy. "Jackson's fine."

"Good to hear."

"But his brother probably killed both women, and it will be hard for Jackson to stay on the sidelines while we build a case."

She nodded. "I'll go see what I can find in their converted garage."

Schak scanned the living room. Jasmine Parker was dusting the front doorknob for prints, but it was obvious the room hadn't been tossed yet. He grabbed the couch cushions and pulled them off, finding loose change and a half-smoked joint. He bagged the roach and labeled it, wondering whether Derrick or his girlfriend had the pot habit. Probably both.

His phone beeped. A text from Lammers: *I want an update!* Schak's shoulders slumped. The sergeant was only getting involved in these cases because the suspect was Jackson's brother. He wasn't about to spend ten minutes trying to text everything with his fat fingers. He called and gave her the rundown, including that Jackson had been inside the crime scene. She would know eventually anyway. Lammers didn't interrupt or ask questions until the end. "When are you meeting next?"

"Five or so this afternoon."

"See you then." His boss abruptly hung up.

Schak tried to regroup, thinking it was time to take a small sip from the flask under his seat.

"Hey, Schak. Come see this!" Evans shouted from the bedroom.

He hustled past the outline where the body had lain, strode through the kitchen, and stepped into the outer bedroom.

Evans stood next to a tall wardrobe closet with both doors open and a drawer in the bottom pulled out. She pointed to a metal box in the drawer that was half covered in clothes. "It's a safe," she said excitedly. "But it's locked and so far, no key." She cocked her pretty head to the side. "What do you suppose they're hiding in there?"

Chapter 25

Wednesday, May 9, 11:45 a.m.

Jackson sat in his car in the Burger King parking lot and ate a chicken sandwich. No fries. Sometime soon he hoped to have sex again—either with his old girlfriend or his new one—and he needed to shave a few pounds off his stomach. It was a little late in the game, but he had to try. His bigger concern though was two unsolved murders . . . and his brother's predicament related to those crimes.

He'd read through his case notes for Holden's homicide but didn't have any new insights. They still had three viable suspects: Barulla, the crazy neighbor; Aidan Emmerson, the pissed-off customer; and FreedomGladiator, the right-wing troll. But if Nicky's murder was connected to Holden's, then all three of those men could be dead ends. Barulla, in particular, might be off the hook because he was still in jail. Where did that leave them?

Derrick.

No! He refused to believe it. Something else was going on, and he couldn't figure it out unless he had all the information from both cases. He called Schak again, who let it ring five times before answering. "Hey, Jackson. I'm busy here. What have you got?"

"Time on my hands. Give me a lead to follow on Nicky's

murder." He had to start thinking about her as *Walker*. The team typically referred to victims, suspects, and witnesses by last names, unless a case involved multiple family members.

A long pause from Schak. "Okay. I need all the help I can get." Another pause while someone talked in the background. "Find out where Derrick and his girlfriend did their banking, then get statements for the last three months."

"Done. Thanks. We need to meet later too."

"Right. Let's say five or so."

"Anything I should know about the new homicide?" Jackson was eager for an update. It felt strange not to be at the scene, right in the middle of everything.

"We just found a locked safe, so there might be something there. But it will need to be drilled."

It had to be Nicky's. "Anything useful on her electronics?"

"They're locked too, so not yet."

Jackson had more questions, but they were about finding a suspect other than his brother. He didn't want to push Schak too hard. "I'll check in if I find something important."

"See you later."

Relieved not to be totally shut out of the new case, Jackson headed to the department. The fastest way to find out where the couple banked was to ask Derrick. He'd wanted to check on his brother anyway, but he'd resisted out of concern for how it would look.

A swipe of his security card opened the holding cell, and Jackson stepped in. Derrick, who'd been lying on the bench, sat up. He looked a little better than he had the last few times Jackson had seen him.

"Wade! Please tell me this is all a mistake."

"I'm working on it." Jackson sat on the bench next to him.

"I need to know where you and Nicky did your banking."

"Pacific Union, the one on Chambers. We still kept separate accounts though."

Jackson remembered Derrick mentioning a charity campaign. "What about the GoFundMe money? Where did it go?"

"Into Nicky's account. She's been handling our bills since I got fired." He winced. "I should have been honest when we talked about it in the hospital."

"When did it happen?" *And why hadn't Derrick told him?*

"Six weeks ago. During my previous hospitalization." He covered his face with his hands, then lamented, "I didn't want to tell you because I'm so ashamed of what's happening to me."

"That's crazy. People get sick. It's not your fault. You know I have RF. Sometimes I'm in so much pain, I wonder if I can keep working."

Derrick let out a hollow laugh. "Our parents were healthy until the day they were killed. What's wrong with us?"

"I don't know." Jackson couldn't let himself think about health issues right now. He had to find Nicky's real killer. "The team found a locked safe in your bedroom. What's in it?"

Derrick's eyes registered surprise. "I didn't know it was there. It must be Nicky's."

What was she hiding? "No clue what's in it?"

"None. Sorry."

"What else can you tell me about Nicky? Does she have family around here?" He'd never asked before because he'd expected Derrick to walk away from the relationship as he usually did.

"She's estranged from her family and never talks about them."

"How long has she been in Eugene and where does she work?"

"She moved here a few years ago, and she's an herbal consultant, but she doesn't have that many clients." Another consultant? An herbalist and a nutritionist might have overlapping clients. Or attend the same conferences or social gatherings. "Is it possible that Nicky and Tayla knew each other?"

Derrick's eyes widened. "Oh man. I never thought about that. Nicky never mentioned knowing Tayla."

"Tell me about Nicky's friends."

"She had a rough childhood and doesn't really trust people, so she's kind of a loner."

That could explain why she didn't have many clients.

"When can I get out of here?" Derrick leaned his head against the wall.

"Schak is running Nicky's investigation, so it's his call. But I'll do what I can to get him to release you."

"Thanks. Can you get me something to eat? I'm actually feeling hungry for the first time in months."

"Sure. I'll send something back here but I have to get going. I can't prove you're innocent until I find the perp." He patted Derrick's shoulder. "Hang in there."

On the drive to the bank, he called Schak but his partner didn't answer. Jackson left him a brief message: "I'm headed to the Pacific Union on Chambers to look at financials." He started to hang up, then added, "Here's a new detail. Both victims were self-employed as health consultants. Maybe they have a mutual client or attended the same conference." He hoped he didn't sound like he was grasping at weak connections just to help his brother. But there had to be some other motive commonality. That was the problem with Derrick as a suspect—no real motive.

The local bank occupied a building that had once been a pizza parlor, but the remodel had been so extensive you'd never know it. Jackson waited at the customer service desk for a woman to get her will notarized, then he stepped up and introduced himself. "I need to talk to your manager right now."

The bank teller, a young man with a beard, took it in stride. "I think she's available."

They walked to a back office with an open door. The teller stuck his head in. "Clara? A detective is here to see you."

The woman excused herself from a call, stood, and stuck out her hand. "Clara Joiner. What can I do for you?" Middle-aged and a little plump, but she was dressed in a stunning red skirt-suit.

Jackson sat down as he explained. "I'm working a homicide case. The woman, Nicky Walker, banked here, and I need to see the last three months of her transactions."

Joiner's expression went from surprise to concern as she thought it over. "Do you have a subpoena?"

"I don't need one. The woman is dead and I'm trying to find her killer." The bank manager could refuse and force him to get the paperwork, but he was within his legal rights to request it.

"Say her name again."

The manager keyed in the information and quickly found the victim's account. "I'll print the statements for you, but I can also email a PDF if that would be helpful."

"Thank you." He pulled a business card from the outer pocket of his satchel and pushed it across the desk. "Here's all my contact information." He waited quietly while she processed the documents, then asked, "How long has Nicky Walker been a customer here?"

After a moment, she responded, "Two years, almost to the date."

A printer on a side wall kicked into action, making a horrific noise.

The manager gave an apologetic smile and retrieved the papers. "Is there anything else?"

Jackson made a quick decision. "Do you have a room where I can peruse these before I leave? In case I have questions or decide I need to go back further?"

A small frown. "Our conference area is available."

She walked him across the hall into a windowless room with a large table and six executive chairs. As Jackson sat, she closed the door and silently walked away. He'd wanted to ask her for a cup of coffee, but he sensed she was uncomfortable with his mission. But that was her job—to protect clients' private financial information.

He skimmed through the first month just to get an overall sense of Nicky's finances. His eyes blurred and he swore at himself for not buying reading glasses yet. But a deposit jumped out at him. The amount, a thousand dollars, wasn't particularly significant, but the source was odd: *The David J. Miller Family Trust.*

Jackson flipped to the next month's printout and found another deposit in the same amount, also on the third day on the month. Nicky was a trust-fund recipient. But if her family name was Miller, where had Walker come from? Had she been married? An ex-husband could be a likely suspect too. Especially if she had moved to Eugene to escape him.

Back on the first page, Jackson read more slowly, his eyes straining. Normal payouts to a landlord, a utility company, and several to a grocery store. A few online purchases as well, from a retailer called Vitacost. Near the end of the month, another deposit showed up. This one from a GoFundMe account in the amount of $854. He searched the previous months and found deposits of $1152 and $796. The online charity campaign was pulling in more money than he would have expected. How long had it been open? Derrick had been sick off and on for about six months.

Jackson hurried across the hall and stepped into the bank manager's office. "Sorry to bother you, but I'd like to see three more months. Can I get statements for November through January, please?"

Joiner nodded, her mouth a grim line.

When he had the paperwork, Jackson did a quick skim. The family-trust deposits were there in the same amount for all three months, but the online-charity money had only started in January. Still, the first GoFundMe deposit had been for nearly six thousand dollars. He strained his eyes looking for where the money had gone, because it certainly wasn't in the account. A chunk had been paid to North McKenzie Hospital, and another thousand had been withdrawn in two separate $500 transactions a few weeks apart in February. Was any of it significant? The Miller Family Trust intrigued him the most.

Jackson gathered up the documents, thanked the bank manager, and strode out. Across a shared parking lot was a dollar store. Still fighting the gut pain, he went across and bought a couple pairs of reading glasses before going back to his car. His phone rang as he climbed in. *Lammers.* He thought about not taking her call, then realized that wouldn't be in his best interest. Might as well get this over with. He put in his earpiece and braced himself. "Sergeant. How are you?"

"Don't polite-talk me. Just get your ass into my office right now."

Chapter 26

Evans took a last look around the crime-scene house, feeling like she'd overlooked something. But it didn't matter at the moment. She could always come back. Right now, she had to take the portable safe to the evidence unit and get it drilled. Often locked boxes just held cash or jewelry, but Nicky had been murdered, so they had to learn her secrets—if she had any.

Evans went back to the bedroom and found Schak searching dresser drawers. "I'm headed to the evidence lab now," she called from the door. It was unusual to report to Schak. They each handled their own assault cases sometimes, but when they worked together on a homicide, Jackson always had the lead.

"I'm leaving soon too. I've got to take the phone and tablet to a tech guy."

"Or gal." She grinned to keep the peace. Schak was old-school, but worth retraining.

"Right." He gave her an exaggerated wink.

"See you at five." She picked up the safe from the bed where she'd left it, surprised again by how much it weighed. Only a foot long and eight inches deep, it seemed small, but whatever it was constructed of would withstand a bomb blast. She hoped Joe's drill would have enough power to bust out the locking mechanism.

The evidence technician was in the middle of a ballistics test for the gun Jackson had dropped off, but he promised to work on the safe as soon as he was finished. Evans drove to a nearby store, bought a protein bar, and ate it, thinking it wasn't enough food. She'd been called out to the new crime scene before breakfast, then had worked straight through lunch. She checked her phone to see what calls she'd missed. Sophie Speranza, a pesky but sometimes helpful reporter, had tried to reach her twice. She needed to talk to her, but it would have to wait.

Ben Stricklyn had also called that morning. Evans' blood pulsed just thinking about the prick. She didn't want to believe he'd actually get Jackson fired, but after what he'd done to her, she wouldn't put anything past him. She obviously didn't really know her ex-boyfriend or who he'd become. A part of her had hoped Stricklyn had just gotten out of control in a bad-drunk-jealous moment and would quietly go away. But his call meant the issue would have to be dealt with. Just not today.

Resisting the urge to drive straight back to the evidence lab and pressure Joe, she drove to a Dutch Brothers coffee stand and ordered a tall Italian roast. As she reached in her shoulder bag for her wallet, she found Nicky's purse instead. She'd picked it up earlier from a hook on the living room wall in the house.

When she had her coffee, Evans drove back to the crime lab, parked in the back lot, and pulled out the little black bag. The contents were minimal: a slim card holder with a driver's license and debit card; a squeeze tube of herbal lip balm; a metal ring with two keys, and a nail file. Evans pulled the license from the card holder and examined it. Nicky was five-seven and 135 pounds, according to what she'd told the

DMV. Even though she wasn't smiling, she was still a stunning woman. Her sleek dark hair and big eyes gave her a foreign look. Yet she seemed familiar. Then it hit her. Nicky Walker resembled Tayla Holden, the first victim. Standing side-by-side, they might look like sisters.

A chill ran down Evans' spine. Were they dealing with a serial killer?

Not likely. Murderous psychopaths were rare. The connection between the women was Derrick Jackson, and the man obviously was attracted to a certain type. But something else on the license struck her as off. The background color of the photo seemed a little dark. Evans pulled out her own license and compared the two. The blue in Nicky's was slightly more of a primary color than the aquamarine in hers. But maybe the DMV had changed the fabric board they used behind photos.

Or was this license a phony? She would take it to a detective in the fraud unit and see what they thought. But not now. More than ever, she wanted to see what was inside Nicky's safe. Evans texted Joe and asked if he had opened the box yet. While she waited for a response, she checked the task list she'd made for the day—then hadn't touched because of the new homicide. Near the top was: *Call Sophie.* The reporter's number had appeared in Holden's call history recently, both as incoming and outgoing connections. Evans had no reason to suspect the reporter of anything but being her usual busybody self, but it would be interesting to know what the two women had discussed. Besides, this might get Sophie to stop calling.

The reporter picked up on the second ring. "Hey, Detective Evans. Thanks for returning my call."

"Sure. I need to know what you and Tayla Holden talked

about on the phone."

"We were setting up an interview. I'm doing a feature on local women-owned startups." Keyboard clicking sounded in the background.

"Did you do the interview?"

"Well, no. It was set for Monday, and when I showed up, the police were there."

Sophie had been at the crime scene? The patrol cop on the street must have turned her away. "When you talked to Tayla, did she tell you anything of interest?"

"That might relate to her death? I don't think so."

"Did she say anything other than when she could do the interview?"

"Not really." Sophie was quiet for a moment. "This probably isn't important to your investigation, but . . . I talked to her mother yesterday, and she said Tayla had been in a motorcycle wreck and had a serious pain problem because of it. Apparently she had trouble finding a doctor who would prescribe her opioids until she went to a pain clinic."

The accident and the clinic were new information. "Do you know the name of the clinic? Or her doctor?"

"No, sorry. It seemed very personal and I didn't ask."

"Thanks. I have to go."

"Wait. I have questions about her murder. I have to turn in my copy soon."

"I can't tell you much, but go ahead and ask."

"Do you have a suspect?"

"We have several."

"Is one of them a guy who goes by FreedomGladiator?"

The mother must have told her.

"I can tell by your silence that he is," Sophie said. "Will you confirm it for the record?"

A tough call. "You can report an online harasser but don't name him. We don't want him to go underground." She didn't really suspect Larry Alder, but they had to be cautious.

"Thanks. Is the other suspect Tony Barulla?"

What the hell? "Where did you get that name?"

"I saw the bomb squad at his house around the corner and I did a little digging. It's my job."

The reporter was smart and tenacious. Evans couldn't help but admire her. "He's a person of interest."

"Can I quote you?"

"Only as someone involved with the investigation. I'm not leading it."

"Who is? Jackson?"

She didn't want to mention Schak because he wouldn't appreciate calls from Sophie. "It's not important."

"Can you tell me how Tayla died?"

"Asphyxiation." Evans had second thoughts about revealing it, but Sophie deserved a few details. She was as dedicated to her job as they were to theirs. "I have to go." She hung up and checked for text messages. Joe had replied: *Soon.* That had been five minutes ago.

Evans climbed out, hurried into the building, and found the evidence tech in the main lab area. He waved at her and went back drilling the lock on the safe. She stayed near the door, watching and pacing. It took nearly ten minutes, but Joe finally put down the noisy power tool. He pulled off his safety goggles and wiped his brow. "Damn, that was a lot of work."

Evans scooted over to the bench where the safe rested. "Let's pop it open."

"You'll probably be disappointed." Joe chuckled. "The last safe I opened had nothing but old family photos and worthless stock certificates." Still wearing work gloves, he tugged on the lid.

Evans peered into the metal container. A bundled stack of cash, a ring with a single key, and a small amber bottle. The key intrigued her most, but she did a quick count of the bills just to make sure the total wasn't significant. Less than $600. She picked up the amber vial and twisted the cap open. Grayish powder.

"Close it!" Joe shouted.

Evans quickly complied. "What is it?"

"I don't know, but I intend to wear a mask when I test it to find out." He shook his head and gave her a scolding look. "If it's not one of twenty common substances, it will have to go to the state lab."

She handed the vial to Joe. "Can you expedite the test?"

He rolled his eyes. "I already put aside a ballistics test to drill this baby on the spot, so don't push your luck."

"Fair enough." He would probably rush it anyway. Evans picked up the key. "My best guess is that this is for a safety deposit box. Nicky Walker seems to like locked containers." She held the key out for the tech to scrutinize.

"I think you're right. Do you know where she banks?"

"I can find out." Evans slipped the key into her jacket pocket. "Thanks, Joe." As soon as she was outside, she called Jackson. The afternoon had heated up and she took off her jacket as she walked to the car. "Hey, Jackson. Can you ask Derrick where his girlfriend banked?"

"Pacific Union on Chambers. I just left there."

"Were they cooperative? I've got a safety deposit box key I want to try."

"Talk to the manager, Clara Joiner. She gave me six months of bank statements without quibbling."

"Excellent. I'm glad Schak is letting you do some grunt work."

"Maybe not for long. I have to go in and see Lammers right now."

Evans wasn't worried. Unless Ben Stricklyn had tried to carry through his threat to get Jackson fired. But he wouldn't go through their sergeant. "You'll be fine. Lammers loves you."

"That's nuts," Jackson scoffed, then signed off in a worried tone. "I hope to see you at the meeting."

Evans checked her phone for the time: *5:03*. What the hell had happened to the whole day? The bank was probably closed now. She called to check and got a recorded message. She would go there first thing in the morning. At the moment, she was due at a task force meeting.

Chapter 27

Sophie hung up the phone, excited that Evans had called and confirmed both suspects. Now she could update her story and get it into tomorrow's paper. It was almost time to go home, but she would work late to make this copy happen. As she made the changes, her supervisor stepped into her cubicle. Balding, pot-bellied, and troll-like, Hoogstad wasn't pleasant to look at, but she was grateful to the editor for defending her when she'd been shoved aside. His presence now worried her though. "Is it my turn?" *Didn't they usually fire people first thing in the morning?*

A woman Sophie didn't recognize followed Hoogstad into her space while he silently shook his head. "I'd like you to meet the new managing editor, Sandy Cabrera." She sported a pink leather jacket.

How bad could she be? "Hello." Sophie stood and shook her hand. Might as well keep her job for as long as she could. "Welcome."

"Thank you. I just wanted to say that I value your experience, and for now, your job is safe."

For now. That was all she heard. "Okay." She couldn't bring herself to express gratitude. She was so tired of living with the daily uncertainty. After a moment of silence, she added, "Nice to meet you."

"Likewise." The new boss walked out.

Hoogstad gave her a disappointed look, then exited too.

Sophie sat down and got back to work. When she finished adding Evans' quotes, she uploaded her copy and turned her attention back to Tony Barulla. As Tayla Holden's back-fence neighbor, he seemed like a better suspect than the online troll. She had checked with the county that morning and found him in jail, charged with possession of a destructive device, a somewhat serious crime if he had, say, a bomb. But no mention of homicide. Prosecutors often held suspects on bogus lesser charges to keep suspects incarcerated while law enforcement built a solid case.

What if she could get an interview with Barulla?

She called the jail again but no one answered. While the phone rang, she opened her browser and loaded the Lane County Inmate Locater, hoping to get more detail. She keyed Barulla's first and last names into the search field and got a *No Results* message. She tried again using *Anthony* and got the same message.

What? He'd been in jail that morning! She hung up and called the same number again. After six rings, a female deputy answered. "Lane County Jail."

"Tony Barulla was in your system this morning and now he's not. Was he released?"

"Sounds like it, but I'll double-check."

Sophie waited, realizing she hadn't even identified herself to the deputy.

The woman came back on. "His mother, Natalie Barulla, posted bail this afternoon for a supervised release. His next hearing is set for thirty days, June 8th at one p.m."

"Uh, thank you." Sophie keyed the details into her note file. The great thing about working the crime beat was that almost all criminal proceedings were public information. She didn't add his release to her story though. She wanted to talk to Barulla and see what he had to say. Getting those quotes might be outside the scope of a normal murder piece, but his *destructive device* charges were a whole separate issue that involved public safety. She checked the time and realized her day was over. Sophie shut down her computer, said goodbye to her cube neighbor, and headed out.

Feeling hungry because she'd missed lunch, Sophie stopped at Market of Choice on the way and bought a container of Asian chicken salad. If Barulla decided to get chatty, she might not be home for hours and wouldn't want to have to cook. In fact, she was so hungry, she'd probably eat half the salad in the car before she talked to him. If he was even home. The deputy had said 'supervised release,' so maybe that meant he had to stay with his mother.

A dented black sedan sat in his driveway. She vaguely recalled the car being there on Monday when she'd been chased off by the police officer at the end of the block. She parked on the street and strode up to the door, her handy recorder in the pocket of her jacket. He didn't answer her knock, but music played inside the house so she figured he was home. Maybe he just hadn't heard her. She knocked again with considerably more force. The door, unlocked, pushed open.

Through the crack, she saw him sitting in a recliner, eyes closed. Was he sleeping? It seemed odd that her pounding hadn't woken him. "Mr. Barulla?"

He didn't flinch.

Sensing something was wrong, she stepped inside and noticed items on the floor by his chair. An empty liquor bottle and an open prescription container. *Oh shit.* It looked like the suspect had killed himself.

Chapter 28

An hour earlier

Jackson sucked in a deep breath, feeling a tightness in his chest, and knocked on Sergeant Lammers' door. "It's open," she called out. Squaring his shoulders, he stepped in and took a seat before she could command him to. He looked her right in the eye. *Show no fear!*

"So you walked into a homicide scene where your brother was the only witness and likely suspect. Do you realize how stupid that was?" She gave him her worst evil-eye stare.

"Yes, sergeant. I do now." He started to explain his emotions in the moment, then stopped. Less was better.

"You're the best detective we have and you've never crossed a single line, so I'm not going to suspend you."

Relief washed over him. "Thank you."

"You're also the only person who called me when I was suspended." Lammers let out a small sigh. "But we're both going to pretend I didn't say that."

"Got it."

"Based on everything I know about both homicides, I'm not sold on the idea that Derrick is the perp. And we're still as shorthanded as ever, so I'm leaving you on the case." She picked up a printout from her desk and seemed to be deciding what to say. "Schak will run both homicides and you report to him. Stay in the background and do legwork only.

175

But I want your full attention on finding *all* the connections between the two women."

Another wave of relief. "Yes, sergeant."

"If Derrick turns out to be the only connection, I'll reassign you for your own sake." She stood. "We have a task force meeting to attend."

When the two of them walked into the conference room, everyone gave a quick glance their way but didn't say anything. Schak was at the head of the table, where Jackson usually sat, and Evans and Quince were across from each other. Jackson was glad to see Quince was back on board. They needed all the help they could get. "Hey, Quince. Good to see you."

As Jackson sat next to him, Quince held out his hand for a fist bump. "I could use the overtime pay."

Everyone laughed. They always worked late without any benefits.

"Let's get started," Schak said. "I've got food coming later, and I'd like to be mostly wrapped up by then."

His tone was so serious, Jackson had to suppress a smile.

Schak launched in with the basic details to update those who hadn't been at the scene. "Nicky Walker died last night between nine-thirty and eleven, strangled by a scarf. We found more scarves in a drawer, so it seems likely the garment belonged to her."

"I think she always wore them," Jackson said.

Evans jumped up, walked to the second whiteboard that had been brought in, and wrote rapidly to catch up.

"There are no signs of a break-in or struggle," Schak continued. "Also, Nicky lived with Derrick Jackson, who once dated the first victim, Tayla Holden." He glanced over his shoulder at Evans. "What else did we learn?"

"Nicky Walker had a small safe in her bedroom that contained $600 in cash, an unknown powder substance, and a key." Evans listed *cash, key,* and *powder* under a heading labeled Evidence. "I think the key is to a safe deposit box, which I'll check out in the morning."

"Derrick claims he didn't know about the safe," Jackson said. He felt compelled to add, "I'm just reporting information contemporaneously." He'd heard the word in the news a lot lately.

Schak stayed focused on Evans. "Anything else?"

"Yes, but it's about the first victim. Are we okay to go back and forth?"

"I think we have to, especially when we find overlap." Schak offered a grim smile.

"Our favorite reporter"—Evans smiled and rolled her eyes—"talked to Holden's mother and found out that she'd had a motorcycle accident that led to her pain problem. The mother also mentioned a pain clinic, which I will try to find."

Jackson had to ask. "Did you find any medications that belonged to Nicky?" The team seemed to have settled on calling her by her first name, probably because he did.

"No. And I searched the house thoroughly myself." Schak finally made eye contact with Jackson.

But only for a second. Was he feeling uncomfortable because of their reverse roles? "We should get Nicky's medical records just to see if there's any overlap," Jackson suggested.

"We can, but I think it's a waste of time." Schak's voice was deadpan.

Jackson remembered another connection, so he pressed the issue. "The victims were both vegans and had similar careers, so maybe they had an overlapping client. We should check that out too."

Schak leaned back with his arms crossed. "We have a viable suspect. Derrick had been involved with both women, and they look enough alike that he clearly has a preference."

"Or someone does," Lammers cut in. "We need to get back to fundamentals. What motive did Derrick have for killing both women? My understanding is that he hadn't seen the first victim in over a year."

Jackson's relief at her support was short-lived.

Evans cleared her throat, and they all turned to her. "I spoke to Holden's mother last night and asked who her daughter had been dating. She said the last she'd heard was Derrick." Evans met Jackson's eyes, her expression pained. "What if Derrick was cheating on Nicky and seeing his old girlfriend? That could cause some problems."

"He's been sick for six months!" Jackson regretted the emotion behind his words, but not what he'd said.

"He's still a big man who could have easily overpowered both women." Schak sipped from his cup, his hand trembling a little. "Here's my theory. The nude photo that Tayla Holden had on her phone caused some kind of problem with Nicky, Derrick's new girlfriend. Or maybe Holden tried to extort money from Derrick with the threat of revenge porn, by threatening to post the image online. I know it's usually guys who do that, but a woman could as well."

"Derrick wouldn't care about that," Jackson argued.

"I'm not done." Schak took another sip. "So Derrick killed Holden to put a stop to whatever was going on with the photo. When Evans questioned Derrick, Nicky figured out that he'd done it. So when Nicky confronted him about it, Derrick killed her too."

Jackson didn't buy any of it. "Derrick was in the hospital Saturday night."

"I checked the records, and he wasn't admitted until almost three a.m." Schak crossed his arms again. "So Derrick could have done it."

Lammers got into it. "What about the other suspects in the first homicide? Do any of them have a connection to the second victim?" She glanced down at her case-notes handout. "We have FreedomGladiator, the online troll. Aidan Emmerson, who was pissed off about Holden's product. And Tony Barulla, the Peeping Tom criminal next door." Lammers looked around the room for follow-up.

"I talked to the troll," Evans said. "His name is Larry Alder and he lives with his mother." She wrote his real name on the board. "He has no record and his mother gives him an alibi for Saturday night."

Crap. Jackson tried not to feel discouraged.

"Barulla's in jail," Schak reminded them. "So we know he didn't kill Nicky Walker."

"Actually, he's not." Quince spoke for the first time. "We're building a solid case against him for the vandalism crimes, but his mother posted bail this morning and he was released."

The room was silent for a moment. They were taken aback by the development, but still, they realized Barulla had been locked up at the time of Nicky's death. Jackson wanted to bring up Emmerson as still viable, but he knew it would seem lame. Especially since the guy had no obvious connection to Nicky, and he'd sent the names of friends who would testify to his presence at a party the night Holden was killed.

"Holden's high-end phone consultations didn't pan out

either," Schak added. "They're both in Europe."

Lammers' phone rang in her jacket pocket. While she checked the ID, Evans mouthed *Sorry* at Jackson. He didn't take anything she'd said personally. She was just doing her job.

The sergeant abruptly stood and took the call, her expression grim. As they waited, a delivery kid, looking sheepish, came into the room with two brown bags. "The sandwiches you ordered." He grinned and glanced around the table. Jackson, closest to him, pulled out his wallet and gave the kid a five. On the side, he heard Lammers asking questions that could only mean one thing.

Finally, she hung up and turned to the team. "We have another death, but it may not be directly related. It looks like Tony Barulla committed suicide."

Chapter 29

Everyone was on their feet, looking at him, and for a moment, Schak felt paralyzed. This was really Lammers' decision, but he wanted someone else to take the case. "Maybe Jackson should head up this one. A suicide shouldn't take much time." Feeling the effects of the bourbon he'd poured into his coffee, he grinned at Jackson. "Pass me a sandwich, please. I need a little sustenance." He hoped his longtime friend wasn't taking his theory about Derrick too personally. Jackson was too close to the suspect to see the scenario clearly.

Jackson blanched, then slid the bag toward him. No one else moved.

Finally, Lammers said, "I want Quince to take this one. He's been working Barulla's other crimes and knows the man best." She clapped the young detective on the shoulder. "I'll go with you." Then she looked across the table at Jackson. "After you eat and get your assignment for the Vegan Girl Murders, I want you at the scene for a while too. Sophie Speranza discovered the body and is still onsite. I'll let you question her because I know how much you like her." She gave Jackson a quirky smile and left the room. Quince grabbed a sandwich and followed her out.

Irritated to lose their help, Schak bit into a ham-and-cheese and gave himself a moment to think. He'd wanted Jackson out of the room so he and the others could talk more freely about Derrick, but that would have to wait. He had to divvy up the tasks and get everyone back to work.

"I'll track down both women's medical records," Jackson offered.

"Let's wait on that." He had to stay in charge of this case. "I'll attend the autopsy in the morning, hear what the pathologist has to say, then let you know."

Jackson nodded, clearly not happy, and reached for a sandwich. "What about Derrick? He's still sitting in the holding cell."

"His home is a crime scene, so he can't go back there. He can either spend the night here or in jail." Schak silently begged Jackson not to suggest Derrick could go home with him. He wouldn't allow it, and he and his friend were already on thin ice.

Jackson stayed silent, and Evans jumped in to cover the awkwardness. "After I check for a safe deposit box, I'll stop at the lab. I'm very curious about the powder Nicky kept stashed. Any ideas?"

"Maybe it's a crushed opioid," Jackson suggested.

Why wouldn't he get off that idea? Schak asserted himself again. "We have no reason to think Nicky had a pain or addiction problem. I want to focus on Derrick's connection to Tayla Holden so we can firmly establish motive. We need to get both of their phone records going back a few months and see if they communicated." He eyeballed Jackson. "I need you to write the subpoena for that."

"We can just ask Derrick to call his phone company and produce his records."

Jackson's confidence unnerved him, making Schak doubt himself. "Fine. Ask him." He turned to Evans. "Did you make any progress with the other images of naked men on Holden's phone? If she was extorting one guy, maybe she was working all of them for cash."

"Not yet. The second homicide this morning derailed my task list." Evans finally reached in the food bag too. "But I'll get on it."

"Is there anything else we haven't covered?" He knew he was missing something, but he just wasn't thinking as sharply as he wanted to. He blamed the conflict with Jackson.

"I looked at Nicky's bank records this afternoon," Jackson said. "She had money coming in from a GoFundMe campaign she'd set up for Derrick and from a family trust fund. But she also had several $500 withdrawals."

Probably not important.

"What if the cash was for blackmail payments?" Jackson added.

"The amounts are too small." Schak finished his sandwich.

Evans jotted the financial information on the board, then turned and said, "Oh yeah." She pulled a plastic bag from her satchel. "I took a close look at Nicky's driver's license, and I think it might be forged." She pushed it toward him to look at. "I'll drop it off with one of the fraud detectives tomorrow."

A fake license? What could that mean? Schak pulled the card free of the plastic and stared. He didn't see anything wrong.

"It's the color of the photo background," Evans said. "I think it's too dark."

Schak shook his head. Like most men, he didn't see color as sharply as women did. "Okay. Check it out. But why would she have phony ID?" He instantly thought of five reasons and felt foolish. "I take that back." He handed the driver's card to Jackson, wanting to give him something that would keep him busy. "Why don't you run her image through the FBI's facial recognition software, then take the license to our fraud guys?"

"Or gals." Evans grinned.

Schak wasn't in the mood for it. "I think we're good to go." He stood, signaling the meeting was over.

Chapter 30

Jackson took his time gathering up his notes, waiting for Schak to leave first. He was worried about his partner, who seemed tense and not as sharp as usual. He hoped it wasn't because he was drinking again. If he was, it was now an on-the-job problem. Schak glanced over at him as he walked out, and Jackson gave him a tight smile. Schak dropped his paper cup in the trashcan by the door.

Evans took her time too, and as soon as the room was clear, she asked, "How are you holding up? I know this focus on Derrick has to be stressful."

"I'm fine. But I'm worried that Schak isn't." Jackson strode over to the trash, pulled out the cup, and sniffed it. A whiff of alcohol. He handed it to Evans for confirmation. She smelled it and nodded. "Yep, he laced his coffee."

"Let's not deal with this now, okay? He'll think it's about me trying to protect Derrick by derailing his investigation."

"When and how are you going to handle it?" Her voice was tense.

"I don't know. But we have to keep an eye on him and make sure nothing on this case falls through the cracks." Jackson thought about the cup Evans was still holding. Should they keep it?

"I'm worried about Schak's focus on Derrick." Evans stuffed the coffee container into her bag. "I mean, this could be a serial killer with a thing for women who look like crypt-keepers. Derrick's connection to both of them could be circumstantial."

"I'm worried about that too. And I still intend to look at medical records and consultation customers for an overlap."

"Good call." She stroked Jackson's arm. "But if the evidence points to your brother, I'll do everything I can to build a case against him."

"I promise not to hate you for it." He gave her a grim smile too. "I have to go. Lammers is expecting me at the scene and my kids want me at home." He started toward the door.

Evans followed him. "What have you done to Lammers? She's lost all her bark and bite."

"Me? I had nothing to do with that."

Evans leaned in and whispered, "Maybe it's her cannabis prescription."

Jackson chuckled. "If it was pain making her so crabby, then I'm glad she found relief."

They stopped outside the conference room and looked at each other. Jackson knew that if they got together as a couple, Evans would probably have to leave the team. But it would be worth it. Had he made up his mind? "See you tomorrow." He moved toward the exterior stairs.

"Call me if anything interesting comes up at Barulla's."

"I doubt it will."

In the car, he called Katie, surprised when his daughter picked up immediately. "Dad, what the hell? It's six-thirty. Why didn't you tell me you'd be late?"

"I'm sorry. We've had two deaths today, and I'm still working. Tell Benjie I'll be home before bedtime to read him a story." *Bad idea.* If anything was hinky at the death scene, he might not be home until midnight. "No, just give him a hug from me."

"And what do I tell Kera?"

"What do you mean?"

"She showed up today out of the blue and said you were expecting her."

Oh no. Panic fluttered in his gut. He hadn't told Katie that Kera was coming because he'd lost track of it while working a double homicide. Or was it just another sign that he wasn't meant to be with Kera? "Sorry again. She called when I was already deep into this investigation, so I was focused on the case. You know how it is."

"You forgot your girlfriend was coming home after being gone for six months?" Katie used an exaggerated Valley Girl voice.

He burst out laughing. "I'll be home as soon as I can."

"Yeah, right." His daughter hung up.

He was still smiling when he drove out of the parking lot. Katie's sense of humor was finally coming back, and the joy of it filled his heart. Relief too, that his little girl was turning out well and that he hadn't screwed her up.

Twenty minutes later, he pulled up near the dead man's home for the second time in forty-eight hours and again, it was hyperactive. Instead of the bomb squad and SWAT guys, this time there were crime-scene techs and detectives.

Inside, Barulla was in a recliner, dressed only in baggy shorts. He looked like he'd fallen asleep after a pickup basketball game. Only he didn't have that kind of body. Gunderson was taking his core temperature and didn't look up. Quince wasn't visible, but he was probably searching the home.

Sergeant Lammers stepped around the corner from the kitchen. "It's about time." She pulled an evidence bag from her pocket and held it out.

Jackson walked over and examined the contents: A empty prescription bottle, this one white with a red lid. "Where did you find it?"

"On the floor next to his body, along with an empty vodka bottle. I saw in the case notes that you'd found a prescription container in the first victim's purse, so I wondered if they had a similar source."

"I don't think so. Let me see the label." Jackson pulled out his new reading glasses and took a closer look. Oxycodone, prescribed by Dr. Potter to Natalie Barulla. *Tony's mother?* "What does Gunderson think?"

The ME yelled from across the room, "He's been dead about three hours and no obvious signs of trauma."

"Thanks," Lammers yelled back.

"Where's Sophie?" Jackson felt compelled to get her part over with.

"I let her leave for a few minutes to go to the store, but she'll be back."

Footsteps pounded up the hallway, and they both turned to see Quince approach. He held out a large flat evidence bag with a piece of paper inside. "It's a suicide note. I found it on the printer tray."

Jackson's first reaction was relief that Barulla was a suicide, which meant they didn't need to investigate. *But a printed suicide note?* Almost unheard of. People always handwrote their final goodbyes. "The printed part seems odd."

Quince shrugged. "Not really. Last time we were here, we picked up all kinds of personal notes and essays. He was a man with a lot of opinions and he crafted them all on his laptop, then printed them. He sent a few letters to the *New York Times* as well."

The relief settled back in. He would question Sophie, maybe chat with a few neighbors, then go home. He needed to see Kera. Knowing she was in his home, waiting, filled him with longing. "What does the note say?"

"That he felt like an outsider and was tired of being mocked and judged. That he'd rather die than spend one more day in jail."

A wave of sadness hit him, and Jackson struggled to shake it off. He knew it wasn't really about Barulla.

Quince wasn't done. "He also confessed to killing Tayla Holden. He called her a tease and said she'd invited him into her home, then rejected him."

Jackson's mind raced. If Barulla had killed Holden, then the two women's deaths might not be related. Did that help Derrick or hurt him?

Lammers echoed his thoughts. "Now we have to rethink the Vegan Girl Murders."

He wished she would quit calling them that. And for the first time, Jackson wondered if Derrick had killed his girlfriend during an argument. So many women died that way.

Sophie slipped into the living room. "I'm back." She held a to-go cup in her hand.

Jackson nodded at his teammates and walked over. "Let's go talk in my car."

When they were settled into the front seats, he realized Sophie looked vulnerable—shoulders hunched forward and eyes pinched. He'd never seen her like this. "We'll make this quick. Why did you come here this evening?" He knew the answer, but he needed her statement on record.

"To interview Tony Barulla. I saw the bomb squad here on Monday, and I knew he was charged with possession of a destructive device. I wanted to hear his side."

"Did you talk to him in person?"

"No. I planned to just show up and see if I could charm him into giving me some quotes."

A typical Sophie strategy. "So you had no reason to think he was suicidal?"

"I was shocked to find him dead." Her voice was quiet.

"Okay." That predictable conversation was over, so now he could switch gears. "I want to ask about Tayla Holden. I know you talked to her mother. Tell me what she said about Tayla's medical problems."

Sophie took a sip of what smelled like mint tea. "She referred to Tayla's motorcycle accident as an event that had derailed her life for a while. She said Tayla had chronic pain afterward and apparently had trouble finding doctors to keep prescribing opioids."

"What about the pain clinic?"

"It sounded like after Tayla started going there, the prescription became a non-issue."

"Did she name the clinic or any doctor specifically?"

"No. Evans already asked me this." Sophie reached in her pocket, hesitated, then pulled her hand back out. "I have a recording of the conversation with Mrs. Holden. I'll transcribe it and send it to you."

"Thanks." He didn't know what else to ask her. "Do you have any background research on Holden that might be helpful?"

"Probably not. I was focusing on her as a business start-up feature. But her personal life seems rather tragic." Sophie shivered. "Did Tony Barulla kill her?"

Jackson decided to be honest with her. "He left a suicide note to that effect." His mind raced again. "So the women's deaths are probably not connected."

Sophie sat up straight. "Deaths? Who is the other victim?"

Oh crap. How was he going to walk this back?

Chapter 31

Jackson walked into the house, a cacophony of emotions tap-dancing in his torso. Excitement to see Kera after months of longing for her, dread about what he had to tell her and how it would make her feel, anxiety that sex with her wouldn't go well because of his guilt, and worry that she wouldn't want to sleep with him after he told her. He wouldn't blame her for that. Maybe he shouldn't tell her about his feelings for Evans. Maybe they would just go away.

He found Kera sitting on the living room floor with the two young boys, building a colorful fort out of Legos. She and Benjie both jumped up and rushed to greet him. Benjie got to him first, and Jackson gave him a quick hug. It was past the boy's bedtime, but this was a special occasion.

"Kera's back!" Benjie announced. "To stay!"

"I see that." Jackson folded Kera into his arms, marveling at how warm and soft she was. And her smell! The jasmine scent of her shampoo mingled with the pure-Kera scent of her skin. "I've missed you," he whispered into her neck.

"Oh yes. This is heavenly."

He hated to let her go, but the boys were both talking, impatient for their attention. "We'll continue this later," he promised. *Oh crap.* What was he saying? He had to tell her about his conflicted feelings.

"Yes, we will." Kera pulled back.

Micah stepped toward him, the shy boy trying to express

himself. Jackson scooped him up and gave him a squeeze. "I've missed you, Micah."

"Me too." The tiny arms around his neck clung to him with joy.

How was he supposed to walk away from all this? Jackson's eyes watered and he smiled so widely his mouth hurt. After a moment, he pried Micah loose. "Let me get my jacket off and I'll join you on the floor."

He retrieved his weapon from the top of the fridge where he'd just left it, locked it up in the bedroom, and downed more anti-inflammatories. Back in the hall, he knocked on Katie's door. She took her time before yanking it open. "Hey, Dad. Make it quick. I've got a lot of homework."

"We will talk about what happened at school yesterday, just not right now."

"There's not much to say. Jason grabbed my ass again, and I punched his gut. I got sent home because another student saw me hit him and reported it." She rolled her eyes. "The only reason I didn't get expelled is because Mrs. Mayfair knows what he's doing. But I don't think Jason will mess with me again."

Jackson worried that the guy might want revenge and would assault Katie outside of school. And what could he do to prevent it? He was a goddamn police officer! He should be able to protect her. He would have a chat with Jason's parents. *Soon!* "Keep yourself safe like we've talked about. Head up and eyes alert. Don't be alone in nonpublic places."

"Yeah, yeah. I'll be fine." Katie closed the door.

Jackson pushed aside his concerns for the moment. He had a family full of joy waiting for him.

After they put the boys to bed in Benjie's room, he and Kera sat on the couch. Jackson held her close as she talked about losing both her parents. "I have to go back, you know," she finally said. "Their house is going to need weeks of work to clear out everything and get it ready to sell. But I had to come home and see you for a while first."

"How long can you stay?"

"A week or so."

Jackson gave her a squeeze. "I'm glad you're here."

"I have an interesting proposal."

Another vacation, he guessed. "What do you have in mind?"

"You could retire from the department, and we could move to Redding and live in my parents' house. It's paid for, so we wouldn't have that expense. Plus, you would have your pension. You wouldn't have to work at all. You could be a full-time dad to these boys. It's what they both need."

She was serious, so he tried not to look unnerved. He took a moment to visualize the scenario in his mind. Building a fort with the boys in the backyard, fishing in the creek, restoring an old car. He would love it! For about a week. Then he would be bored and restless and probably full of self-loathing.

Kera laughed softly. "Did I scare you?"

"Yes and no." Jackson tried to find exactly the right words. "I love the idea in theory. But I know myself. And I'm not ready to retire. Even if I left the department to cut back on my hours, I'd still want to work for the prosecutor's office as an investigator."

"I know." A deep sigh. "But I had to try."

Now. He had to tell her now. "Kera."

"Oh, I don't like the sound of this."

"It's been hard for me while you were gone. I started to

think you were never coming back."

He waited for her to respond but she was quiet.

"To protect myself from feeling lonely and abandoned, I think I subconsciously shut down some feelings."

She twisted to look him in the eye. "You don't love me anymore?"

"Of course I love you." This was the part he dreaded. Could he say it? He had to! "But I've started to develop feelings for Evans. I don't know what it means, but I had to tell you."

The pain on her face was hard to take.

"Did you sleep with her?"

"No, but I think I want to." There. He'd said it. And probably killed his relationship with her.

"So go sleep with her. Get it out of your system." Kera scooted away from him, but took his hand at the same time. "Then come back to me. What we have is real and mature and based on mutual priorities. What you feel for Evans is only physical." Kera let out a gruff laugh. "I hope it's only physical. I know she's your friend, but I suspect she's not someone you can actually build a life with."

Stunned, Jackson didn't know what to say.

Chapter 32

Thursday, May 10, 7:05 a.m.

Schak woke with a headache—and a mouth so dry his tongue felt sticky. He sat up and the room spun. *Shit!* He'd forgotten to take aspirin and a glass of water before bed. That was the only way to not feel like this in the morning. *Or quit drinking again.* The little nag in his head started to annoy him.

He heard the shower running. Tracy was already up. Please let her have made coffee. He stumbled into the kitchen, smelling the fresh brew and trying to remember how much he'd had to drink once he'd gotten home. The evening was a blur, except for the part when he'd said something to make his wife mad. *Damn.* He would apologize first thing.

Coffee in hand, he went to the table and gulped it. He didn't have much time and he still had to shower. Nicky Walker's autopsy was scheduled for eight, and he'd slept in. Beyond that, he was running a double homicide with deaths that may or may not be connected and a perp that might be his best friend's brother. He was so burnt out on this job. But he didn't know how to quit.

The water shut off and a few minutes later, Tracy came into the kitchen. She didn't look at him or speak as she pulled a breakfast bar from the cupboard. Schak pushed to his feet, his lower back pinging with the pain of too much time in the car yesterday. He shuffled over to his wife. "I'm sorry, Tracy. I was out of line last night."

She glared at him. "Do you even know what you said?"

Oh boy. "No. I was pretty tired."

"You were drunk. And we've been here before. I have less patience now than I did then, so either quit again or I'm done." She spun away.

He would stop drinking as soon as the stressful part of these cases wrapped up. No problem. He wasn't going to lose his marriage over it.

Fifty minutes later, he stood in the underground hall outside the autopsy room. Schak couldn't make himself go inside. He could not watch another dead body be cut open and peeled back. To witness her being probed and rolled over like a carcass.

The elevator doors opened and Rich Gunderson rushed toward him. "We'd better get in there. You know how Konrad is if we're five seconds late."

"I can't do this. I have too much else going on." He had plenty of valid excuses. "We had another death last night, and the guy left a suicide note with a confession for the first victim. So we have to start over on motive for the second victim." Sort of. He still thought Derrick had probably killed his girlfriend. "Will you call me when the autopsy is done and give me the highlights?"

"Sure." The ME didn't move to go in. "Are you all right?"

"Of course." *Damn. Did he look hung-over?* "Why do you ask?"

"Nothing serious. You just look, uh, worried."

"I am. Our suspect in the second case is Jackson's brother, and Jackson is not on board with that."

"Yeah, I can see why that could be a problem." Gunderson gave his shoulder a push. "Good luck with that." The ME opened the door and went inside.

Schak headed back to the elevators.

On the drive to the department, he stopped for a box of doughnuts. Once he was in their work area, he dropped his briefcase on his desk, and walked over to Jackson's cube with the pastries. "Hey, buddy. I got you a maple bar."

Jackson turned and tried to smile. "Thanks, but I've got to lose a few pounds." He had dark circles under his eyes and looked like he hadn't slept well.

Was he that worried about his brother? "Everything okay?"

"Not yet, but it will be."

What the hell did that mean? "What are you working on this morning?" Schak had just meant to change the subject, but realized he sounded like a boss.

"Doing a search for the David J. Miller Family Trust, but the name is so common I'm getting nowhere."

"I'm not sure it's important."

"I plan to call the state lab too and see when we can expect toxicology reports." Jackson shifted and looked away. "We've got Barulla now and we need to know what's in his system."

"You have doubts about his suicide?"

"Maybe." Jackson let out a frustrated breath. "He left a printed suicide note. That's pretty weird."

"Yeah, but Barulla was a weird guy."

"That's a fact."

"I skipped the autopsy, but as soon as I have a report, I'll send it to you." Schak took the doughnuts down the hall to the other end of the building. Two tech people were at their desks and both looked up. He held out the box to Officer Fredricks, a new guy they'd imported from LA. Oversized and dark-skinned, he looked more like a defensive lineman than a computer nerd, but Schak was learning not to make assumptions based on physical appearance. He knew the guy was good.

"You saved my morning!" Fredricks took a glazed pastry and pushed half into his mouth.

Schak offered the box to the woman, Delarosa "The Hack," who was even more talented. Her weird hair bugged him, but this morning he didn't care.

She shook her head, then handed him Nicky's phone and tablet. "I stayed late last night to pop these, so they're both open for your reading pleasure."

"Thanks. Did you look at any files?"

"A few. I ran an email search for keywords like *afraid*, *stalking*, and *blackmail*, just to see if anything obvious came up, but no luck." Delarosa rubbed the shaved sides of her head. "But you need to check the Messenger account on her phone."

He'd heard of the chat platform, but it hadn't been a factor in any of their homicides yet. Young people were rarely murder victims, at least not in Eugene. He needed help accessing it, but he didn't want to ask the young woman.

Fredricks stepped over and took the phone. "Let me show you where to find the app." The big man clicked on a weird-looking square, and a list of chat messages appeared. They looked like a Facebook feed, which both confused and reassured him. "Thanks." Schak took the devices back to his desk.

He left the phone app open but decided to glance at the victim's computer files first. The tablet was new for him too, and he couldn't find any personal files. Feeling frustrated, he picked up the phone and scanned through messages. Most just mentioned the names of new people that were now on Messenger. Not helpful. His own phone rang in his pocket. Relieved, he pulled it out. *Gunderson.* "What have you got for me?

"There are no useful highlights from the autopsy. She was definitely strangled, with a crushed hyoid bone, but we knew that. The only oddity was some strange scarring on her body. Walker's neck, for example. She probably wears the scarf to cover a tracheotomy scar, which is a rare thing. Also, the bone scan revealed that she has pins and plates in one of her ankles, plus surgery scars there too. I'll send the full report after Konrad writes it up and uploads it."

"Thanks." Schak started to hang up.

"Oh, and I just remembered. She's had a lot of work done on her teeth. They're almost all crowns. With women, that usually indicates either a history of bulimia or drugs."

Bulimia? Was that a puking thing? "Thanks for the call."

Schak rubbed his head, wishing the ache would subside. He had so much to think about. The pins and plates and surgery scars could indicate chronic pain. Which meant Nicky's dental issue could be about opioids. That meant Jackson might be right about the victims both having a chronic pain problem. But so did millions of people. He had to question Derrick and see what he knew about Nicky's health history.

Schak jumped up and stepped toward the cubicle opening. The walls seemed to waver and lightheadedness overcame him.

Chapter 33

Schak stopped, held still for a moment, and waited for the sensation to pass. *Just a blood-pressure shift*, he told himself. He'd had a heart attack on the job a few years back, but it hadn't felt like this. Had it? No, this thing hadn't been painful. Just stupid. Too much alcohol, not enough water, and getting up too quickly.

When he felt better, he headed downstairs, moving slowly. In the kitchen area, he forced down a cup full of water. A front desk officer came into the room. "Hey, Schak. Are you all right?"

"I'm fine. How's my detainee?"

"Better than when you brought him in." She grabbed a water bottle from the fridge. "I was just going to take him this."

"I'll do it. I'm headed back there now." He took the water and hustled out, embarrassed that she'd noticed something was off. Was it his color? Or was he sweating already?

At the holding cell, he changed his mind about going in and sitting down. Instead, he called out, "Hey, Derrick."

From his stretched-out position on the bench, the man sat up, wide-awake. "What now?"

"I have some questions. Come over here."

Derrick pushed up and lumbered over. "What do you want to know?"

"About Nicky's scars. The tracheotomy, for example."

"What? I didn't know it was a trachea scar." He scowled. "She told me she fell on a rake when she was kid."

"And the pins in her ankle? What happened there?"

"An ice-skating accident. Why is this important?"

"Was she taking pain pills?"

"Just prescription anti-inflammatories."

"Did she ever mention opioids?"

"No, she hardly even drank."

Irrelevant. "Who's her doctor?"

"I have no idea. What's this about?"

Schak ignored the question and tried to remember what else he wanted to ask. Oh yeah, the driver's license. "We think Nicky's ID is fake. Do you know her real name?"

Derrick's shoulders slumped and his hands went to his head. "I am so confused by all this. But you can't get me to confess by making up a bunch of shit."

A waste of his time. Schak handed him the water bottle through the bars and walked away.

"I'm hungry too," Derrick called after him.

Back at his desk, Schak thought about taking Derrick a doughnut. *Nope. Not his job.* He grabbed one for himself and took a big bite. The dizziness episode flashed in his mind, and he tossed the pastry in the trash. Staring at the garbage, he realized what he'd forgotten. Everything else could wait. He grabbed his briefcase and hurried out. He had to search Nicky Walker's home again.

At the now-familiar cottage, he climbed from his car, relieved that they had cloud cover today. It was still too warm for him, but at least he wasn't sweating. The house still had two vehicles taking up the driveway. The techs had processed both, but so far, the team had no reason to haul them into the bay at the evidence building. He walked past, retrieved the key from under the mat, and pulled the crime-scene tape down from the door.

Inside, the place smelled musty, and he suspected it was the carpet. He and Tracy had torn all theirs out years ago and loved the cleaner feel. Schak pulled on gloves and headed straight for the garbage container in the kitchen. Nearly empty, he didn't have to dump it. He sorted through and found an empty creamer carton, a filter full of coffee grounds, and some eggshells. Breakfast stuff. *From Tuesday morning? Or Wednesday?* Had Derrick calmly eaten breakfast before calling Jackson in a panic? That made no sense, unless he was guilty. Schak took photos of the garbage contents, then pulled the bag to take as evidence.

He set it by the front door, then moved toward the bathroom. The plastic trash container held only empty toilet paper rolls, so he left it and stepped into the hall. He really didn't want to dig through the large trashbin outside, but that was next. Unless they had a container in the office. He went into the next room and looked around. At first, he didn't see any receptacles, but finally spotted a round black one under the desk. Schak squatted and reached for it. He pulled a chocolate wrapper from the top—and found what he was looking for.

An empty amber pill bottle with no label—just like the one Jackson had found in the first victim's purse.

Chapter 34

Jackson called the state lab again. No one had answered the first time, and he intended to be tenacious. Finally, a weary female voice came on the line. "Oregon State Forensics Division."

"Detective Jackson with the Eugene Police. I know how swamped you are, but we're waiting on a report for an unidentified bottle of medication sent in Tuesday morning. Has it been processed?"

"What's the name and case number on the evidence?"

"Tayla Holden. I'll get you the number in a moment." He reached in his satchel side pocket for one of the pre-numbered evidence labels used with this investigation. Just as he grabbed it, the desk person at the state lab said, "Never mind, I found the file. Our report hasn't been sent, but the medication is methadone, a fifty-milligram dosage."

Methadone? That was usually given to people trying to curb their cravings for more-harmful substances like heroin but it was addictive in itself. He was glad he hadn't taken one of the pills in his moment of extreme pain.

Jackson noted the drug, then asked, "Are any of the other reports for the same case number finished? We're waiting on a tox screen too." At this point, he assumed Holden's blood work would come back positive for methadone. But what else?

After a minute, the weary clerk said, "The toxicology

report is scheduled to be released today, but I can't seem to access it, so someone is in the file."

"Okay, thanks." Jackson hung up. It was too soon to push them about Nicky's tox screen, which had just gone in the day before.

A Google search of methadone revealed that doctors prescribed it for chronic pain too. He tried to read the information about the drug's half-life and the need to let it build up in the body, but it was too much information for the moment. The detail that stood out was its intensively addictive nature and the need to carefully monitor dosages and titrate slowly when coming off the medication. The lack of a label on Holden's bottle indicated the meds were a black-market purchase. Even if the drugs weren't connected to her death, someone in the department had to track down the source.

He grabbed his phone and sent Schak, Evans, and Quince a shared text update about the methadone. But before following up on his own lead, he had to be a good team player and complete the assignment Schak had given him. He scanned Nicky's ID, saved the file as an enlarged jpg, and called a friend at the FBI.

"Jackson. Good to hear from you. I hope it's not bad news." Agent Rivers sounded happy and unrushed.

He envied her. "Unfortunately, it is. We have two dead women and a possible black-market drug connection." He didn't know yet if Nicky had taken meds, prescription or not, but his gut told him that she had.

"Overdoses? That's out of your normal scope, isn't it?"

"Both homicides. What I need help with is an ID. We think it's fake. Can I send you the image and have you run it in your facial recognition software?"

"You know you can. But if you bring the ID itself, our expert can tell for sure if it's a forgery."

"If we were still across the street, I would." Another disadvantage to their new location. They'd lost their close proximity to the FBI's resources. "We have a fraud guy here who can usually spot them."

"Okay. Send the image and I'll get right on it."

"Many thanks."

After sending the email, he hustled down the hall, ignoring his gut pain. He'd loaded up on Aleve before leaving the house so it wasn't as intense, but he knew that was temporary. In the area where the three fraud detectives worked, Jackson found Bisson sleeping at his desk. *Good grief!* Was the whole department on overload?

He leaned in next to him. "Bisson. I need your help."

The older man sat up, blinking. "I was at the hospital with my wife last night, and it's catching up to me."

"Is she all right?"

"Not really." His mouth was grim. "Tell me what you need."

Jackson respected the man's privacy and handed him Nicky's license. "Evans thinks this one might be fake. She claims the background color is off."

"It's definitely too dark. And the font is wrong." Bisson handed it back. "It's a good one, but not issued by the state."

"Okay. Take care."

Nerves pinging, Jackson went back to his desk. Something inexplicable was going on with the victims, but he couldn't see the whole picture yet. Figuring out who Nicky really was just might be the key. He called Agent Rivers and she picked right up. "I was just going to call you."

"You've got a match?"

"No. I'm sorry. Neither her name or face is in CODIS."

"Thanks anyway." Disappointed, Jackson hung up. If Nicky wasn't a criminal, why had she moved away and changed her identification? The answer was out there. Someone, somewhere, knew who she was. He would run a nationwide media search for her, but those calls would take time, and he might as well start local. He reached for his phone again.

Sophie answered cheerfully too. "Hello, Jackson. I hope this means you've decided to tell me the name of the second victim."

"I intend to. Then I need you to do something for me."

"I will if I can. What's her name?"

"Nicky Walker. Only we know now that her ID is phony. We need to find out who she really is."

"You want me to get her photo into the paper and ask the public?"

"Yes. I'll send the image I have of her driver's license. You can use that image."

"Ick! Find a good picture of her, please. Something we can run at high-rez."

"I'll try. But I'll go ahead and send what I have and you may have to just use it. We need this ASAP."

Sophie paused, and he heard computer keys clicking in the background. Jackson started to hang up, but Sophie asked, "What else can you tell me about the victim? Is she connected to Tayla Holden?"

"We don't know much."

"Where did she come from? Our new publisher owns a chain of newspapers everywhere. We could go out of state with the story if I had more to work with."

They didn't have anything else. That was the problem. He

remembered the trust deposits. Maybe the bank could track the source of those. Could it hurt to tell her?

"Just tell me."

How long had he paused? "We do have one odd detail: the David J. Miller Family Trust. But you can't mention the trust publicly or indicate anything financial."

"So why tell me?"

"You can ask members of David J. Miller's family to come forward. Just don't mention the trust. It's private."

"Got it." More clicking keys.

He knew something else too, but it took a moment to surface. "I think Nicky told me she was from Arizona, but she apparently lied about everything else, so I don't know that for sure."

"You knew the victim?"

"Sort of. Don't use that and don't ask how."

She laughed softly. "You know I'll find out. I do like a challenge. So how did she die?"

"Strangled. I have to go."

Jackson hung up and wondered if he should have mentioned the pain meds or pain clinic. Probably not. They didn't know that about Nicky yet. Just Tayla Holden. He googled *Eugene pain clinics* and found a short list.

A moment later, Schak called. "Hey, Jackson. I think you might be right about chronic pain being a common denominator. I just found an empty pill bottle under a desk at Nicky Walker's home. It looks like the one found on the first victim, and I can't believe I missed it yesterday."

A tingle went up Jackson's spine. This was the lead they needed. Before he could respond, Schak cut in. "Has Derrick ever had a drug problem? Or made money dealing?"

"No." *This was not about his brother!*

"I'm going out on a limb here, but unless Derrick was supplying both women with pain meds, I think we can release him."

Yes! The tightness in Jackson's chest finally loosened. "Can I do that now?"

"But he can't go to the house just yet. We may need to spend more time there. Also, he can't leave town. He's not completely clear."

"I understand." Jackson stood, eager to give Derrick the news. "I'll start calling pain clinics and see if I can find out where Holden went for help. This may lead us to a doctor or underground source."

"We need Evans and Quince on this too. We have to search both women's medical records if we can get them."

"Let's start with phone records and see if we can find any calls to doctors or clinics." He hadn't seen any on Tayla's phone, but he'd only gone back a few weeks. "Do you have Nicky's phone?"

"It's on my desk. I got it from the tech gal this morning and started to look at the Messenger stuff, then suddenly realized that no one may have searched the garbage at the last scene."

An oversight, for sure, but he'd missed Holden's purse on the first search too, so he couldn't judge. "Where are you?"

"I'm driving to the evidence lab to get this pill bottle shipped to the state. I'm sure they can test the dust particles to determine the contents. Maybe get a fingerprint too."

"Speaking of which, the methadone Holden had can be prescribed for chronic pain."

"Maybe we're finally on track."

Jackson struggled to suppress his frustration. He had tried to get Schak moving in this direction yesterday. "I'll

grab Nicky's phone from your desk and see what I can find."
He hung up.

First he had to release his poor brother. *Then what?*
Schak had driven Derrick to the department, so he didn't
have a vehicle. Nor could his brother go home yet. Jackson
called a taxi for him. Derrick could either go to a hotel or to
his house. But with Kera and Micah there, his place was
already jammed. After their talk last night, he suspected Kera
would look for other accommodations. But maybe not. She
had stayed and slept on the couch after blowing him away
with her openness. But he still didn't know what he would do.

Jackson took the stairs down to the holding cells. A
scruffy young man lay on the floor in the first one. Jackson
glanced in to make sure he was all right. Eyes open and
breathing. In the next cell, Derrick paced back and forth.
When he saw Jackson, his face crumpled in relief. "Please tell
me I can go home."

"Not home, but you're free to go. I called you a cab." He
flashed his ID at the security lock.

"Why not home?" His brother had a little more color in
his face now.

"It's still a crime scene." The door slid open. Derrick
rushed out and hugged Jackson. Startled, he stiffened and
hoped the encounter would be brief.

His brother stepped back. "Sorry. I'm just tired and
hungry and still freaked out about finding my girlfriend dead."

Jackson walked toward the front of the building, and
Derrick followed, still talking. "Sleeping on the bench was the
shits too, but I actually feel less nauseous than I have in
months."

When they were outside, Jackson handed Derrick a
twenty. "For the cab. You can go to my house, but Kera and

Micah are there, so it's full."

"Oh right. You told me she was coming."

"You're not entirely in the clear, so don't do anything stupid." Jackson clapped his brother on the shoulder. "I have to go back to work. You do whatever is best for you." Knowing Derrick, his brother would head straight home, despite the warning not to re-enter the crime scene.

Back upstairs, he hustled into the cubicle next to his and grabbed the small phone. A personal tablet sat next to it. He took both to his own desk and sat down, wishing he had coffee. Schak had mentioned Messenger—a first from his Luddite team member—but he was not likely to find texts from a real doctor or clinic in the app.

Jackson tapped the computer tablet. A customized home screen appeared, but he recognized the Mail icon. He opened it, disappointed to see only a few messages. One from her bank, one from her mother, and a product-purchase follow-up. He read the mother's note in case she had mentioned a doctor, but she had simply expressed a desire to visit. He checked the Deleted folder, and it was nearly empty too. More marketing ads. He looked for subfolders where she might have stored important emails, but Nicky had clearly not saved any.

After perusing a folder marked Letters, he found a personal note she hadn't finished. No name or date either, but the two sentences were revealing: *This can't continue. I have moments when I'd rather be dead than ever see you again.*

A sick feeling landed in his gut. Who had she written that to? For a second, he worried that it was Derrick. Even so, what did it mean? That their relationship was unhealthy? Nicky hadn't finished writing the letter, so whatever was happening had passed. Maybe it wasn't about Derrick, and maybe it hadn't passed. Did Nicky have a stalker? His sense of urgency intensified. Jackson hit print, so he had a copy to share with his team, then got back to work. He had to keep checking sources until he found a mention of a doctor, or clinic, or prescription. He searched her browser history and found a list of websites recently visited. Most were Pinterest pages with fashion and health items.

Frustrated, he picked up Nicky's phone and tapped on another icon that looked like it might be an email app. A dialogue box opened and there were two messages: One from SexySeth@Hotmail.com who was bluntly hitting on her and another from RioMan@Yahoo.com. The message had arrived Tuesday afternoon: *Time for an exchange. The usual.*

An exchange? A chill on the back of Jackson's neck this time. The email account and message were anonymous . . . unless they could convince the tech company who'd developed the app to track down the computer that had generated the Yahoo account, then share the information with them. That could take weeks, if it could be done at all.

The words *exchange* and *usual* indicated a meeting with a preset time and place, and the cryptic nature of the communication indicated a need for secrecy. Why was it *time*? Schak had said the pill bottle in the garbage was empty. Maybe Rio was a cautious dealer notifying Nicky that her next drug supply was coming soon. Tuesday night? When she had been killed?

Chapter 35

Thursday, May 10, 8:45 a.m.

Evans drove toward the Pacific Union bank on Chambers, still smiling from her effort that morning to identify the naked men on Tayla Holden's phone. It sure beat staring at financial records or chasing down unhelpful witnesses. She'd taken a moment to give Derrick's photo extra scrutiny. Would Jackson be built the same?

Her phone rang, startling her, and she grabbed it up, assuming it was Schak or Jackson with an update. The voice in her ear was neither. "Hey, gorgeous, it's time to stop avoiding me." *Stricklyn!* He sounded calm and pleasant this morning, compared to the nasty message he'd left yesterday, but that worried her even more.

"I'm busy! We have two homicides." She hadn't decided how she would deal with him yet.

"Come over tonight or say goodbye to your boyfriend's career. I'm either—"

She hung up, not wanting to hear more. The bastard had lost his mind if he really thought she would give in to this. Just because he'd seen her having a drink with Jackson? Maybe standing too close to him in the parking lot? Instead of learning from other men's downfall during the Me-Too movement, Stricklyn seemed to have been inspired to think he could get away with it. *Idiot!*

Light drops of rain hit her windshield, adding to her foul

mood. Where the hell had their brief sunshine gone? They'd had the wettest, ugliest winter ever, and she was ready for outdoor fun. She'd promised she would get out into the beautiful Oregon landscape this summer. Maybe hike Smith Rock for the first time—even if she had to go by herself.

By the time she reached the bank's parking lot, the spring shower had stopped, and she was surprised to see people standing near the front door. She joined the group and bounced on her feet while she waited.

A clerk unlocked the glass doors, and everyone hurried inside to stand in the teller line. Relieved, Evans went to the customer service desk and asked for Ms. Joiner.

"I'm sorry, but she's not here this morning." The clerk didn't look sorry.

Evans showed her badge. "I'm with the Eugene Police and I have a key to a safe deposit box. The owner of the box was murdered and I need to know what's inside."

"Another detective was here about that customer yesterday. I can take you back." The young woman led Evans to a small room. A waist-high narrow table took up the center, and the walls were lined with locked compartments and drawers. A few at the bottom were large enough to hold a suitcase, but most were the size of small post-office boxes.

"Do you need anything else?" the clerk asked.

A sudden realization left her feeling stupid. "Yes, in fact, I need to know which number."

"I can get that for you."

Evans stepped into the hall to wait. The tiny space reminded her of elevators and other places you could get trapped inside. The clerk took her time, and Evans had to take long, slow breaths. She couldn't shake her sense of urgency about this information—or maybe it was just the case itself. Barulla's suicide felt wrong as well, maybe too convenient. A thought that had been lurking in her subconscious abruptly surfaced. What if the neighbor had been murdered and framed? What if Holden's killer was still out there and another woman was in jeopardy?

The bank clerk came back, a troubled look on her face. "Nicky Walker doesn't have a safe deposit box here."

Oh hell. "You're sure about that?"

"Of course." A nervous smile. "I'm sorry you wasted your time."

So was she. Evans thanked her and left the building. What the hell was the key for? A dozen possibilities came to mind. Nicky might have a deposit box at another bank. If her driver's license was fake, she could have a deposit box right here at Pacific Union, but under a different name. Or the key might open a lock on a storage unit. Had anyone asked Derrick? Did it even matter?

In the car, her phone beeped with an incoming text. No, two, and they had downloaded at once, making her think they were late in arriving. Both were from Jackson: the first saying Holden had been taking methadone, and the second reporting that Nicky's ID was fake and her face wasn't in the system.

Damn! How the hell could they solve her homicide if they didn't know who she really was?

Chapter 36

Surprised by Jackson's request for help, Sophie switched gears. She'd been working on her women's piece for the ad-supported supplement, but it could wait. Right now, she had to find out what she could about Nicky Walker and the David J. Miller Family Trust.

Why did the name sound familiar? There had to be hundreds of guys with that moniker. The only more common names in the U.S. were Steve Smith or Michael Johnson. Still, she sensed she'd heard the reference, and now she had a vague feeling it was associated with medicine somehow. Maybe he was a surgeon who'd pioneered a new procedure or conducted a breakthrough clinical study. She kept up with medical news in her free time, just because it was interesting and sometimes useful. Jackson had also said Nicky Walker might be from Arizona, and Sophie had grown up in Tucson.

Amused, she got up to make tea before she started a deep dive into the research world. Her focus and fascination, even as a college student, had been on crime. She'd taken sociology classes to study deviant behavior and had read bizarre crime stories from across the country just for entertainment. So if she'd heard of David J. Miller and he'd stuck in her mind, he was likely either a doctor or a bizarre criminal.

Sophie stopped at her editor's desk on the way back. Hoogstad waved her in. "What's the word?"

"I want to write a posthumous profile on Tayla Holden. She was an interesting woman with a lot of ambition who got derailed by a motorcycle accident and chronic pain." Sophie paused to let him process all that. "Then she made a comeback and started the vegan sausage business, only to be murdered."

"A good story." Her boss thought for a moment, then said, "Write it. Just don't spend a lot of time." He pulled his lips back in what he thought was a smile and waved her away.

Back at her desk, she keyed *David J. Miller Family Trust doctor Arizona* into the search field. The results populated with a bunch of links to law firms who specialized in setting up trusts. She tried again, without the reference to the legal documents. This time, the search results included links to articles from *Psychology Today* and a dozen listings for individual physicians. An orthopedic surgeon, a neurologist, and a family doctor. Sophie scrolled past them to the next page, looking for something more distinctive. On the third group of listings, she spotted a reference to a *David J. Miller Family Trust*.

She clicked the link, and the search engine took her to an obituary. She scanned the text, which was longer than most people's write-ups. David J. Miller, a retired trauma surgeon, had died and left several heirs who would benefit from the trust fund he'd set up. He'd lived in Phoenix, Arizona and had been temporarily famous for treating Jean Garrison as a child.

Weird memories popped into Sophie's mind, and her stomach clenched. Jean Garrison had been an abused child. Something bad enough to make the news. *Shit!* She hated those stories. Adult crime was different. Sophie opened a new tab and keyed the name into the search bar.

A page of old news articles loaded, and some of the

details came back to her. The child, Jean, had been the victim of her mother's mental illness—a syndrome known as Munchausen Syndrome by Proxy. Sophie took a sip of tea to pause and calm herself. She'd heard about the case when she was a kid herself, then had studied it in detail for a paper she'd written in college. The poor girl had been repeatedly poisoned and injured in her crazy mom's attempt to garner attention and sympathy for herself. One of the girl's doctors, an ER physician named David Miller, had finally figured it out.

Sophie leaned back, cradling her hot cup for comfort, but too upset to drink any tea. It was possible that Nicky Walker was one of the doctor's children, which would explain why she was receiving a monthly payment from the trust. But it didn't explain why the woman had changed her name. That behavior indicated some kind of shame or reason to hide. And in this story, the doctor was the hero.

What if . . . Nicky was Jean Garrison? And the ER doc had included her in his trust out of kindness or pity? Sophie scanned down the screen, looking for recent stories about Garrison. What she found stunned her.

Chapter 37

Jackson called New Way Pain Management first. He identified himself and asked to speak with the person who had the most authority.

The request seemed to confuse the receptionist. "What do you mean? The clinic is jointly owned by three doctors."

"Put one of them on the phone, please."

"They're with patients."

"Two women have been murdered, and I need information immediately. Can you please tell me if Tayla Holden was ever a patient there?"

"We can't violate her privacy. Federal law doesn't allow it."

He was familiar with HIPAA rules. "As I mentioned, the women are dead. There is no confidentiality issue."

"Give me your name again and your phone number, and I'll try to get back to you."

Feeling impatient, Jackson gave her the details. "The other name I want you to check is Nicky Walker."

"Tell me the first one again."

He spelled both names, knowing he sounded irritated, then got off the phone. He went back to his search page, ignoring the physician listings. Lots of doctors specialized in pain, but they worked for hospitals or other family-medicine practices. According to Sophie, Mrs. Holden had specifically said 'pain clinic' so, for now, he had to keep his focus narrow.

He skipped a listing he suspected was a cannabis shop and opened Women's Health Center: Pain Management and Autoimmune Disorders.

As he listened to their phone ring, he heard someone behind him. Jackson shifted in his chair and saw Schak in the doorway.

"Let's all meet." His partner gestured toward the conference room.

"Five minutes," Jackson said, pointing to his earpiece.

A woman came on the line. "This is Women's Health."

"Detective Jackson, Eugene Police." He decided to try another approach this time. "One of your past clients, Tayla Holden, was murdered a few days ago. I need to talk to her doctor."

The receptionist made an odd murmuring noise. "I have to put you on hold."

After a long wait, the line went dead. *Crap!* He started to call again, then remembered he'd told Schak five minutes. They all needed to confer and get refocused.

As he crossed the hall, Evans came up the stairs. "We're meeting now," Jackson called to her.

"Be there in a moment." She kept moving toward her cubicle.

Feeling thirsty, he headed for the stairs to get a soda from the machine on the first floor. He'd learned not to drink the coffee in the break room. When he got back to the conference space, Evans and Schak stood near the board talking.

She looked up at Jackson. "The key was a bust. Nicky doesn't have a safety deposit box at Pacific Union."

"Did anyone ask Derrick about it?"

Silence.

"I'll give him a call." Jackson let his brother's cell phone ring four beats, then left a message: "Nicky had a key inside the safe in your bedroom. Any idea what it's to?" He sat down, took a long drink of his cold, sweet caffeine, then said, "I doubt if Derrick has any idea. He claims he didn't even know about the safe."

"Quince is talking to Barulla's mother and won't be here, so let's get through this quickly." Schak took a seat. "We have two main priorities. Figure out who Nicky really is, then find out where the victims were buying their street medications."

"I'm making calls to pain clinics," Jackson reported. "I'm hoping a doctor will talk to me, and we can springboard from there."

"What is your thinking?" Schak asked. "Someone on staff is dealing on the side? With ready-made customers walking in the door every day?"

"Wait! What did I miss?" Evans spun to face them.

"I went back to the scene and found an empty pill bottle in the trash under Nicky's desk." Schak looked sheepish. "It matches the one the first victim had."

"That's a solid connection." Evans wrote it on the board, then jotted down *methadone* too. "I wonder if they're taking the same drug. Someone who works in a pain clinic might have access to a variety of meds."

"Until today, I didn't know methadone was used for pain management." Schak rubbed his head. "But I know it's highly addictive."

Jackson had a worrisome thought. "What if the clinic is prescribing methadone to most of its patients? That seems like a problem."

"We should be able to find out." Evans bounced on her feet. "I think doctors have to be specially licensed to prescribe methadone. Same for suboxone or any kind of opioid treatment drugs."

Jackson hadn't known that. "The bottles aren't labeled, so I don't think it's a doctor. The source could be a patient at the clinic, someone who's prescribed more meds than they need. So they make money selling what they don't take."

"All of this is interesting," Schak said dryly, "but remember, the women are dead. Why would a dealer kill clients?"

Jackson had put his phone on the table, and a call was coming in. He leaned toward it. *Sophie.* "I need to take this." He pressed the speaker button. "Hey, Sophie. Did you find anything?"

"Yes, but it's weird."

He remembered to tell her she had an audience. "We're in conference and both Schak and Evans are here."

"Hi, guys. Sorry to interrupt but you might want to hear this."

Was she being dramatic? "So tell us."

"The name of that trust, David J. Miller, struck me as familiar, so I did a little research."

Schak gave Jackson a wide-eyed look.

Crap. He'd forgotten to mention that he had talked to the press to take their search public. He usually led the investigations, so it was habit to call the shots about what they released to the media. He mouthed *Sorry* at Schak.

Sophie was still talking. "I had a feeling the name was associated with medicine, so I googled doctors and hospitals. Believe me, there are plenty of physicians named David Miller."

The mention of doctors made him snap to attention.

"It was a news story I had read, so I started thinking about hospitals in terms of patients. Then I narrowed it down to Arizona, where you said Nicky had lived, and I found Dr. David J. Miller's obituary." She clicked her tongue. "He was a trauma surgeon at Maricopa County Hospital in Phoenix and, in his trust, he'd included a previous patient. A young girl named Jean Garrison. She had been harmed and poisoned repeatedly by her own mother for the attention."

"What?" Schak's expression was priceless.

"It's called Munchausen by Proxy," Sophie explained. "It's when people make a family member sick so they can go to a hospital where they get attention and sympathy. I heard about the case as a kid because it happened in my home state and was big news at the time. Then I researched and wrote about the syndrome in college, so it was familiar to me."

A load of queasy dropped into Jackson's stomach. "What are you saying?" It was all so long ago.

"What if Jean Garrison changed her name to hide from the notoriety?" Sophie's voice grew animated. "She could still be getting trust payments from the doctor who'd treated her as a child."

"You think Nicky is Jean Garrison?" Schak looked even more confused.

Jackson understood, but he wasn't sure about the money. "Why would the doctor pay the child for a lifetime?"

"Guilt. Love. Pity. But that's not important." Sophie sounded impatient now, as though they were all rather stupid. "The child grew up to be like her mother. I sent you a link to a news article about how Jean poisoned her boyfriend in college. The judge felt sorry for her because of her childhood and—"

Jackson cut in. "Thank you for the information. We have to talk about this privately now." He closed the call, dread filling his stomach.

Evans came over and stood near him, a hand on his shoulder. "Derrick has been sick for months with an ailment they can't figure out. What if Nicky is Jean Garrison and she's repeating her mother's behavior? Again."

Jackson had already taken the next step. What if Derrick found out his girlfriend had been poisoning him? And caused him to lose his job? Had he killed her in a rage?

"I have to call Joe," Evans cut into his thoughts. "We need to find out what the hell that powder is that Nicky was keeping secretly locked away."

Chapter 38

Jackson forwarded Sophie's link to Evans, who then opened it with the mail function on her tablet. He and Schak watched over her shoulders as Evans loaded the page. A news article from ten years ago. The gist was that the woman, Jean Garrison, had poisoned her boyfriend for attention. A judge had taken pity on her and sentenced her to a one-year suspended sentence and five years of probation—with the condition that she get extensive psychiatric counseling to stay out of prison. Evans took time to absorb the details, but all he could do was stare at Jean Garrison. Slick black hair, intense dark eyes, and a thin face. She looked just like Nicky, only younger.

"I think this confirms Sophie's theory." Schak gave a mock shiver. "This is even freakier than our locals usually get." He reached for his thermos.

Jackson hoped it was just coffee. "Knowing this will probably speed Derrick's recovery, but it doesn't help us solve these murders. Or at least, I'm not seeing it yet."

"Me neither." Evans pushed back from the table. "I think I need some coffee. Anybody want something from the break room?"

Jackson shook his head and Schak ignored her, still staring at the image online.

His phone, still on the table, rang again. He reached for it and didn't recognize the number. He answered anyway, hoping it was good news. "Jackson here."

"This is Dr. Ezrow from the Women's Health Center. You called about a former patient."

Former? Damn. "Yes, Tayla Holden. I'm sorry to report that she was murdered." Jackson put the doctor on speaker.

"I had already seen that in the newspaper. It's heartbreaking, but I don't know how I can help you."

"Tell me what you were prescribing her and why she left the clinic."

She hesitated longer than he expected. "Normally I would never do this."

"I know, but it's necessary." *Just tell us everything!*

"I prescribed Vicodin to Tayla. It's a mix of oxycodone and Tylenol, a 500-milligram dose. I allowed her sixty pills every thirty days, and she was supposed to limit herself to two a day. But she couldn't keep to it and would call me in the middle of the month to pressure me for more. Sometimes I gave in to her, but it violated our policy, and the situation became a problem."

"Did you kick her out?"

"Not exactly. I told her I wouldn't take any more calls from her, and I encouraged her to check herself into a treatment center. Maybe even go to a methadone clinic."

"Did you prescribe her methadone?"

A small gulp of air. "Of course not! It's too addictive and too toxic to the body. We try to treat pain with healthy alternatives and keep the opioids to a minimum."

"Did you ever suspect any staff members of dealing meds on the side?"

Another pause. "I hope you're not implying that we don't keep accurate records of all medications that come into our clinic."

"Not at all. I'm just trying to find a connection between Tayla Holden and Nicky Walker."

A sharper intake of breath. "Is Nicky dead too?"

"Yes."

"She was also a client here for a while."

As he'd thought! "When did she leave the clinic and why?"

"Only a few months ago. She had a similar problem."

He knew he was wasting his breath but he had to ask. "Can my team peruse your records? We have to figure out who they both saw at the clinic."

"No, sorry. Not without a subpoena. Our clinic may not be the only connection between the women. I'm looking at the dates of their appointments, and Tayla had left the clinic before Nicky had her first visit."

Jackson glanced at Schak to see if he had any ideas. His partner shrugged.

Evans had questions. "Did either patient come with a referral? Do they have anything in their personal details that overlap?"

"Let me look these files over and get back to you." The doctor abruptly hung up.

"We need to rethink this." Schak started to pace. "Barulla confessed to killing Tayla Holden, so maybe Nicky was murdered for another reason and there is no connection between the deaths. They both took pain meds. So what? Millions of people do."

"Illegal drugs," Evans reminded him. "Always a potential for related crime."

"And what other motive do we have?" Jackson countered, looking at Schak.

"Derrick found out his girlfriend was poisoning him and strangled her. End of story." Schak looked intractable. "He was at the scene, for Christ sake."

Evans cut in. "Here's a new idea. Maybe Nicky's other boyfriend figured out where she is and killed her in revenge."

"Ten years later?" Jackson didn't buy it, but a new sense of urgency flooded over him. "There's so much overlap in these women's lives. They look alike, they have similar careers, and they both took street drugs for their chronic pain." He locked eyes with Schak because he needed his buy-in. "I still think there's something going on with the pain clinic. I want to go check it out and meet the staff."

Schak glared at him. "You can't. Derrick is still our best suspect and you're too close to this to be objective."

"I'll go," Evans offered. "I have a thought about Barulla. He spied on Tayla Holden. What if he saw something over the hedge? Such as the killer?"

A moment of quiet while they processed the theory.

"Maybe the real killer framed him," Evans added.

"You think the perp silenced Barulla as a witness, then got himself off the hook for Holden's murder by forging a confession?" Schak's mouth twisted with skepticism. "Even if all that is true—and I'm doubtful—it still leaves Derrick as our best suspect in Nicky's death."

"So why did you release him?" Jackson asked.

Schak rubbed his head, his face tight with stress. "Because the street drugs are still a lead we haven't followed."

Jackson's phone rang, startling them. He snatched it up. The same number again. He answered the call, pressed the speaker button, and put the phone back on the table. "Detective Jackson here."

"Dr. Ezrow from the Women's Health Center." She hesitated. "I know this may not be relevant, but one of our staff members didn't show up for work today. She didn't call in either."

A tingle ran up the back of Jackson's neck. The dealer knew they were investigating and had left the clinic.

Schak leaned toward the phone. "It doesn't sound relevant. Unless you've got something else."

"We called Samir, of course, but she's not answering. She's been here a year as a receptionist and never done anything like this." Ezrow's voice trembled with concern.

Jackson's thoughts shifted in a whole new direction. The doctor was reporting a missing woman, not a suspect, but he didn't know what her disappearance had to do with their investigation. Still, his instinct told him this was important. "Have you tried calling her friends or family? She might have been in an accident."

Schak cut in again. "If you think she's missing, we can give you the name of a detective who handles those cases."

"This is the part you might find interesting," the doctor finally blurted. "Samir, our receptionist, has long dark hair and a delicate face. She looks so much like Tayla, it's uncanny."

Chapter 39

Evans drove across downtown, pushing the boundaries of safety. For the moment, the receptionist's failure to show up at work could be nothing, especially since Samir was only nineteen. That meant she was young enough to simply blow off a job. Her age also didn't fit the killer's MO, but her physical appearance did, so they had to check her out. Which was why Jackson and Schak were headed to the missing woman's house. Her task was to learn whatever she could about the clinic's employees and their access to medications.

The facility was located on the south end of Willamette near a busy retail intersection, and the last mile of the drive took forever. Evans finally parked in the back lot of the new building and hurried inside. She passed a patient who was waiting for attention and strode to the reception desk. "Detective Evans, here to see Dr. Ezrow." She intended to talk to everyone on staff, but she wanted to see the owners first.

"I'll take you back." The heavyset clerk apologized to the patient who was waiting, then walked Evans to a small office on the building's street side. "Wait here while I'll get Dr. Ez. She's with a patient."

Evans stayed on her feet, making a mental guess at how many employees the clinic had. Three doctor-owners, maybe three or four physician assistants or nurses, and a couple receptionists? They might even have part-time phlebotomists. This mission could take all day.

A minute later, the doctor came in, a white coat hanging on her tiny frame. Her mannishly short salt-and-pepper hair matched her stern expression. She took Evans' hand in a surprisingly tight grip as she introduced herself. "I hope I'm not wasting your time."

"If you are, it will be a best-case outcome for your employee."

"Right." She moved behind her desk. "What can I tell you about Samir Thibault?"

The missing girl wasn't Evans' focus. "I need to know who has access to your medications."

The doctor sat and encouraged Evans to do the same. "Just the three physicians who own the practice."

"Tell me about them."

"Besides myself, there's Risa Archibald. She's an orthopedist and physical therapist who specializes in pain management. Plus Vance Kettering, an immunologist who specializes in fibromyalgia and chronic fatigue syndrome."

The immunology element surprised her. So did his gender. "Why Kettering? Don't women come here to see female doctors?"

Ezrow scowled, her brow creasing in the smallest movement. "Patients come here because they're in pain and want to be taken seriously. So many women suffer in silence because their PCPs don't take them seriously. Dr. Kettering is a compassionate physician, and our patients love him."

"Is he here?"

"No, he's on vacation this week."

"Were Tayla Holden and Nicky Walker his patients?"

"No. They were mine."

Evans couldn't visualize the ninety-eight-pound doctor strangling anyone. "Give me his name and phone number. I have to talk to everyone here eventually."

Ezrow dug around in a desk drawer, then handed her a business card. "You don't have to disrupt his vacation. He'll be back to work Monday."

Evans slipped the card into her pocket. "When Detective Jackson asked if you ever suspected an employee of dealing pain meds on the side, you hesitated. Tell me who you suspect."

Ezrow's narrow shoulders slumped. "We caught a lab technician stealing pharmaceutical samples and had to fire him. But that was six months ago."

"He might have been dealing those drugs on the side—and he could still be in business. Tell me his name and where I can find him."

"Aaron Chase. I can give you the address we had for him, but no guarantee it's still correct."

While she waited, Evans processed the new lead and kept coming back to the same question: Why would a dealer kill his clients? It made no sense . . . unless they'd threatened to turn on him.

The doctor wrote the ex-employee's information on a sticky note and handed it over. "Aaron had a drug problem, obviously, but I can't imagine him hurting anyone."

That's what friends and relatives almost always said about murderers. Some women were married to serial killers for decades and claimed they never knew. Sociopaths were good at hiding their true nature. "Show me where you keep medications."

"We don't have any here except a few samples dropped off by pharma reps and injectables like cortisone." The doctor stood. "We write scripts and our patients take them to pharmacies."

Evans had thought so, but it was still worth asking. A clinic that catered to people in pain was fertile ground for a dealer of any kind. "I'll check out Aaron Chase. But I also need you to look through patient files for someone who might be selling or trading the medications they're prescribed."

"I'll try, but our patients are mostly women over the age of forty."

"Don't rule out anyone based on gender or age." A good reminder for herself as well. "The perp might not be male." Evans stood to leave. "I'll be back to question more of your employees later. This lead seems too important to postpone."

"Good. I'm worried about Samir."

In her car, she texted Jackson: *Checking out Aaron Chase, caught stealing meds from clinic.* Evans headed toward the fired employee's old address near campus, hoping Jackson would check in soon. The case was starting to feel explosive.

Chapter 40

Jackson offered to drive, and Schak didn't resist, even though this was his case. He'd had a little Baileys earlier just to take the edge off. He preferred bourbon, but the sugary stuff blended well with his coffee and smelled like any other creamer.

They walked out to the parking lot, and Schak sensed that his partner was trying not to limp. He was moving slower than usual himself, and the thought of how rundown they were getting was funny and sad at the same time. They reached Jackson's car, which looked just like the twenty-year-old piece of shit the city had issued him. This one smelled better though. Schak buckled up. "Sorry if I seemed argumentative in there. I think I'm overcompensating for the fact that our most likely suspect is your brother."

"I understand. It's weird for me too."

They pulled out and saw Evans' car down the road ahead of them. She was on her way to the clinic where he hoped she would find some answers. "What do you make of this new development?" he mused. "Samir Thibault is so much younger than the other victims." *What the hell kind of name was that anyway?*

"It's worrisome." Jackson's expression seemed locked in a permanent scowl. "The physical similarities wouldn't mean much if the girl didn't also have the clinic as a connection."

"Maybe she's the one who supplied drugs to the others,

then got the hell out of the clinic when we started asking around." Schak wasn't sold on the idea, but this was how they brainstormed.

"I had that thought earlier, but I don't see her as killer," Jackson said. "Maybe she's working with a criminal boyfriend."

They were quiet as Jackson weaved through the heavy downtown traffic. The university area where the missing girl lived was only another mile. When they were on Pearl Street and briefly out of the congestion, Jackson turned to him. "Schak, I know you're drinking again and I'm worried."

Goddamnit. He didn't want to have this conversation. "It's just the stress of this case. I'm going to quit as soon as we have this guy locked up."

"I think you should go to a meeting tonight and start sobriety again tomorrow."

It wasn't his business! Yet Jackson was right. Schak knew how hard it had been for his friend to bring it up, but he still couldn't make himself respond.

Jackson changed the subject back to work. "I hope we find this girl sprawled on the couch, stoned, and watching TV."

Schak chuckled at the image. "But we'll still ask her if she knows either Holden or Nicky."

"Of course. Her criminal boyfriend might like women of all ages, as long as they're his type."

"The Morticia look."

Jackson chuckled. "I thought that when I first saw Holden, but she was probably too young to even know who the character is."

A moment later, they parked in front of an old Victorian-style house that had likely been divided into units. The campus area had once been filled with them, but slowly they were being torn down and replaced with apartment complexes that cost renters twice as much money.

They knocked, but no one answered. Footsteps echoed somewhere in the house, so Schak stepped inside. "Anybody home?" A tangy, lived-in smell enveloped the space—sweaty clothes, bathroom mold, and fried onions. Maybe a little pot smoke.

A young man danced out of the kitchen wearing headphones. Startled to see them, he yanked out his earpieces. "What are you doing?" He was thin, shirtless, and strangely pretty—for a guy.

"Eugene Police. We're looking for Samir Thibault."

"Haven't seen her today."

Jackson held back, so Schak took the lead. "What about yesterday?"

"I saw her leave for work, but not since." The guy came toward them, no longer dancing.

"What's your name?" Schak asked.

"Justin Clark. Why? What's going on with Samir?"

"We were hoping you knew."

"I don't. We're just roommates, so she doesn't owe me a report on her activities. But we try to keep each other informed. We all do."

"Who else lives here?"

"Zoey Inslee. She's a student."

"Does Samir have a boyfriend?"

"I don't think so. She's a receptionist at a medical clinic and she reads a lot. That's most of what I know about her." He grinned. "And she moved here from Portland."

No help. Schak handed him a business card. "If you hear from her, call me."

"Is she in trouble?"

Jackson cut in. "No, but she might be in danger, so this is important. Let us see her room, please."

The roommate fidgeted for a moment, then said, "Okay, but let me check it first. In case she has a stash." Justin took a step toward a hallway.

A stash? Schak visualized a pill bottle like they'd found at the other crime scenes. He grabbed the kid's arm. "The meds might be what got her into trouble. We have to see her room as is."

Jackson hurried past Justin as Schak detained him. "We don't want to bust her for drugs. We're trying to save her life. Which room?" He let him go.

Justin pointed down the hall. "The end. I think it's open."

Schak followed Jackson into the small room. Behind him, the kid stopped in the doorway. A narrow bed, a small table with a folding chair, and a beat-up tallboy dresser. The pink blanket with little cartoon cats reminded Schak of how young the missing girl was.

Jackson started to search the dresser.

Schak turned to the roommate. "Call her phone."

"I already did, and it's not in here."

That was a good sign. If Samir had her phone, her decision to be unavailable was probably voluntary. "Does she have a laptop?"

"No, but Samir was saving for one." Justin looked worried now. "What's going on?"

"We're not sure." Schak squatted and dug through the little trash container, not wanting to make the same mistake again. Just empty candy wrappers and wadded-up paper. He unfolded one of the crumples. Just a handwritten list of things to do. A young person who still used old-school methods. He pulled the other crumpled wads out of the trash and dumped them on the table. He would look at them in a minute. Finding a prescription bottle—if it existed—was the priority.

He searched the high shelf in her small closet. No drugs, no keepsakes, and no books, except a high school yearbook. As Jackson got down and looked under the girl's bed, Schak glanced at the inside cover pages. Samir had graduated from a school in Portland the year before. Out of the corner of his eye, he saw Jackson lift the top mattress.

Schak glanced over at Justin, who was still in the doorway, watching. "Where is her family? Portland?"

"Yeah, but she was adopted and says she never really bonded with the people who raised her." With one eye on what Jackson was doing, the roommate kept talking. "Then when her adoptive parents split up, she started searching for her real mom. That's why Samir came to Eugene."

Chapter 41

Jackson's pulse raced. Not only did he have the girl's handwritten diary, but her roommate had just told them who she was. But he needed confirmation, so he got up close to the young man. "Did Samir find her mother? What's her name?"

"Uh, yes and no." Justin took a step back. "This is personal for Samir, and I'm not sure I should talk about it."

"It's also the key to finding her. Just tell us." Jackson tried to keep his voice calm, but his body pulsed with adrenaline.

"I can't remember her mother's name."

"How did Samir find her?"

"I'm not sure."

"Come on, this is important."

Schak broke into the conversation. "How did Samir get her job at the clinic?"

"I don't know!" The roommate's voice shook. "All I know is that when she found her biological mother, she rejected her. Samir was devastated, but she got the job at the clinic right afterward and decided to stay in Eugene."

"Okay. That helps. Do you have a photo of Samir?" The clinic had one on file, but this would be faster. "A headshot preferably."

"Sure." The kid scrolled through his phone, then turned it to Jackson. "Is this one okay?"

A beautiful young woman at her desk, looking back at the

photographer, smiling. Her face was broader, but still, a younger, prettier version of Tayla Holden. "Send it to me." He handed Justin his business card. "At this number. Do it right now."

"I'll try, but you've got me shaking."

Jackson met Schak's eyes. "I have to put out a statewide alert."

"I'll contact Zapata in Missing Persons and get him on it too." His partner seemed clear-eyed and sharp now. *Thank goodness.* It had been painful to bring up Schak's drinking, but he wanted his partner to stop before he screwed up or lost his job.

"Can I help?" the roommate asked.

"Does Samir have a car?"

"No, she rides a bike. It's a blue Specialized."

"Thanks. Call us if you think of anything useful." He headed for the door, the diary in his hand.

Once they were in his car, he and Schak made their phone calls. Jackson then sent Samir's photo to the head of the dispatch center. She would get the image out to every law enforcement officer in Oregon.

Schak, still on the phone, asked, "Where was she last seen?"

"So far, we know that she worked her shift at the clinic yesterday, and no one has seen her since."

Schak repeated the information and hung up. "What now?"

"The clinic. Something is going on there." He started to check in with Evans and realized he'd missed a text from her. A flash of fear streaked through his gut. He read the message out loud: "Checking out Aaron Chase, caught stealing meds from clinic."

"He sounds like a viable suspect," Schak said.

"I don't want Evans questioning him alone. He might have already killed two women."

"Maybe three," Schak reminded him. "Call her."

Putting the phone on speaker, he made the contact. In a moment, Evans came on. "Hey, Jackson. Did you get my message?"

Relieved, he glanced at his partner. "Yes, and I have you on speaker with Schak. Where are you? We want to be there when you question Chase."

"I've already been to the address I got from the clinic. It's an apartment and someone else lives there now. Also, Aaron Chase is not in the system."

"Put out an alert for him, then head back to the clinic. We have to question everyone." He gave her the new information about Samir, then added, "I think she met Tayla Holden at the clinic, but I'm not sure how their relationship plays into this."

"Maybe it doesn't," Evans said. "Except that she probably looks like her mother, so she's the perp's type too. See you there."

Jackson cranked the engine and raced out Willamette Street.

When they reached the Women's Health Center, the parking lot was empty.

"Crap!" Jackson checked his phone and realized it was nearly five. "Let's meet and strategize. Maybe what we need is in the girl's journal."

Schak grabbed his arm. "You released Derrick, didn't you?"

"Yes, why?"

"What if he grabbed that poor girl?"

Chapter 42

On the drive back to the department, he and Schak argued about Derrick. "He's not well enough to pull it off," Jackson repeated. "And unless he's suddenly turned into a serial killer, he has no motive for kidnapping or hurting Samir."

"If she's Holden's daughter, maybe she knew about the drugs Derrick was supplying her mother and threatened to report him."

Using his earpiece, Jackson called Derrick again, but still no answer.

"The fact that he's not reachable makes him guilty too," Schak insisted.

Jackson made a sudden left and drove toward River Road.

"Where are we going?"

"His house."

"Huh." Schak was quiet on the rest of the ride.

Ten minutes later, the familiar cottage came into sight. Both vehicles sat in the driveway in their same spots. Jackson parked behind them. "I put Derrick in a cab this morning and suggested he go to a hotel," Jackson said, climbing from his sedan. "But Derrick has never done what he's told. I'll bet you he's in there sleeping."

"We'll see."

Jackson moved as quickly as he could without wincing, then pounded on the door. "Derrick! It's Wade. I'm coming in." The door was unlocked, so he pushed in, and Schak followed.

A pizza box lay open on the coffee table with half the pie gone, and the TV blared with a news report. Derrick was nowhere in sight. Jackson jogged through the kitchen and shoved open the door to the converted garage.

Rhythmic snoring filled the room. Derrick lay sprawled on the bed, still wearing the pajama pants he'd had on when Jackson arrived early the morning before. Beside him, Schak said. "So you won that bet. Let's get back to work."

"We should tell him he's been poisoned," Jackson said. "He may need to go back to the hospital."

"Maybe he just needs rest. Your call." Schak shrugged. "I'm going to take a quick look around just to cover the possibilities."

Jackson almost laughed at his partner's sheer stubbornness. He decided to let Derrick sleep for now. His body was probably starting to recover, and they had a missing young woman who had to be their priority.

Jackson parked in the department's back lot, eager for Schak to get out of the car. "Go order food and coffee," he told his partner. "I need to make a private call."

"Will do." Schak climbed out, groaning as he did.

Now that Derrick wasn't their suspect, they'd unofficially switched back to their usual roles, and his world felt right again. Almost. Jackson called Kera, needing to talk to her, but also hoping she wouldn't answer. She did. "Hello, Wade."

"Hey, Kera. Sorry I've been out of touch."

"I know. You're working a homicide." Soft and supportive.

Guilt flooded him. She was such a good woman! Even after he'd told her he had feelings for someone else. "Two homicides actually. And now we have a missing young woman. We think the cases are all connected."

"Oh no! I hope the poor girl is still alive."

Jackson sensed that she might be. Otherwise, why hadn't they found Samir's body in her own home like they had with the other women? "I'm hopeful, so we have to keep searching. Which means I'll be working around the clock until we find her."

"I understand. I've been through a few of these with you."

"It frustrates me not to be there with you after all this time apart."

"That's not what you said last night."

There it was. The reminder. But he didn't blame her. "I'm sorry."

"Don't worry, we'll have time together. Meanwhile, I'm catching up with friends and getting stuff done that I put off for months."

"Yeah, like what?" He didn't really have time to chat, but he owed her some attention.

"Getting a last will and testament drafted and notarized."

"That doesn't sound like fun."

"No, but when you watch both your parents die, it suddenly seems like a good idea."

His parents had been murdered when he was fairly young, and he still didn't have a will. But other than his retirement account, he didn't have an estate to leave anyone. "You're still at my house, right?"

"No, I'm staying with a friend. You need to resolve your issue with Evans, and I'm not going to get in your way while you do."

He didn't know what to say. "I don't deserve you."

She laughed. "I can't argue with that." A pause. "I'll take the kids to dinner so you can get back to work and not worry about them. But send Benjie a video on my phone, please.

That boy gets despondent when you're gone all day."

"I will. Thanks. Love you." Was it wrong to say it to both women? He did love them both. Was this how some divorced people felt? As if they would always love their ex, even if they couldn't make the relationship work?

"See you later, Wade." Kera hung up.

Without saying she loved him. He didn't blame her for that either. She was probably protecting herself. He tried to put himself into her position and couldn't. If she had another man in her life, he would be irrationally upset, maybe even want to confront the guy. But he couldn't deal with personal stuff now. A young woman was in danger, and his team had to work this investigation until they found her.

He started to get out of the car, then remembered his promise for Benjie. Jackson held out his phone, pressed record, and said a fun hello to his son. After he sent the video, he forced himself to hurry inside.

Schak and Evans were already in the conference room when he got upstairs. Schak hadn't taken the spot at the head of the table so, out of respect, Jackson left it empty and sat next to Evans. They were all just teammates, brainstorming how to find Samir and nail down the killer.

He spoke to Evans first. "Tell us what you learned at the clinic." Jackson wished he had his computer in front of him to take notes. He would do his best with shorthand and his old-school notebook.

"Other than the new suspect, I didn't find out much. Once I had his name, I tried to find him. With the receptionist missing, that felt like a priority."

"It was. And still is." There had to be other avenues to pursue. "Do any men work there now?"

"One of the owners, an immunologist, is male. But the

245

other two doctors are women."

"We can't rule out women," Jackson said, mostly for his own benefit. "Tell me about the immunologist."

Evans went to the board and wrote three names, the last one Vance Kettering. "He's on vacation this week, and neither of our victims were his clients."

"I want to talk to him anyway. Do you have contact information?"

Evans handed him a business card. Jackson stared at the text, something niggling his memory. He'd heard the name recently but couldn't remember where. And it started with a K! He looked up excitedly. "Remember the K scratched in the floor in Holden's kitchen?"

"We have to find this guy," Schak said. "The K could mean killer, but everything else points to the clinic."

"He's definitely our focus," Jackson concurred. "Do we know where he went on vacation?"

Evans shook her head. "No. I asked. But we have the girl's journal. Has anyone looked at it?"

"Not yet." Jackson handed it to her. "I'll let you do that."

Evans chuckled. "Are you afraid of young-girl angst?"

"Maybe." He reached for Evans' tablet. "I'll check Samir's social media pages."

"Anything for me?" Schak sat forward, eager to work the new lead.

"Here." Jackson pushed the tablet over to him. "You check Facebook and see if Samir's friends know where she is. Or if she posted anything about Kettering. I'll call Dr. Ezrow and see if she'll open up the clinic and let us look at employee backgrounds."

"Hah!" Evans scoffed. "Besides the privacy issues, it's after hours."

"If we do get Ezrow's attention," Schak said, "let's show her photos of the victims' pill bottles and see if she recognizes the source."

"Excellent idea." Jackson found the doctor's earlier call in his phone and hit redial. If the number was connected to an office line, no one would answer. And no one did.

A pizza guy arrived and dropped off their order. Schak tipped him and he left. Jackson's stomach growled at the aroma, but he wasn't ready to take a break yet. "Where will I find Dr. Ezrow's private number?"

"Try calling the clinic's after-hours number." Evans picked up a slice but put it on a paper plate without taking a bite. "The answering service will know how to contact her."

"Another fine idea." Jackson googled the clinic on his phone, found the number, and called.

A recorded message played. "This is the Women's Health Center after-hours line. If you have a medical emergency, please call 911. If you've seen a clinic doctor in the last forty-eight hours and have a follow-up issue or question, please leave a message and someone will get back to you."

Jackson kept it brief. "This is Detective Jackson and I spoke with Dr. Ezrow today. I have several follow-up issues, and I'd like her to call me ASAP."

Feeling better, he ate a slice of pizza with the works. He loved it when Schak ordered food. He could indulge without too much guilt.

They were all quiet for a few minutes as Evans skimmed the missing girl's journal, and Schak looked at Samir's Facebook page while chowing down.

"Samir tracked her mother to Eugene," Evans announced, "then followed her around until she worked up the nerve to confront her. But Tayla Holden rejected her, claiming the guy she was dating would freak out if she suddenly had an adult-age kid."

That had been a year ago, so she meant his brother. "Yeah, Derrick is like that. But still, it's a bullshit excuse to turn your own kid away."

"I agree." Evans kept reading.

"The girl's Facebook stuff is private and I can't see her posts." Schak shoved the computer tablet back at Evans. "I wonder if any of the tech people are still here."

Jackson's phone rang and he snatched it up. A local number he didn't recognize. "Detective Jackson here."

"It's Dr. Ezrow returning your call."

"Thanks. I have a huge favor to ask." He put her on speaker.

"Don't count on it."

His hopes fell. "We need to see your employee files. Can you meet us at the clinic and give us access?"

"No. I'm in the middle of something and can only give you about three minutes." A rush of impatience.

"Tell me how Samir Thibault came to work for you."

"She applied and got hired. Why?" A slight pause. "She must be seriously missing."

"Did you know she was Tayla Holden's daughter?"

"What? No. That's weird."

"Did anyone in your office know that?"

"I doubt it."

"Who interviewed her?"

"Dr. Kettering. He does most of the hiring."

Jackson knew he had to tread lightly here. "How well do you know Dr. Kettering?"

"Well enough. He's my ex-husband."

Chapter 43

Evans' pulse raced as she listened to the exchange. If Kettering had hired Samir, maybe he was the one with the crypt-keeper fetish. She cut into the conversation, too impatient for diplomacy. "Does your ex have a type of woman he's attracted to?"

"What are you asking?" A note of fear in Dr. Ezrow's voice.

"Does he like actresses, for example, with long dark hair, fair skin, and delicate features?"

A long silence. "That's what those women looked like, both Tayla Holden and Nicky Walker." Her voice shook. "But what you're suggesting is ridiculous! Vance is a healer. He cares more about his patients than any other male doctor I've ever known." Ezrow hung up.

"Damn. I had more questions." Jackson stared at her. "That was a little more blunt than I planned to handle it."

"Sorry." She'd been thinking about her own situation with Stricklyn all day, and her nerves were shot. "She didn't deny it."

Schak stopped eating and pushed his plate aside. "But what motive would the doctor have to kill these women?"

Ideas had been crashing together in her head for the last hour, and they finally made sense. "To silence them."

"About?" Jackson cocked his head.

"Sexual coercion. Think about this scenario." Evans took a breath so she could spell it out calmly. "The women both got kicked out of the clinic because they'd become addicted to pain meds, thus making them needy, vulnerable, and in withdrawal. Kettering, who already found them attractive, approaches them with an off-book supply of powerful opioids, which they happily take, making them more addicted. Now comes the catch. To keep the meds coming, they have to sexually service him, or he threatens to cut them off."

The men were silent, so she finished her thought. "Then something spooked him. Maybe a colleague was accused of sexual assault, or one of the women threatened to go to the police, or check into rehab. Afraid of losing everything—like so many other men in this me-too era—Kettering decided to clean up his problem by killing the women."

"Holy shit." Schak shook his head. "It makes total sense . . . and yet it's unbelievable."

"I'm with you," Jackson said, "but what about Samir? How does she fit in? We didn't see any sign of drugs in her room. She's also been showing up for work every day for a year. I don't see her as an addict."

Evans was still mulling that over. "Maybe she witnessed something."

"Like Barulla, who spied on Tayla over the fence," Jackson remembered. "Maybe he saw the doctor at Holden's house the night she was killed and had to be cleaned up too."

Schak stood and belched loudly. "Sorry. I had to get comfortable." He rubbed his chest.

"Oh shit. Do you have chest pain?" Evans asked at the same time Jackson did.

"No! Just some trapped air." Schak seemed worked up. "We need to call that woman doctor back—and make her tell us everything she knows about her ex."

Jackson was already reaching for his phone. "I hate sexual predators," he said, shaking his head. "Every day that a new one is announced, I get more pissed off. I had no idea so many women had to deal with this."

"I'm pissed too," Schak chimed in. "There's a lot of good men in this world, and we're all getting tarnished."

Evans loved these guys for their decency and their support. "I have to tell you something," she blurted, surprising herself.

Jackson let go of his phone and Schak sat down.

There was no stopping it now. "Captain Stricklyn has been sexually coercing me." She blushed, a new experience. "I mean, he's been trying. He says if I don't sleep with him, he'll fire Jackson."

"What the hell?" Jackson was on his feet.

"Stricklyn saw us in the Grill's parking lot. We weren't doing anything wrong, but he says he'll claim we were fraternizing as a couple." Evans glanced at Schak. "Sorry to bring you into this."

"It's okay. I just don't know how to help."

Evans regretted her timing. "We don't have to talk about this now. Samir comes first. I get the feeling she's still alive out there, and we have to find her.

Jackson came around the table, put an arm around her, and squeezed. "No one is going to fire me or you. I will do whatever it takes to get Stricklyn booted from the department. Let's think about this later and strategize a way to bring him down."

"Hell yes!" Evans felt better than she had all week. "Call Ezrow back. I'll bet she knows where her ex is right now."

Jackson tried, but the doctor didn't answer.

"I'll go to her house. She can't avoid this." Evans grabbed

her tablet and loaded the department's database of individuals, which included everyone who'd ever had contact with the police, even as witnesses or citizens. She found Ezrow listed with a south Eugene address. "Got her." She grabbed her bag and stood, ideas still popping into her mind. "While I'm gone, you guys can find Kettering's home, in case he didn't actually go on vacation. And you can try to figure out where he's getting the methadone. It has to be a pharmacy. If he has hospital privileges, I would start there."

The surprised looks on their faces made her realize she'd just hijacked the investigation. Right now, seniority didn't matter. Evans grinned. "Let's do this." She hurried out before they could argue.

As she crossed the parking lot, the sunshine and warm air surprised her. The earlier rain clouds had disappeared, leaving a warm pink glow in the sky. She loved daylight savings and the extra hours of productivity it allowed. The trip up College Hill to the top of Lincoln Street only took twelve minutes. At this point, every minute could count. Evans didn't see a car in front of the stately house, but the vehicle was likely in the garage—if Ezrow was even home. The doctor had claimed to be in the middle of something, but it had sounded like bullshit. The woman was obviously struggling to come to terms with her ex-husband's true nature.

Evans pounded loudly, but no one responded. She pressed the bell for a long moment too. Impatient and super-charged on caffeine, she pushed open the front door and called out, "It's Detective Evans! We need to talk."

A muffled response from deep in the house. Evans entered the foyer and scanned the house. The decor was so immaculate and showroom-beautiful, the home looked unoccupied. Soft crying came from somewhere. Evans crossed the kitchen and, through glass French doors, she spotted the doctor sitting on a back courtyard. Concerned about startling the woman, Evans called out again, more softly this time.

As she stepped out on the patio, the doctor looked up. Ezrow's eyes were bloodshot and watery, and a nearly empty bottle of red wine sat on the tile near her feet. "After I cut my hair, he never slept with me again," she wailed, her speech sloppy and self-pitying.

"You mean your ex, Vance Kettering?"

"Yeah, that's why we divorced. He was careful, but I'm sure he cheated on me."

Evans wanted to cut to the chase, but she needed this woman to be cooperative. "I'm sorry for your pain. But I need to know where Kettering is."

"How the hell should I know? We're just colleagues at this point. He didn't discuss his vacation plans with me."

Vacation? Evans shuddered. The doctor had taken time off work to commit three murders and another as-yet-unknown crime. "Does he own a weekend property?" She visualized poor Samir in some remote cabin, being pumped full of opioids and sexually assaulted. "This is important. Samir's life could still be at stake."

"He's probably just fucking her, and she's letting him, hoping for a promotion." Ezrow grabbed the bottle for another slug.

The possibility of a consensual affair hadn't occurred to Evans. "Why do you think that?"

"I'm just bitter." The woman hiccupped. "And horrified that the man I was married to might be a killer."

Evans was losing her patience with the drunk woman.

"Where does he normally go?"

"We co-own a condo in Sun River with another couple. He might have gone there."

Eastern Oregon and a five-hour drive. They would have to ask local officers to check it out. "Text me the address."

Ezrow let out a bitter laugh. "I'm not sure I can, but I'll try." She picked up the phone next to her on the cushioned chair and keyed in the information, swearing as she started over a few times.

"Any other ideas where Kettering would go?" If he had left town at all.

"He got the RV in the divorce." Ezrow dropped her phone and grabbed the wine again. "He said he planned to buy a quiet spot by a lake where he could park it and chill out."

That sounded more isolated . . . and more likely. "What lake?"

"Don't know, don't care." She downed the rest of the wine.

"Who is his real estate agent?"

"That couple on TV." Ezrow was barely coherent now.

Evans had no clue who she meant. "I need a name."

The woman was in her own world now. She leaned back and mumbled, "The bastard used to write scripts to himself on my account."

For his own consumption? Or for his victims? "What pharmacy does he use?"

She mumbled something incomprehensible. Evans leaned closer. "Say that again."

But the woman had passed out.

Damn! As Evans walked back through the house, she called Jackson. He didn't answer, so she texted him and Schak: *We're looking for a recent RV property purchase by a lake and a pharmacy where Kettering filled prescriptions to himself.*

She sent the text and climbed in her car. Who would know which real estate agents worked as a couple and ran ads on TV?

Chapter 44

Sophie drove along the expressway, squinting into the bright sun on the horizon. She'd worked late and the rush-hour traffic had thinned, but it was still moving slow. When she neared the Valley River exit, she had to brake hard to keep from rear-ending the stopped car in front of her. When her phone buzzed a moment later, she pressed her earpiece to answer. "Sophie Speranza."

"It's Detective Evans and I have a weird question."

This wasn't the callback she was expecting. "Ask me."

"What is the name of the realtor couple who runs ads on TV?"

An easy one. "I don't watch network programming, but I know who you're talking about because they run ads in the paper too. Lucy and Galen Burton."

"Thanks." The detective was clearly done with the call.

"Wait! What's happening with the investigation? Did Tony Barulla kill Tayla Holden?" She'd written a piece about Barulla's suicide, but so far nobody would confirm that his final message had been a confession.

"Probably not. We have a new suspect, but it's too soon to talk about him."

"What about the missing woman? Jackson sent over a photo and asked us to run it." The image had come in a few hours earlier, and she'd worked late trying to dig up something to run as copy with it. "Is Samir Thibault connected to the other victims? She sure looks like Tayla Holden."

"I can't tell you unless you promise to hold the information until we find her."

"I promise." She could always renegotiate the agreement. "Tell me. Maybe I can help."

"Samir is Holden's daughter. She gave her up for adoption at birth."

Whoa. "But why is she missing? Has she been murdered too?"

"I have to go." Detective Evans hung up.

Someone behind her honked loudly, and Sophie looked up to see that traffic was moving again. She took the VRC exit and briefly considered going back to the newspaper to update her story. But she'd promised to hold the information, and she would. For now.

Inside her apartment, she kicked off her shoes and unhooked her bra. She left it hanging loose because she might have to go back out soon. Sophie poured a small glass of white wine and sat down at her window-side dinette table with an amazing view of the river. She skimmed through her recent calls, found Mrs. Holden, and pressed the connection.

The grieving mother took her call, sounding calmer than she had a few days ago in front of her daughter's house. "Hi. It's Sophie Speranza again. How are you doing?"

"About how you would expect. By the way, I want you to send me a copy of the feature you write about Tayla."

"I intend to, but it may take a few more days. The investigation is still going on."

"I'm not sure why. I called the department's spokes-person and she told me Tayla's neighbor had killed her, then committed suicide."

Apparently the issue was still unresolved. "I don't think that's right. I just talked to a detective who said they had a new suspect." *Damn.* She regretted telling her. The mother would probably call Jackson and ask him about it. "Forget I said that, please. There's something else going on that's more important."

"What could be more important than my daughter's murder?" A weary drag on her voice.

Sophie had a moment's hesitation, then shook it off. "Your granddaughter's disappearance."

A sharp intake of breath. "What are you talking about?"

"The baby girl that Tayla gave up for adoption is here in Eugene."

"Oh my god. What's her name? I want to contact her. "

Sophie hated to crush her spirits, but she was still hoping for information that could help. "Samir is missing, and the police are looking for her. Do you have any idea where she might be?"

The woman burst into tears. "What is happening? First my daughter, now my granddaughter."

Sophie kicked herself. "I don't know yet, but I'll find out what I can. Jackson and his team are the best. They'll find her."

Chapter 45

Jackson pulled into Vance Kettering's driveway, and exterior lights came on around the house. The response was automatic, and he instinctively knew the man wasn't home. No RV was in sight either, but the neighborhood probably had rules against them. The whole subdivision at the top of Skyridge had been built in the last few years, but the doctor's house was only one of several that had a view of the city below.

After going through the motions of knocking and calling out, Jackson got back into his vehicle. He called Schak, who was in the department, searching property records. "Find anything?"

"Sort of." In the background, his partner shuffled papers. "Kettering bought a tax lot near Fern Ridge Reservoir, but there's no actual address. I'm trying to find the lot number on the county map, but no luck so far."

"Stay with it. This could be our break." Jackson started the engine, unsure of what to do next. "I'm headed back."

"See you."

He exited the driveway and rolled down the winding street. He wanted to find the pharmacy Evans had mentioned in her text, but he had no idea where to start. He'd already called the hospital, but their in-house drugstore was closed. It seemed unlikely that Kettering would risk filling scripts to himself where he worked anyway. Jackson still wasn't clear about the doctor's process for getting medication to the victims, but it was obvious he hadn't wanted his name on their prescription bottles. Maybe he used pharmacies all over town, picking up the methadone in a new place every time. That would have been smart.

At the bottom of the hill, Jackson turned right, heading back into town. He passed a mini-mall that had been there for decades, noticing a laundromat, a lottery parlor with video poker machines, a Mexican restaurant—and a hole-in-the-wall pharmacy.

Jackson braked hard. He might as well check it out. Kettering had to drive right by it every time he left his home. He had missed the entrance and had to circle back. When he neared the small shop on foot, an older man was locking the glass front door. "Hey!" Jackson shouted, hoping to get the owner's attention before he disappeared.

The old guy looked up but waved him off.

Jackson pulled his badge and held it up to the glass.

The man's eyes went wide and he stepped back.

"Open up! This is important."

Clicking sounds followed as the owner unlocked the door. Jackson pushed it open, introducing himself as he stepped inside. The cluttered space was about the size of his living room. No lights were on except for those over the prescription counter in the back. "What's your name?"

"Kenneth Poling." He had sunken cheeks, heavy-rimmed glasses, and frizzy gray hair.

"Are you a pharmacist?"

"Of course. I also own this business, as I have for decades."

"Do you know Dr. Vance Kettering?"

Wariness in his eyes now. "I know the name from filling a few prescriptions."

"Kettering may be in a lot of trouble. I suggest you protect yourself by telling me everything about his transactions here."

For a long moment, they stood silently in the dim light, between aisles filled with cold medicine and condoms. Finally, Poling spoke. "Dr. Kettering owns a pain management clinic so he prescribes and dispenses a variety of opioids. I fill prescriptions for him and his patients."

"He writes scripts to himself?"

"Yes, he needs medications on hand." The pharmacist's voice quivered. "With some patients, he doses them daily, like at the methadone clinic. It keeps them from taking too many and getting addicted."

Or at least that's what Kettering had told this guy to explain why he needed handfuls of pain pills all the time. Evans' theory was probably true. The doctor had dangled those drugs in front of desperate addicts and demanded sex as payment. He obviously didn't need money. "How many pills at a time? Per week, for example?"

The old guy blinked rapidly. "Hundreds."

Jackson's gut tightened in a painful squeeze. How many woman had Kettering victimized?

Chapter 46

Evans pulled into the department and drove past all the new SUV patrol units to park in back. Her brain was still firing on all cylinders, but when she climbed from the sedan, her body began to drag. She'd been working this investigation fourteen hours a day since Monday. The guys, being older, had to be even more tired. As she trudged up the outer stairs, the callback she was expecting finally came through.

"Lucy Burton of Burton Realtors, returning your call."

"Great, thanks. As I mentioned in my message, we're trying to find a missing nineteen-year-old woman. We think she's with Dr. Vance Kettering, and we'd like to locate the property he recently purchased."

"Is she in danger?"

"Yes, that's why I'm asking."

A moment of silence. "This is an unusual request. Can you give me a minute?" Her muffled voice could be heard talking to someone else.

Consulting with her partner? Still on hold, Evans trudged into the conference room. Schak looked like he hadn't moved, but Jackson was still out. She put her phone on the table and switched to speaker.

Lucy came back on the line. "The property isn't developed yet, so I'm not sure why they would be there."

"You've seen the lot?"

"We took Vance out there before he bought it."

"Is it cleared and level? Could he park an RV there?"

"Yes, that's why he wanted it. But it doesn't have utilities yet." She made an odd noise. "I shouldn't assume that. Maybe Vance pulled some strings and got the power company out already."

"Can you tell me how to get there?"

"Sure. From Fir Butte, you turn down Corliss Lane. It's a private drive that turns into a narrow gravel road. A half-mile past that, you turn off to the left. You can see the water at that point.

"Thank you." Evans hung up and looked at Schak. "Does that jive with the lot number and location you found on the county website?"

"Yes, indeed." He handed back her computer tablet. "Dr. Kettering is not on social media, but he *was* accused of sexual misconduct in med school."

"No surprise." Itchy to keep moving, she glanced at the time. Jackson had been gone nearly an hour. "Should we head out to his property?"

"Let's give Jackson ten minutes. Text him the directions in the meantime."

Evans' phone rang in her pocket and she grabbed it, thinking it was Jackson. Instead, it was the evidence lab. She'd almost forgotten about the items she'd dropped off. "Hey, Joe. What have you got?"

"That gray powder in the locked box you brought in? It's thallium."

Nicky's possessions. "It's poison, isn't it?"

"Only if you consume it."

"Does it have long-term effects?"

"I'm not an expert in this field, but if someone had been consuming this, I would take them to the hospital for charcoal treatments immediately."

"Thanks, Joe." Evans got up and started to pace. "Derrick was being poisoned with thallium. He needs to go back to the hospital." She called his number and waited while it rang.

Schak's brow creased. "He was sleeping when we checked on him earlier. Maybe you should go get him up and take him in."

Was that guilt? For holding him overnight when he was sick? She'd never seen that expression on Schak's face before.

Derrick didn't answer and her concern escalated. "I'll check on him now, then head out to Kettering's property after I drop off Derrick. Unless you call and tell me otherwise."

"I'll keep you posted." Schak stood and stretched. "I'm not optimistic that we'll find the doctor there. Or convict him of anything. He seems to have covered his tracks and not left any trace evidence at either crime scene."

Evans had started for the door, but spun back. "Don't say that. It's obvious that neither Tayla nor Nicky were admirable women. But they had chronic pain. And they were victimized. They need justice like everyone else."

"Hey! I'm not arguing that point. I'm just worried that we don't have anything but a theory and circumstantial factors."

"We also have a missing woman, so maybe you should get going."

Jackson strode into the room. "Going where?"

"To Kettering's property out by the lake." Schak scooped up his papers and shoved them into his briefcase. "It's off Fir Butte."

"Good work finding it." Jackson stopped next to Evans. "I found the pharmacy Kettering used to fill prescriptions written to himself—hundreds of various opioids every week."

"That's intense!" A new worry hit her. "Was he taking

some himself or are there more victims?"

"We don't know yet."

Evans had second thoughts about spending her time helping Derrick.

"What?" Jackson tried to read her face.

"Derrick was poisoned with thallium, and I thought I would take him back to the hospital. Joe seems to think it needs to happen right now."

Jackson closed his eyes for a second, then squeezed her arm. "Thank you. I've been worried. He's at his house, by the way."

"I'll get it done quickly and meet you at Kettering's property." She headed for the door, and her teammates followed her.

Chapter 47

Vance Kettering popped another 500 milligrams of Oxy, then jogged into the little store. Damn, he felt good. Liberated, actually. He'd often fantasized about strangling his wife—especially when she'd nagged him about the little stuff. But he'd never thought he would actually kill a woman—or two—and get away with it. What was actually liberating, though, was how he felt. No guilt at all. He had suspected his own sociopathy since college, but the psychopathy had surprised him. When Tayla had mentioned getting into rehab and filing a complaint against him, he'd known it was time to shut down that sideline. Too many men had lost everything in the Me-Too era, and he wouldn't let it happen to himself. Tayla and Nicky were drug whores and no one would miss them.

In the store, he picked up red wine, French bread, butter, and eggs. The supplies in the RV were running low, but he didn't want to overstock the small fridge either. On Monday, he had to go back to work. He stopped and considered the thought. Did he really? If he sold the stupidly expensive house he'd bought after the divorce, he could live on his investments easily and never have to listen to whiny patients again. But where would he find women he could sexually control? The clinic was such a great feed source.

He had to be careful for now. Samir's disappearance would eventually be questioned. He didn't think the cops would ever connect Tayla and Nicky though. Their lives hadn't had any overlap except their visits to the Women's Health Center, and they hadn't been patients at the same time, or even recently. He smiled to himself as he walked to the check stand. Tony Barulla had conveniently confessed to killing Tayla, so that bought him a lot of space. That cleanup had been a lot more risky and challenging than the women. But necessary. The little fuck had been watching Tayla over the fence, and who knew what he'd seen?

Waiting for the cashier to be ready, Kettering relived the moment and realized it hadn't been all that challenging. Barulla had been halfway through his own bottle of vodka, so he hadn't even had to use the one he'd brought with him. Getting in close to inject him with fentanyl had been fairly easy too. People tended to trust doctors. The suicide note had taken too long, making him nervous about being in the house, but Kettering was confident the cops would believe it. People facing long prison sentences often killed themselves. The little fuck had also had a bottle of his mother's meds in the bathroom. Plus the bomb stuff? It's almost as if Barulla had wanted to die.

Kettering paid for the groceries with cash and didn't speak a word to the clerk. The less he interacted, the safer. He jogged back to his Audi convertible, tossed the supplies into the backseat, and fired up the engine. Speeding down the empty road into the sunset filled him with another burst of joy. He loved these moments, with the wind on his face and a sense that he could go anywhere and do anything!

Grabbing Samir had been pure impulse—born of frustration. Sex had become an intense addiction, and a man could only go so long without getting his cock sucked. But taking what he wanted had become necessary. In today's climate of asking permission and women whining publicly about men's sexual needs, what other choice did he have? The old coercive way wouldn't work anymore, and he'd wanted to fuck that girl since the day she walked into the clinic. She had perfect hair, flawless porcelain skin, and those luscious ruby lips. She was young and vulnerable too—as if she'd been made just for him. How long could he keep her? Unlike with the other women, he had momentary flashes of empathy for Samir. But the Oxy made them easy to ignore.

At Corliss Lane, he eased off the accelerator, but not much. He made the turn, fast and wide, and for a split second, he sensed the car could spin out of control. But it never did. Another great feeling. At the end of the asphalt, he slowed, not wanting to hit the gravel hard and spin out. It would be tragic to die in an accident when he had the perfect woman waiting for him at home.

Chapter 48

Samir swallowed the spit she had worked up, but her throat was still dry. Rage burned in her belly and all she could think about was escape. After the bastard had finally left, she'd sobbed in relief from the constant sexual assault. But she was done crying now. She had to get free while he was gone.

Samir forced herself to sit up and look at the handcuffs on her wrists. They were tethered with a rope to one of the short posts under the bed. Her ankles were bound together too, but the rope between them was slack. Could she walk into the bathroom? It was right there. He'd let her use it several times, but with the door open while he watched her intently. She'd been too horrified to notice anything, except that it was a tiny space, connected to this closet-sized bedroom. He'd left the other door slightly open too, and she could see a slice of the whole RV. It seemed new, like it had never been used before.

Her mind clouded and she struggled to focus. He'd been shoving tiny white pills under her tongue to keep her calm—while he raped her. But she had to be sharp now. He was gone and this was her chance. To do what?

Find something sharp! Then cut through the rope at her feet and also the one tethering her to the bed. She choked back a sob. She didn't have enough slack to get into the kitchen, and her chances of finding something sharp, or anything at all, in this little bedroom were slim. Samir

269

scooted to the edge of the bed, her body aching everywhere. *Feet on the ground. Now walk.* She coached herself along, feeling more focused as she moved. The rope between her feet was awkward, but she was mobile.

The bathroom held a toilet and a funky little shower. That was it. No drawers to search. No medicine cabinet. She caught sight of herself in the mirror and quickly looked away. She didn't recognize the terrified woman in a stranger's T-shirt. Samir backed out of the little room and moved toward the door leading into the next area. She could step through, but that was it. The rope on her handcuffs pulled tight, and the metal cut into her wrists. The next space had a sink and cabinets on one side and a closet on the other, but she couldn't reach any of it.

Despair washed over her. How long did he plan to keep her? Some women were held as sex slaves for years! How did they keep from going crazy? She'd only been here for a day or so and she was ready to kill herself.

What if he wrecked his car and didn't come back? She could die here, slowly starving, in this isolated spot where no one could hear her scream. She had to find a way to get loose and get the hell out. Samir shuffled back around and stared at the ridiculous space. The bed took up most of it, leaving a narrow walkway on both sides. And nothing else. The small window opposite the bathroom had been blacked out with something on the outside. Could she break the window and use the glass as a cutting tool?

Samir shuffled over, raised her cuffed hands, and smashed into the glass. The window vibrated but didn't show any sign of weakening. Hands hurting now too, she collapsed to the floor and fought back tears. *Deep breaths,* she coached herself. *Keep thinking.* There had to be a way. The rope tethering her to the bed was tied right there on the short corner post.

Tied! Not locked or fused in any way.

She scooted across the carpet on her naked butt until she was right next to the metal bed leg. Her hands were shackled together but her fingers were free—and she was good with knots.

Painstakingly, she worked the thin cord, pushing and pulling the loops and double loops until her fingers ached. She rested for a moment, then started again. Finally, the rope came free. *Yes!* Her heart leapt with joy. She could escape! Her ankles were bound together, but she could shuffle. Did she have time to work through the other knots? How long had the doctor been gone?

Get out! Instinct told her to skip the mess at her ankles and get free of the RV. She didn't know exactly where she was or what was outside, but there had to be a place to hide. The reservoir was around here somewhere, and that meant people who could help her. Samir shuffled through the narrow home on wheels, glancing around for her pants. He'd ripped them off her when they first arrived the night before, but she didn't see them. Her heart pounded in her ears and she had trouble focusing.

In the kitchen, she glanced around for her phone. He'd taken it from her in the car at one point, but she didn't remember arriving here. She still couldn't believe this was happening. She recalled leaving work the day before. Dr. Kettering had stopped and offered her a ride home when he saw her walking her disabled bike. Stupidly, she'd climbed into his sweet little convertible, thinking he was a nice guy. When the doctor insisted on taking her for a ride around the lake to enjoy the sunshine, she'd been flattered by his attention. It couldn't hurt to have the boss as a friend. He'd given her a small bottle of flavored water and soon after, everything had started to go wrong. Through a haze, she'd watched him transform from the nice doctor she worked for into a monster.

Where the hell was her phone?

The sound of a fast-moving vehicle hummed in the distance. *Oh shit!* He was coming back. Samir yanked open a drawer next to the sink. A few pieces of silverware, a spatula, and a corkscrew. Where were the knives? She needed to free her damn legs. She yanked open another drawer. *Empty! Shit!* She glanced at the small countertop. Nothing.

The engine roar drew closer.

Panicked, Samir grabbed the corkscrew and power-walked to the outer door, taking short steps to accommodate the rope. She pushed down the handle and leaned in, expecting the door to open. It didn't move. Had he locked her in? *Fuck!*

No, it had to be locked from inside—to keep it from flying open as the RV rolled down the road. She scanned the doorframe and mechanism and found the latch. She popped it up, hit the handle again, and pushed open the door.

The fresh air hit her with the taste of freedom. Tears of joy rolled down her cheeks as she stepped down the metal rungs and glanced around. Trees everywhere. Except for the gravel road—where he was coming from. Samir guessed the lake was in the opposite direction and started through the trees. She kept her steps short and quick, like football players did during practice. Maybe she would find a path.

Chapter 49

In the distance, the RV came into view and Kettering eased off the gas. Just thinking about the girl, sprawled naked on his bed, made him hard again. The blue pills were a miracle, allowing his cock to keep up with his desire—enhanced by a drop of sativa oil on bread. He'd finally found sexual nirvana.

The exterior door abruptly flew open, and Samir shuffled down the steps.

What the fuck?

How had she gotten loose? Kettering pressed the accelerator.

He watched in panic as the girl shuffled off, the rope between her ankles the only thing slowing her down. He raced down the gravel to the RV, slammed to a stop, and jumped from the car. He willed himself to stay calm. She couldn't get very far. Beyond the woods lay an isolated shoreline, with the nearest house miles away. He could easily overcome her. But what then? Getting her back into the RV would be challenging. Her last benzo had obviously worn off. If she yelled, he didn't think anyone would hear, but he hated screaming. He liked dominating women, not terrorizing them. That tended to ruin the mood.

He'd wanted to keep her and enjoy her for a while, but obviously his confinement method had failed. Maybe he should just kill her and get it over with.

Chapter 50

Samir heard the sports car slam to a stop, and her heart missed a beat. The doctor would run her down like a cougar after a wounded rabbit. Unless she found somewhere to hide. It would be dark soon, making it harder for him. Eyes darting everywhere, she tried to pick up her pace. But the forest was thin with little undergrowth, and the ground was flat. He was probably watching her right now.

She glanced over her shoulder and saw him climb from his car. He would catch her in moments. She couldn't even fight him with her wrists cuffed together. All she had was the corkscrew. If she tried to attack him with it out here, she might wound him, but probably only his arm or his face. The pain would enrage him, and he might beat her this time as well as rape her. Or maybe just kill her. She had to be smart and patient. She would hide the weapon and wait until he was close in and unsuspecting.

Samir slowed her pace and tucked the corkscrew into the garter belt around her waist. She vaguely remembered putting on the black lacy lingerie sometime last night after he'd threatened to hurt her. She had woken up earlier wearing one of his T-shirts, and the length fell to her hips, covering the weapon.

Footsteps crunched on the forest floor behind her, and her pulse hammered. Samir couldn't catch her breath, and she thought she might have a heart attack. Powerful hands grabbed her hair and yanked her to a stop. The doctor jerked her around and forced her to her knees.

Looking down at her with maniacal black eyes, he gave her a choice. "Do you want to die right now or come quietly with me for more good times?"

Hatred burned in her chest. "I don't want to die."

"Good girl." He yanked her up by her hair.

Samir winced in pain.

As he walked her back to the RV, he taunted her. "Your mother wasn't much of a fighter. She willingly sucked my cock every time I wanted her to. All I had to do was offer her methadone."

He'd done this to her mother? Samir didn't really know the woman who'd rejected her twice, but she felt strangely protective anyway.

The doctor laughed, the evil sound echoing through the trees. "More honestly, I threatened to take the meds away. But even in the end, she didn't fight very hard."

What was he saying? "You killed my mother?"

They reached the door, and he held it open for her. "Tayla was a drug whore who didn't have much of a life. She tried, but the truth is, she wasn't a nice person. Why else would she give you away?"

Whatever anger Samir had felt for her mother vanished, replaced with a white-hot need to retaliate. For herself, she just wanted to escape. But for Tayla, she wanted to hurt him. To stick that corkscrew into his neck and watch his eyes panic as he bled to death.

But first, she had to let him get close to her again.

Chapter 51

Jackson pressed the old sedan hard, pushing eighty on the drive out Highway 99, the only stretch of the drive where he could get up to that speed. In the passenger seat, Schak worked the phone, calling Lammers to update her. The boss didn't like to hear about important developments after the fact.

"Sergeant, I have an update on the Vegan Girl Murders."

Jackson didn't correct him.

Schak continued, "We have a new suspect. Dr. Vance Kettering, who runs a pain clinic where both victims were once patients."

"I know him. He has a nice smile and a cold heart." Even on speaker from a small cell phone, Lammers was loud and clear. "He's an immunologist, correct?"

Jackson realized where he'd heard the name—Derrick's hospital room. Kettering had stepped in for a few minutes as a consult. He kept his eyes on the road, letting his partner do the talking.

"We think he was providing the women with non-prescription methadone," Schak explained.

"Taking advantage of their pain?" Lammers' voice was bitter.

"Yes." Schak elaborated. "A young receptionist at the clinic is missing, and we're headed to Kettering's rural property to take a look."

"What can I do to help?"

"Get us a search warrant to go inside, in case we meet with resistance."

"On what grounds?"

Schak glanced over at Jackson.

He leaned toward the phone in his partner's hands. "The girl who's missing looks just like the other women, and is, in fact, Tayla Holden's daughter."

"For fuck's sake." Lammers made a worried sound in her throat. "Do you think she's still alive?"

"Maybe," Schak said. "We've been to her home and didn't find her dead."

Jackson made a quick left turn on Clear Lake Road, realizing he'd overshot the destination—because Fir Butte didn't connect all the way through to the highway.

"Do you need backup?" Lammers asked.

"Evans is following us out here, so we're probably okay."

"Unless it all goes south," Jackson added. His gut coiled into a tight fist and his nerves pinged with anxiety.

"Don't say that!" A car door slammed in the background. "I'm headed back into my office now to start the paperwork. I'll call Judge Cranston to make sure he's available."

"Thanks." Schak hung up and glanced his way. "Is Lammers getting more mellow?"

"She definitely is." Jackson let out a weird laugh. "I'm not sure I like it."

"I know what you mean."

The road was deserted and the sun had started to set, so Jackson pressed the speed again. Two minutes later, he spotted the Fir Butte junction. After he made the turn, he said, "We're watching for Corliss Lane, and it's on your side."

"I know. It's coming up soon. I looked at this area on

Google Maps."

In a few moments, he made the final turn. The private lane was smoother than the county road so he kept up his speed. In the twilight, he didn't see the transition, and suddenly they were bouncing hard on gravel. Jackson eased off the gas. "Crap. Sorry about that."

"It's okay. Just keep moving. I have a sense this girl is in trouble."

"Yeah, me too. I've felt that way since we saw her photo."

They rounded a gentle curve and saw lights in the distance. Jackson shut off his own headlamps, then killed the engine. The sedan coasted to a stop next to a big RV. The occupants might have heard their tires on the gravel, but he hoped they still had some element of surprise.

He climbed from the car and jogged around to the narrow door, with Schak right on his heels. For a moment, he considered knocking and giving a warning shout, then changed his mind. He yanked open the door and took a long painful step up into the mobile unit. Muffled sounds came from a room in the back of the narrow space. He pulled his weapon and ran through a kitchen area toward the partially open door. Behind him, Schak was sucking wind, so he knew his partner had his back.

At first Jackson didn't see the girl—just the big naked man face down on the bed. Then details came into focus. Small feet were visible between the man's legs, and there was blood everywhere.

Please let her be alive! "Samir?"

Jackson stepped into the room, his weapon ready. No, the blood wasn't everywhere. It was all coming from the man's neck where something metal stuck out. But he wasn't dead. The naked man reached for the sharp thing as he rolled over onto his back, crying out in pain.

Dr. Vance Kettering.

Now visible was Samir Thibault, eyes open, her breath rapid and her wrists bound. Side-by-side with Kettering, he saw the resemblance between them. "He killed my mother," she panted.

With his free hand, Jackson reached for his cuffs. "We know."

Chapter 52

Friday, May 11, 3:35 p.m.

Jackson stopped at Dutch Brothers for coffee but didn't drink any until he reached the department. Still in the car, he took a long gulp while the temperature was just right. The stuff was always too hot when he first bought it, then it cooled off so quickly, it was usually blah by the time he got to his desk. He waited a moment, then took another long drink before heading inside. The team was meeting in a few minutes, and he wanted to be sharp. In addition to a crazy-busy morning, he'd been up late, transporting Kettering to the hospital and checking on Derrick while he was there. His brother was recovering physically, but he was still in shock that his girlfriend had poisoned him for money and attention—then had been murdered by one of his doctors.

While Jackson updated his case file, he heard the others gathering outside the conference room. He still had reports to fill out, but they could wait. He picked up his now-cold coffee and walked over to the meeting, not caring that he was the last person to arrive. Lammers and his three teammates had left the chair at the head of the table for him, even though he wasn't officially the lead on this investigation. At this point, it didn't matter. What they had left to do was take Kettering's life apart minute-by-minute over the last few weeks and try to build two cases of premeditated homicide. Even if they failed—because most of the evidence was circumstantial—the doctor would still face a long prison sentence for kidnapping and sexual assault.

A box of muffins sat in the middle of the table, and he helped himself to a chocolate one before sitting down. His teammates greeted him, but they were all exhausted and subdued.

The district attorney hurried in and apologized for being late.

Thanks for joining us, Trang." Jackson tried to smile, but he wasn't feeling it.

"It wasn't optional. I'm still missing crucial details, and I didn't want to wait for your report."

"Then that's where we'll start. What do you want to know?"

"Trace the links for me. I need reassurance that your intrusion into Kettering's home had a solid basis."

Before Jackson could answer, Schak blurted, "We were there to check out a lead, and I heard a cry for help."

Jackson didn't recall it that way, but he would back his partner in court—if it came to that. He spelled it out for the DA. "Leading up to that moment, we have a solid chain. Both victims were in possession of medications that didn't have prescription labels. We discovered that each had been a patient at the Women's Health Center, a pain clinic where Kettering worked. Both had opioid-addiction issues. The doctor was reportedly on vacation during the week of the murders, so that meant he'd had the opportunity to commit both crimes."

"And the missing young woman? How did she fit into this scenario?" Trang was still taking notes.

"She looked just like the murdered women. Then we discovered that she was the first victim's daughter."

"And they all looked like the doctor," Schak said. "He was attracted to women in his own image."

A moment of silence.

The DA's tone softened. "And how is Samir doing?"

"As well as can be expected." Jackson had spoken to her earlier. "She left the hospital with her grandmother this morning and seemed to be in good spirits."

Evans smiled. "They met for the first time last night when I brought Mrs. Holden to the hospital to see her."

Trang looked amused but didn't ask for clarification. He glanced at his notes. "So we have Kettering for two murders, plus kidnapping, sexual assault, and sexual coercion. Not to mention illegal drug distribution."

"Maybe three murders," Jackson corrected. "Tayla Holden's neighbor was killed too. The perp tried to make it look like suicide, but the pathologist found an injection site in the back of his knee. Our theory is that Tony Barulla witnessed something, and Kettering gave him an overdose to silence him."

"No loss to society," Quince blurted. "Barulla had a room full of explosives, and we think he planned to set them off. Kettering may have accidentally saved a few lives."

"He really went off the rails." Trang shook his head. "With this list of charges, I think I can get him to accept a plea that gives him a shot at parole someday."

"You want to plead this case?" Jackson was stunned, even though he'd seen it happen before.

"I want to avoid a prolonged trial, and so will he."

"Don't plead it just yet," Jackson argued. "The lab says Kettering's prints match the partial on Holden's necklace, so we have something solid on one of the murders."

Trang stood. "Send me full reports when you have them."

The DA hurried back out.

Jackson took a bite of his muffin, then pushed the rest aside. He had no appetite. Kera had given him a Vicodin tablet that morning for his pain—with the condition that he make an appointment with his surgeon. He would do it before the day was over. "What else have we got?"

"A roomful of exhausted detectives," Lammers said. "Go home and get some rest. I've got an officer stationed outside Kettering's hospital room, so he's not going anywhere."

Jackson had tied a T-shirt around the man's neck the night before to stem the bleeding. Part of him had wanted to just let the doctor die, but it wasn't in his nature. Besides, death was too good for someone like Kettering. A long life in prison—without access to women or drugs—would be much more of a punishment.

Lammers stood. "I mean it. Take the rest of the day off."

They all laughed. An afternoon of comp time would never make up for all the hours they put in. The sergeant left and Quince stood. "I don't have to be told twice. I'm out of here."

"Me too." Evans got to her feet as well. "I have to go see Stricklyn."

"Do you want us to come with you?" Jackson offered.

"No. I got this." She held open her jacket to show a recorder tucked into an inner pocket. "I'll take it straight to Chief Owens afterward."

"Good luck." Jackson wondered if they would ever have their time together—and what would happen to their lives if they actually did. He'd woken up thinking that the more he was around Kera, the more he wanted to make their relationship work.

He turned to Schak. "Let's all get out of here."

They stood, and Schak reached for his arm. "Hey, buddy. I

want you to know I went to an AA meeting before work today. I'm sober now and I intend to stay that way."

Jackson held out his hand for a fist bump. "Good to know. I'm here for you if you ever need support."

"Don't go all Mr. Sponsor on me," Schak grumbled. "I've got this."

As the three of them moved toward the door, Kera hurried into the room. She was holding Micah's hand and carrying Benjie. The boy looked distressed. "I'm sorry to interrupt, but I thought you might be done and I need Jackson's help."

He rushed toward her. "What's going on?"

"Benjie drank some pink paint we were playing with, and I think he needs his stomach pumped." She glanced at Evans near the door. "But I don't have legal permission to sign for that."

"Let's get to the ER." Jackson took Benjie from her, kissed his head, and prayed the boy would be all right. He turned to say goodbye but his teammates had left.

Chapter 53

Evans walked down management hall, her heart aching and her nerves pinging. If anyone ever needed a drink . . .

Kera had just pulled a bold move to keep Jackson in her court. The woman had wanted Evans to see the boys, to see the responsibility Jackson had. Kera wanted her to understand why their relationship was important. *The bitch!* Yet Evans didn't blame her. Kera was not only fighting for Jackson, she was fighting for those kids to have a father. She was a good woman.

Evans realized she could never take Jackson away from those boys. He and Kera weren't married and hadn't been together in months, but they were still a family. And she wasn't a home-wrecker.

At Stricklyn's door, she steeled herself but knocked softly, then clicked on the recorder inside her jacket. The captain called her in, smiling widely when he saw who it was. "Lara, you've come around."

"Maybe. I need to understand what you really want in exchange for not getting Jackson fired. A relationship? Sex on demand? For how long?"

"Let's think of this as a relationship, only I'll set the terms and you'll be the acquiescent slave."

Her body tensed and she forced herself to stay calm. "What if I can't follow through?"

Stricklyn shook his head. "It's not optional. I'm either

going to have the pleasure of you, whenever I want, or the pleasure of seeing Jackson gone."

"But we didn't do anything wrong."

"I have a picture of you with your arm around him."

"So? He's my friend and teammate." She decided she had enough on the recording and had to get the hell out. "I still have to think about this. I may leave the department myself." She turned toward the door.

"Don't do it. I'll still get him fired," Stricklyn called after her.

Evans hustled down the hall and knocked on Chief Owens' door. He called her in, surprised to see her. "Detective Evans. To what do I owe the pleasure?"

"I'm sorry, but this won't be pleasant." She pulled her recorder and put it on the desk. "Captain Stricklyn has been sexually coercing me." Evans pressed the play button.

When he'd heard the conversation, Owens stood. "Before I fire Stricklyn, tell me the truth, Evans. Are you romantically involved with Jackson?"

With a broken heart, she responded. "No, sir. I am not."

L.J. Sellers writes the bestselling Detective Jackson mysteries—a five-time Readers Favorite Award winner. She also pens the high-octane Agent Dallas series, the new Extractor series, and provocative standalone thrillers. Her 24 novels have been highly praised by reviewers, and she's one of the highest-rated crime fiction authors on Amazon.

Detective Jackson Mysteries:

    The Sex Club
    Secrets to Die For
    Thrilled to Death
    Passions of the Dead
    Dying for Justice
    Liars, Cheaters & Thieves
    Rules of Crime
    Crimes of Memory
    Deadly Bonds
    Wrongful Death
    Death Deserved
    A Bitter Dying
    A Liar's Death

Agent Dallas Thrillers:

    The Trigger
    The Target
    The Trap

Standalone Thrillers:

L.J. resides in Eugene, Oregon where many of her novels are set and is an award-winning journalist who earned the Grand Neal. When not plotting murders, she enjoys standup comedy, cycling, and zip-lining. She's also been known to jump out of airplanes..

Thanks for reading my novel. If you enjoyed it, please leave a review or rating online. Find out more about my work at ljsellers.com, where you can sign up to hear about new releases. —L.J.